THE GRANDDAUGHTER PROJECT

SHAHEEN CHISHTI

Nimble Books LLC

Ann Arbor, Michigan, USA

www.NimbleBooks.com

Subsidiary rights inquiries: wfz@nimblebooks.com

Copyright © 2021 Shaheen Chishti

All rights reserved.

Printed in the USA.

ISBN-13s:

9781608882373 (case laminate)

9781608882380 (paperback)

9781608882397 (Kindle)

DEDICATION

To my Baba, Syed Arif Hussain Chishti.

CONTENTS

ACKNOWLEDGMENTS

To all the wonderful women in my life: Safina, Nayer, Yasmeen, Saima, Zeba, Mamta, Ashima, Babara, Susanne and so many more.

CHARACTERS

MAYA: A plucky Indian woman living in London sent on a mysterious quest to India by her grandmother, Kamla.

RONNIE: Maya's boyfriend.

KAMLA: An elder in Calcutta, determined to pass on the wisdom of generations before she dies.

GITA: Kamla's mother, who learned to read and write at an early age in their home village of Kamalgazi.

MOHAN LAL: Gita's childhood sweetheart, a Big Man in the village ... and a threat to every woman.

ESHA and BIJAL: Kamla's sisters, who suffered with her in the great Bengali Famine of 1943.

SHAKTI: Gita's husband, a drinker.

JAGAT: Kamla's cousin, who brings her treats.

ANISH: Kamla's fiance, who once burned another's girl's face off with acid.

RAJEEV: a gentle, funny man who comes into Kamla's life, and respects her intelligence.

ANITA: Rajeev's fiance.

RAJIKA: Kamla's daughter.

LYNETTE: West Indian, meets Kamla via a lucky break at a cricket match.

TANYA: Lynette's granddaughter, living in Manchester, very pregnant, and craving Coke.

ALICIA: Tanya's mother, Lynette's daughter.

REBECCA: Stand-up comic and author living in New York city.

HELGA: Rebecca's grandmother. Wednesday's child, full of woe.

PAM: Lynette's Mam. Born in the West Indies, migrated to Notting Hill.

THOMAS: Pam's man.

DURGA: the goddess known for her invincible power and impenetrable compassion.

MAYA

"I said my grandmother wants me to find a tree," shouted Maya into the phone. The phone reception was a bit crackled since she was talking to her boyfriend in London, and she herself was in a taxi heading out of downtown Calcutta. "A tree," she repeated, in case he didn't understand. Anyway, she laughed to herself, she herself hardly understood why she was in cab looking for a tree, never mind why anyone else would.

"But that's insane. What kind of a tree?" she heard Ronnie shout back.

"A tree with a hole in it. My grandmother's drawn me a map."

"What? Of a tree?"

"Well, a road leading to a tree in a forest next to a field."

"Maya, it sounds like you are bloody mad. Like you are all mad. What's going on over there?"

"I know it is mad but she is gone and I loved her and it was her dying wish, Ronnie, and I have to respect that."

"Yes, you do and I respect that you have to respect that, Maya." "Thank you, Ronnie," she said. "And you're right," she laughed, "it does sound daft. "

"Any idea how long it is going to take to find this tree?"

"About a week. I haven't booked a return flight yet but I will when I've found it."

"A week?"

"It's a big country, Ronnie. Maybe more, maybe less. I know roughly where the tree is."

"What? I can't hear you," he said.

"I said … oh never mind. Got to go."

Maya settled down in the back of the taxi and yawned. She had been in India two weeks already but was not sure she was over her jet lag. Or maybe it was grief. Jet lag and grief have similar symptoms. At least, she'd been able to sit by her grandmother Kamla's deathbed and had the opportunity to say goodbye to her. Her grandmother was an idol of Maya's, had given her so much love. Such an independent spirit and then she had always encouraged Maya's independence. But now she had this bizarre errand to do. Find a tree. Good God.

"Kamalgazi for holiday, ma'am?" asked the taxi driver. "Visit family?"

"Er, kind of," replied Maya.

"Kind of," replied the taxi driver, laughing. "Kind of holiday. Ha-ha. Either holiday or not holiday."

"In that case, holiday," said Maya, dispelling the image of all the work that would be piling up on her desk in London. Her fingers twitched on the keypad of her telephone. She was tempted to call Andy, just check in to see if he was coping with her strategy report but she knew it would be a mistake. He would only moan that he had been given all her workload and make remarks like, "When are you coming back, shirker?" or "Can't believe you've thrown me in it." Anyway, what could she do to help them? Canary Wharf was 3000 miles away.

Maya took a deep breath and closed her eyes. This was about her grandmother. "I am in a period of mourning—compassionate leave," she told herself putting her phone away in her bag and looking, for the first time, out the window.

The road into Kamalgazi was narrow due to the long line of trucks parked up on the dusty sidewalk. India, Maya thought, where everything is chaotic. Trees, scrubland and empty bottles ran along the central aisle between the two carriageways.

It was a foggy day, endless grey sky interrupted by half built white tower blocks. If Kamla had just died a couple of months later, it would not have been the monsoon season and Maya could have simply gone back to London, completed the report that was giving her such a headache, got married to Ronnie and come back when her mind was clear. But no. Rajika, her mother, was adamant, "Your nani-ji wanted you to find the tree before the rains come, Maya, so you have to do it now."

The map inside Maya's pocket was hand-written, neatly drawn. Kamla had used a ruler but it was a map nonetheless. If Kamla had not been such a sane person, she might have considered it some kind of eccentricity, madness, leaving behind a map to a tree.

And now what? There may not even be a tree where Kamla pinpointed it. Considering all the cranes Maya was seeing, the field and forest that Kamla laid out on her map could easily have been transformed into a housing unit overnight.

Maya had never before questioned her grandmother's sanity. Kamla had always been to her a rock, a comfort, someone who knew exactly what she wanted from life and how to achieve it. Well, perhaps not *her* own life, but certainly Maya's life. It had been her, more than her mother, who had pushed Maya every step of the way.

"You must make something of your life, Maya," she said from when Maya was the tiniest child. "Never let others make your life for you."

Yet, just when Maya had the chance to make something of her life, get married, advance in her job, she gets sent off on a relative's dying wish for her to find a tree.

"What am I going to find at the tree, mam-mi?" Maya had asked her mother.

Rajika shrugged. "Don't ask me, this is between you and Nani-ji."

It was as if her grandmother had forgotten that Maya had grown. Did she still think of Maya as the little girl who used to clamber onto her lap requesting treasure hunts and fairy tales?

"Yah mam-mi, but what was Nani-ji thinking? I have a job and a fiancé. How do I find the time to go play hide and seek in a forest?"

"I know darling," said Rajika. "But as I have said, this is Nani-ji's wish, not mine."

"What destination for your journey ma'am?" asked the taxi driver abruptly halting the cab, causing Maya to jerk back.

"Where are we?" asked Maya, unfolding the map from her pocket and staring at it for some road names.

"Ahead of us we have the Kamalgazi Mosque, the largest mosque in the district," the taxi driver announced momentarily adopting the role of proud tour guide. "You want to alight here? First stop for your holiday, ha-ha?"

"Umm," said Maya. "No, it looks like we need to go left at the end of the road and then right."

"You show me the map," said the driver. "I help you."

"No, it's OK," said Maya reluctant to hand such a precious piece of paper across.

"You hold it up and I look," said the driver. "Taxi fare ticking."

Maya held up the map. It was drawn on a piece of A4 paper and the road names clearly written, but the taxi driver squinted.

"Upside down please," said the driver. Maya turned it the other way.

"This house? This is where you're going?" The taxi driver pointed a grubby finger at a house that was now upside down. "It's an important house."

"Is it?" asked Maya. She had clocked the house but not really paid it much attention, focusing mainly on the tree located a little way down the path.

"Yes, important to map maker."

Maya looked closely. The taxi driver was right. Of all the effort Kamla had put into presenting the map, including the mosque and the new flyover and shiny shopping complexes, it was to the house with its pitched roof, shutters and wide veranda, that Kamla had devoted the most time. She had even shaded around the wide front door.

"I take you to the house," said the taxi driver. "And you walk to this red dot, your destination, right? The treasure, ha-ha."

Maya followed the taxi driver's route along the map with her finger until they pulled up outside the house so perfectly depicted by Kamla's artwork.

"Apologies to upset," said the driver, pulling up to a pair of closed black gates, "but this house is bloody ugly. Not British design. Important maybe but not a lucky house."

As Maya closed the taxi door, two barking ridgeback dogs appeared from either side of the black 4x4 parked up in the driveway. They had obviously figured out that closed gates meant no exit so they opted to show their mettle by breathing heavily through the ironwork.

"I wait up the road," said the taxi driver nervously. "As I said, apologies but bloody ugly house."

"Maybe so, but this is apparently where I am meant to be."

She got out of the taxi and felt like she was moving back in time. It was, in its way, rather exciting to be an adventuress, she thought. Just like Kamla to bring that out in me.

KAMLA

December 2013

Kamla was surprised at how still her hand was as she drew the map. Everything else she touched seemed to shake or quiver with the effects of old age, but, as she did this, her hand was composed. This was just as well as she wanted to draw the house exactly as it was, as it had always been except for the addition of the gate and the deletion of the fruit trees.

She had to draw it in the finest detail for Maya so that Maya noticed it, held it in her gaze. Maya would be reading about it in due course, it was a part of her history so it would help if she had a mental image.

It really was a very ugly house for its age, Kamla decided, as she sketched the square lines copied from the photographs she had taken when she made her final visit to Kamalgazi three months before. No finesse, no charm, how had she ever thought it grand?

Such meticulous reproduction of such a haunting place caused Kamla's back to hunch and her eyes to ache as she sat at the desk at her home in Calcutta. She removed her spectacles and rubbed over her eyelids with a thumb and forefinger, just allowing her head to rest motionless on her hands. This drawing project will take me to my dying day, she said to herself. A batty project by all accounts. Instructing my granddaughter to locate a tree. She will curse me when I am gone. I can just hear her now.

A tree? Has Nani-ji gone mad? Kamla smiled remembering the high-pitched voice Maya produced when irate. What a pest I am. Let God hope she will understand my motives otherwise she will forever consider me just a mad old lady.

Kamla returned to the drawing. She was looking forward to adding in the next part. She had allowed five centimeters for the track down from the house along the field by the row of small brick houses with the bright orange tiled rooftops, which had once, when Kamla inhabited them, been mud huts.

The Kamalgazi of today was nothing like the village Kamla grew up in. Now there were shopping malls and tower blocks, road networks and sports grounds but the overly zealous city planners had not yet honed in on the field surrounding the tree. This was because the Goddess preserved it. It endured due to the spirit of the Durga, creator and protector. No amount of machinery could bulldoze the supreme power.

Kamla had spent much time wondering how best she should depict this section on the map to incorporate the tree that grew on the outer rims of the forest behind the wooden houses.

It was a sacred tree, so should it be adorned? Or maybe it should be larger than all the other trees, except that might confuse Maya. She had considered drawing the goddess onto the map, sort of hovering around the tree but decided that might put Maya off. Maya was a pragmatist; a floating goddess would not cut it with Maya. Maya liked numbers and hard facts. If you couldn't back it up, forget it.

In the end she disguised the goddess as a red dot. That way Maya could interpret the tree whichever way she liked.

Three months earlier, the goddess had been sitting inside the tree waiting for Kamla on her final visit, just as Kamla knew she would be. At every turning point in Kamla's life, the goddess was there. No wind or rain or flood disturbed her presence. She was no longer the work of beauty she had been seven decades ago because, in respect to womanhood, she altered with time. Look how ravaged *I* have become, Kamla reminded herself unwrapping the leaves around the statue. The statue, as she held it in her hands, was not much bigger than her own hands. The paintwork was chipped off and the left arm missing but the dip of the eyes and the strong forehead leading down to the mouth still set in a smile of compassion. These were all intact.

Kamla wrapped the goddess up in a fresh handful of dried leaves and around this she wrapped the documents so that the whole package created a stubby tube. She secured the package in an elastic band and placed them in a plastic bag. "You will meet my granddaughter next," she said sticking her arm into the tree and patting the package. "Guide her wisely and, unlike me, perhaps *she* will listen."

MAYA

June 2014

Maya followed Kamla's finely drawn dashes along the track past the small homes dressed with colorful saris drying on the rooftops. Women waved from doorways, men on bikes stared sizing Maya up, the rarity of an Indian businesswoman in urban clothing.

"Namaste," Maya said politely, not wishing to draw attention to herself but realizing it was an improbable wish.

She followed the track around the back of the houses towards the small forest of trees. The ground was wet and she kicked herself for wearing her delicate leather pumps.

Eyes hungry with curiosity bore into her back, observing her every step from all angles, but she ploughed on up the increasingly muddy track towards the forest. There was no doubt in Maya's mind which tree it was that she was looking for, as there was only one large tree on the outer rims of the forest and Kamla had drawn it well. Beside it stood a smaller tree, but it was the big one that had the hole in the trunk. It was not much wider than an arm and there were green shoots growing out of it, but it was a hole nonetheless.

Maya was not used to the eyes of India, always watchful, clocking every activity someone took. She wished she had snuck in during the dead of night, while hungry eyes slept. Cautiously, she folded up the black sleeve of her blouse and stuck her arm in.

The inside of the tree was warm and the base of the hole covered with a carpet of rubbery toadstools. Maya could not feel anything at her first attempt, not that she knew what to expect. Pulling her sleeve up further, she shoved her whole arm deep into the thick, aged trunk. At the back her fingers came upon plastic. Maya pulled it all the way out, a folded plastic bag. There was no need to look in the bag, she identified it the moment she saw it, as it was Kamla's yellow shopping sack with the faded lion on the front.

It was not until she was back in the taxi listening to the driver's playlist of Hindi-pop played at full volume that she snuck a peek into the bag. Inside wrapped around a half dollop of clay were three A4 envelopes. The first addressed to Maya, the second to someone called "Rebecca" and the third to a "Tanya."

A scribbled note lay on the top.

My dearest Maya,
  You have to know the past to understand the present.
  God bless and good night.
  Nan-ji
  PS: I entrust to you the beautiful goddess, Durga. She is not at her finest but she is the embodiment of all goodness for women. She is on our side, treat her well.

Nan-ji must have written this note and made this packet recently, she thought. It didn't seem that worn. Maya examined the dollop of clay. Yes, there were signs of beauty in the statue, but she was not convinced of its divine virtue, since she was not superstitious. To her it was just that, a statue. Still, if Kamla wanted it cared for, she would do her best.

She bundled the statue back into the plastic bag and opened up her envelope. Then, on a whim, she said to the driver, "Take me back to that tree."

He did and she paid him and got out. It was such a beautiful day, she thought, and I need time to read this. It's such a long letter.

She sat down next to the tree, enjoying the warmth and shade, so unlike England's grey and dampness. How long since she had actually sat down next to a tree? How delightful. Another unexpected gift from Nan-ji.

KAMLA'S LETTER TO MAYA

-1-

2012

Dear Maya,

The first indication that I was wrestling my way into the world came on the first day of the Durga Puja festival 1934, the most important day of the Hindu calendar. To be born on such an auspicious day meant that my mother's prayers were at last being answered and my family was about to be blessed by the son they had hoped and prayed for, ever since the births of my three sisters.

When it was apparent that their prayers had not reached the correct ears and I was yet another baby girl, my father, your great grandfather, Shakti, a permanently grumpy man, drank too much Cholai and took to slapping Bijal, Esha and Leela, my three sisters and cursing the days they were born.

My mother, Gita, blamed herself for failing yet again.

"What is wrong with me? Have I not been grateful enough to the goddess Durga? Should I pray more?" she cried in despair.

Shakti, who cared little for prayers or goddesses, bypassed the religious theme completely.

"You are worthless. You have one purpose in life and that is to give me a son."

She might have felt worthless but Gita knew the moment she glanced into my newborn eyes that I had a fighting spirit inside me.

It was a spirit that seemed to thrive on very little for, despite food being sparse, I grew fat and hearty with cheeks as plump as cushions.

We lived in Kamalgazi, the village of my mother, Gita's, birth because it was here that Gita found employment for Shakti, cultivating the paddy fields of the wealthy landowner Mohan Lal Raju.

Gita and Mohan Lal had grown up alongside one another since Gita's mother worked as a domestic servant for the Raju family. There were even rumors that Mohan Lal had feelings for Gita but because he was high caste and she low, any thoughts of marriage were out of the question.

Having been an attractive child, Mohan Lal matured into a fat young man with a greasy complexion who paid his laborers the minimum wage yet always expected thanks for his generosity whenever he passed by.

His home towered over our mud brick hut two paddy fields away. As we gazed over at its pitched roof, wooden shutters and wide verandah, my sisters and I imagined how muffled the noises of the roosters and doves must be through the solid white walls.

My father, thin and wiry and black from eking out his existence under the hot sun, rewarded his hard life by drinking away three quarters of his meagre pay packet. Despite the lush green fields, the pure air and cleansing monsoons, which kept the Raju family nourished, we scraped by, living off the remaining quarter of the money, sustained by cold rice, salt and chilies.

What we lacked in food, though, we made up for in education. No peasant children were educated, particularly not peasant girls, but Gita, as a child polishing teak, found books in the Raju home and taught herself the basics of reading and writing, which I am eternally grateful she passed on to us.

She was not advanced, she knew how to read simple words and do basic arithmetic by counting on her fingers but it gave my sisters and me the foundation and, more importantly, the passion to learn.

I was the quickest to absorb information, which came as no surprise to my mother. She believed absolutely that I had received a special blessing from the goddess Durga who is known for her invincible power and impenetrable compassion. We all felt her powers accounted in some form for my chubbiness.

We were taught how to pray fervently to the goddess and give thanks for every scrap that passed our lips and, like our mother, my sisters and I became devotees of Durga. We found through her, calmness in our hearts and harmony, which was necessary for facing up to Shakti, for as we grew increasingly pious, he grew increasingly angry and violent and drunk.

"You must be kind to your father," Gita used to tell us. "His mother did not give thanks enough to the god Shani for his safe birth, thus he has been rendered permanently blighted by Lord Shani's quick tempered wrath."

Shakti took to disappearing for days on end leaving us not a rupee. It was during one of his leaves of absence when we were scraping around on our hands and knees for grains of rice and roots that Mohan Lal appeared amongst our huddle of shacks gorging on a handful of dates. Clearing his throat as he always did before he spoke, he announced that he was sacking Shakti.

"He is a waste of space on my land," he said, spitting out a half chewed date stone, which my elder sister discreetly retrieved and popped into her mouth.

"Please Mohan Lal, don't do this. Does our childhood friendship mean nothing to you?" Gita cried, throwing herself at his knees, grubby fingers soiling his crisp white linen.

"It does indeed, Gita, which is why I will offer you the same wage if you come and clean in my house."

"Sahaab, I can start now."

"You can start cleaning my house tomorrow but you will clean my trousers now. I cannot go into the town with muddy kneecaps."

When Shakti returned late that night, bleary-eyed and staggering, he kicked Gita awake.

"Is it true what the Sahaab tells me, he is to employ you, not me?"

"We need the money," said Gita sitting up and wrapping her sari around her.

"It is me who gets the money, not you," Shakti said attempting to swipe Gita but he tripped over my sisters and myself and crashed into a faded picture of Vishnu.

"It should not matter who gets the money, so long as we have some."

"It matters to me," said Shakti banging his chest. "I am the man, I earn the money. You make me sons."

"Not now," said Gita, settling back down on her straw bed.

Gita was a master sleuth at detecting the level of Shakti's drunkenness. Tonight he was all words, no violence, so it was safe to return to sleep.

-2-

What a beautiful letter writer Kamla was, Maya thought, as she began to unravel the second letter. I wonder where she is going with all this. Maya looked up at the beauty of the sun, still warming her. Such peace. How hard Kamla and her great-grandmother's lives were. She turned back to the letter:

Kamalgazi was a beautiful place. It is a shame you will never see it as I saw it. It is getting built up with "dream homes' and skyscrapers so now it most probably is a metropolis. In my day, it was just green fields and trees and swooping birds and croaking frogs and the fragrance of jasmine and, because it was so flat, it looked like it stretched on and on forever. It was hard to imagine Calcutta was less than 20km away, because our world was so peaceful.

We knew everybody living around the paddy fields outside Mohan Lal's home. Women in their doorways beating rugs and hanging out lungee waved to us as Gita and I set off the next morning.

"Going to barā ghara?" they called out, the "big house" as Mohan Lal's was known. One of my bigger friends, an eight-year-old boy called Shambu, ran over to show me a snake he had caught inside the red and white bougainvillea. It was dead and shriveled but he wore it around his thin, black neck like a hunter parading his spoils.

"Don't get too grand," Gita's friends said, patting us as we passed, in the hope we might bring them the kind of luck that Gita had been granted. In Kamalgazi, anyone permitted to enter the Raju home was important, servant girls and dignitaries alike.

"Can I see the library?" I asked Gita as we approached the paved pathway leading up to the house.

"No, you will stay by my side all the time, Kamla. Do not get into trouble."

Our entrance was not the wide front door but the servant's entrance to the left, shaded by a jujube tree.

"Chalo," my mother called, shooing away the crowd of curious children who had followed us into the grounds. "Go home."

The kitchen was wide and long with a small window and a narrow wooden table, shiny pots and pans and jars of multicolored chutneys. There were two cooks peeling vegetables and grinding spices. They did not smile as we entered. Their faces were lined and their eyes sad. They just nodded and Gita nodded back removing cleaning products from a door at the far end of the kitchen. She knew her way around well.

"Come Kamla. We are to start in the dining room."

Once in the center of the house it felt so much smaller than it looked from the outside. Perhaps this was the effect of pictures shrinking the walls and the rotating fans suspended from the ceiling. Heavy wooden doors separated the rooms from the hallway and everywhere smelt like overly ripe fruit.

The dining room was dark with a heavy table running its full length.

"First we must polish this table, Kamla," said Gita handing me a cloth. "And after this," she pointed to the wall behind me, "the library." I spun around and gasped. I had never seen a book before and certainly not ten books sitting side by side along a wooden shelf protected by a pane of glass.

"Can I look at one?" I whispered, sidling up to the bookshelf.

"Quickly," said Gita. "But don't touch the glass."

"Can you see your favorite here?" I said.

"It's the brown one, Panchatantra, in the middle," said Gita.

"Can I look at that one?"

"Hurry and keep your nose away or it will make a cloud on the glass."

Gita had taught us to read by drawing shapes in the dust and she told us stories she had picked up by looking at the pictures in Panchatantra of frogs and tortoises and geese, although the stories were always a little confused. Due to her limited learning she had to guess at a lot of what the words might be saying.

"Clean well and perhaps Sahaab will let you touch it one day."

I like to think I worked hard helping Gita clean windowsills and dust down chairs but I am sure I was more of a hindrance. I wanted to look at every small detail, run my fingers along the fabrics on the walls, prod the china figurines on the mantelpiece. It was perhaps because I was so absorbed in an oil painting that I did not hear Mohan Lal enter the room, that is, until he cleared his throat.

"Why have you brought her?" he asked, snarling at me like I was an insect burrowing beneath his nail.

"My apologies, Sahaab, but she is too young to leave alone."

"If you want to earn more money, she will have to be left."

"I want to earn more money."

"Come with me then, there is something more for you to clean," said Mohan Lal. "You," he pointed at me. "Stay here…. Alone."

He strode out of the room leaving a lingering aroma of garlic and sweat and Gita followed waving a reproachful, "Do not even think of disobeying' finger my way.

I stood still in the silence waiting for Gita to return. It was cold in Mohan Lal's dining room, as no light penetrated the heavy linen drapes. I perched on the edge of the dining table now slippery with polish and calculated my options.

Remember, I was known to be a spirited child, which I believe was just a polite way of saying, naughty. The only idea that popped into my head sitting all alone in the cold, dark room was to sneak a glimpse at the brown book. My fingers were twitching to open the glass cabinet. I could not begin to imagine what the pictures that Gita described could possibly look like, as I had never seen illustrations before. I knew only the drawings of gods on the walls of ours and other mud huts I

*visited, distorted by time and weather and, just now, the
horses and soldiers and guns adorning Mohan Lal's walls.*

*I snuck over to the cabinet and, taking care not to breathe
on the glass, I pulled the small metal handle. The glass door
rattled but did not open. I tried it again. I might have kept
trying it, unaware that doors like this have keys to lock them if
I had not heard my mother's normally calm placid voice,
raised almost to a shout.*

*I tiptoed into the hall. It was silent again except for a tick
tock ticking through one of the adjoining doorways and the
ordered sound of chopping in the kitchen.*

*"No, Sahaab, I thank you for your offer but I do not accept
it," Gita said, this time more quietly.*

*I followed her voice into the room opposite the dining
room, a brighter space with comfortable chairs as opposed to
the stiff wooden ones we had spent half an hour buffing. The
windows in this room overlooked the paddy field and, in the
far distance, I could see the thatched roof of my home.*

*There was a thick heavy curtain hung from the floor to the
ceiling, screening off half of the room. My mother and Mohan
Lal were behind this.*

*"How can you resist twenty-five paise? Fifty paise perhaps?
Fifty paise and you show me beneath your sari?"*

"I am not comfortable with this Sahaab."

*"This is about more than comfort. It is about friendship,
have we not known each other our whole lives?"*

"Yes, as acquaintances."

"Yah, as friends, Gita."

"I have my honor."

*"And I have my appetite. Damn you, Gita why else have I
brought you into my house?"*

"I am sorry, Sahaab."

*"You will be sorry when you are begging on the streets with
no rupees in your pocket!"*

At the sound of the commotion, I ran forward and slid into the thick heavy fabric curling my body up as small as it could go so that I could glimpse behind the drape.

Mohan Lal was stripped down to his white vest and had undone the catch at the top of his trousers. He was constraining Gita with a fat hairy hand on her shoulder.

"Here, Gita, I have 50 paise, it will feed your family for two days."

I watched Gita relax her taut frame.

"As you wish, Sahaab."

Mohan Lal spun Gita around to face him. He pushed her down on to the long, low bed.

"Sahaab?"

"It is this or no job, Gita," Mohan Lal said, climbing on top of Gita and enveloping her in his flab.

I cannot tell you what he did to my mother on this day but it was certainly enough to earn us a hot meal of potato and red lentil curry.

Gita went every day to clean the house of Mohan Lal but no longer permitted me to go with her. This did not stop me secretly entering into the house and hiding in either the dining room or the colorful room with the drapes. I got to know the downstairs of the house inside out but never dared to venture upstairs. I had never been that high up before and I was nervous about how rapidly I could escape should I need to.

Most days Mohan Lal came to find Gita and took her off with him to their special place behind the drape. Normally I hid in the drape or just outside it. I did not like what I saw inside. Gita always resisted but Mohan Lal offered her money and threatened her with losing her job and begging on the streets if she did not let him have his way. I could not tell whether what they were doing was acceptable. I tried to understand it for I had never seen Shakti touch my mother

*other than to swipe her with the back of his hand or kick her
shins. This was not what Mohan Lal was doing to Gita but he
too looked like he was hurting her. Sometimes he pulled Gita's
hair and slapped her face and he hated her looking miserable.*

*One time he produced a long knife from beneath the bed
and held it to Gita's throat.*

*"Smile or I will cut you a smile across your cheeks." This
day was an angry day. He had no patience with Gita. I was
scared because Gita's voice was pitched higher than normal.*

"Of course, Sahaab, I can smile."

*I have never forgiven myself for the day I forgot to watch
out for Gita. It was such an exciting day and it all happened
so quickly. I was with Gita in the dining room. In the weary
way mothers of spirited children have, she had come to accept
that there was no point in forbidding me about following her
to the big house, as I would do it anyway. What she did forbid
me to do was to enter the colorful room.*

*She was polishing the glass book cabinet and I was hiding
under the table when Mohan Lal entered.*

*"I have some more cleaning for you," he said as he always
did. I watched Gita prepare to leave but then stop.*

*"Sahaab, there…there is a book inside this cabinet I
remember reading as a child. Your father permitted it, the
brown book just there. May I be allowed to unlock the cabinet
so I may refresh my memory of the book?"*

*An ant walking across his sandal would have incited more
interest for Mohan Lal. He would have flicked away Gita's
question completely had she not stood firm.*

*"I've never opened the cabinet but I imagine there is a key
somewhere in one of those drawers," he said carelessly,
pointing to a set of drawers to the left of the cabinet. "You can
look if you like… after the other cleaning job."*

He stuck his hand in his pocket and jangled some coins.

As soon as Mohan Lal and Gita were out of the room, I flew out from under the table. There was nothing in the drawers except for the key.

Cautiously, perhaps overly cautiously, I turned the thin metal key in the lock and the glass door popped open. Ignoring all the other books, I went straight for the brown one removing it from the shelf.

I shut the glass panel, returned the key to the drawer and resumed my hiding place under the table. The title was embossed in gold, PANCHATANTRA. This book will mean little to you, my dear, as you have all your life been swamped with books to read but I had never held a book before or smelled its musty pages or examined in depth so many drawings of creatures in one place. I was absorbed in turning the pages.

I do not know what I would have done to intervene had I been hiding in the colorful room on this day, instead of surreptitiously leafing through a book. I like to think I would have raced behind the drape and rescued my mother from her oppressor but, as well as being spirited, I was also a hungry child and the fear of missing rice for disobeying Gita was overwhelming. For on this day, as I was hiding beneath the dining table reading of hunters and doves, my mother ran into the room calling to me.

"Kamla, Kamla, hurry, we must leave now."

I leapt up, and shoving the book beneath my tunic, followed Gita out of the servants' quarters and up the path to home. She was staring straight ahead.

"What is it?" I asked, running to keep up.

"I—I killed him," Gita cried, clutching her cheeks. "He had a knife and..."

She began punching her head with her fist. "What was I thinking, what was I thinking?"

"What did you do?" I grabbed hold of Gita's arm for her to keep it still.

23

"I dropped a heavy chair onto his head. He was going to kill me, oh what have I done?"

"Did he look dead?"

"Yes, Kamla, most dead. He was on the floor with his eyes closed and blood on his forehead."

As we approached the first paddy field, Gita threw herself to her knees. "Sarvasvaroopey Sarveshev Sarvashakti....keep running Kamla... Samanvietey Bhayevbhyah Traahi No Devi Durge Devi Namostutey."

I could not leave Gita mid prayer so I waited, keeping my eyes on the big house in case someone came out to catch us.

"Go Kamla, keep running."

Gita hauled herself up and ran with me, pulling up her sari to free her stride.

"What is it Mam'mi?" asked Bijal, a look of puzzlement on her face as we panted up the muddy path into our home.

"Mam'mi has killed the Sahaab," I said with a little glimmer of pride at knowing the story first. "There was blood and he fell to the floor," I added.

"What?" cried all three of my sisters.

"But why, Mam'mi?

"How?"

"He hurt me," said Gita. "And he had a knife and it all happened so fast. I..."

The hut was dark in comparison to the glare of the midday sun. We had not noticed Shakti asleep in the corner.

"You stupid, worthless woman," he said suddenly, clambering off the straw bed and thumping Gita in the chest. "What for us now?"

"She didn't mean to, Pita, he was hurting her," I said pushing myself in between my parents.

"Of course he was hurting her because she is stupid and stupid people get hurt," said Shakti, grabbing a broom from inside the doorway and jabbing my mother with it.

"You need to get out. I don't want the police here. Leave us, woman."

Clutching her head in her hands, Gita backed out of the doorway, tears rolling down her cheeks.

"I'm going too," I said.

"No, Kamla, you have to stay," said Esha.

"No I don't," I said. I ran out of the hut after Gita who was blindly zigzagging off through the soggy paddy fields.

"Wait for me," I called.

"Go home, Kamla," said Gita.

"No Mam-mi," I said. "I know what Mohan Lal did, I saw him hurting you."

Gita spun around, "No, Kamla, you didn't."

"I did. Not today but other days. He hurt you and you didn't like it."

"It doesn't matter anymore."

"Why did you let him do those things to you?"

"You are too young to understand that I had no choice, Kamla. Men can be very demanding, especially rich men like Mohan Lal."

"I would rather we had nothing than Mohan Lal hurt you."

"That is good then, Kamla, because now we have nothing."

We trampled along beside one another, Gita moaning away and every so often telling me to turn back, but only half-heartedly. Her mind was jumbled.

As we left the first paddy field for the next I remembered the book. It was no longer in my tunic. My heart dropped to my feet. It had been the best object I had ever held in my hands.

"Mam-mi, I need to go back, please, wait here for me. I'm coming."

Gita gave a small nod and carried on walking.

I retraced my steps back to the hut and found the book just outside the doorway of the hut, in a patch of shrubs. Grabbing it, I stuffed it back under my tunic and was turning to race back to Gita when I bumped almost comically into Mohan Lal. He was very much alive, very sticky faced with nothing but a small cut above his left eye.

I gasped.

"Where is Gita?" he asked me.

"Er, nowhere," I replied, clutching the book tightly, unable to remove my eyes from Mohan Lal's pimpled face. Even though I knew it was best for Gita that he was alive, deep down I wished he had died.

Shakti and my sisters hearing Mohan Lal's voice came out from the hut, alarmed.

"You are all well? Thank Vishnu for your safety and please, Sahaab, one hundred of my most sincere apologies to you," said Shakti bowing so low the top of his head scraped his calloused toes. "My wife, she has a temper and she is stupid so many times."

"I do not care about your wife. Although you can inform her that for the upcoming puja, as employer of all peasants, I will be erecting the pandal and providing all patima of the Goddess Durga, something I am sure you will all be most grateful for."

"Thank you, Sahaab," said my sisters clapping their hands together with excitement.

"And you can tell your wife that I expect her at my house to continue her cleaning employment first thing tomorrow morning."

"But..." I cried.

"Yes Sahaab," said Shakti pushing me out of the way. "I will certainly inform her of this most gracious news."

[My dear, I do hope you are getting the irony of this situation. Mohan Lal and my father, Shakti, are discussing their reverence for the goddess, Durga, the most revered goddess in the Hindu faith and slayer of evil, but where is their reverence for women in their earthly form?]

As soon as Mohan Lal was gone, Shakti shoved me. "Go find Mam-mi, now."

Clutching the book, I hurried into the rice paddies.

I found Gita sitting beneath a chatim tree nervously twitching at the thread of her headscarf.

"Mam-mi," I cried. "Everything is fine, Mohan Lal is alive."

"He is?"

"Yes, he has only a small cut and a fat spotty face."

"Hush, Kamla, don't be disrespectful."

"He wants you back tomorrow and he is going to provide all the patima for the puja."

"Oh, thank God," said Kamla exhaling dramatically. "I must watch my hot temper."

"It is not you, Mam-mi. It is him," I said sitting down beside her.

"You be quiet, Kamla, you do not know anything."

"I know that I hate Mohan Lal and wish he was dead," I said sulkily.

"Yah and what then? We starve on the streets?"

"Perhaps."

Gita swiped me around the side of my head.

"You know nothing."

"Shall we look at this book together?" I asked removing the brown book from beneath my tunic.

"What is this, Kamla? What have you done? This is not our book."

"The Sahaab doesn't care," I said.

"This is stealing. You may not have this book."

"But Mam-mi..."

"Kamla, it goes back, tomorrow." Gita grabbed the book, stood up and headed back to our hut.

I did not approach my 8th Durga puja with the same level of excitement I had experienced in previous years. Ever since the "incident" with the knife and the chair, Mohan Lal had become abusive and cruel to Gita withholding her pay or making her work extra-long hours and depriving her of food or water. He no longer spoke in the friendly way he had behind the curtain, instead he was brisk and matter of fact.

Mohan Lal had also become abusive to me after discovering I was hiding out in the colorful room behind one of the long, comfortable chairs. After shouting and pointing his finger at me, he bent me over, pulled up my tunic and slapped me so hard on my bottom that I had deep red welts. He told me that he had had a patima personally carved for me to give the deity but, because I was a "bad girl," I would not be permitted to have it.

[My dear, I am sure the Durga puja will be as big an event in your lifetime as it has been in mine but, just in case it is not, let me briefly explain a little bit about it. The puja is to celebrate Durga, our most important goddess, slayer of the demon, Mahisashura, who was terrorizing the earth. Goddess Durga preserves moral order and righteousness. The puja lasts for ten days and is a time of cleansing with fasting and prayer. On the sixth day, shrines are erected on behalf of the goddess known as pandals and these are filled with patima, red sundried mud of Bengal carved and painted into icons of our goddess. For three days we worship at these pandals offering rice and fruits, garlands of marigolds, chanting and prayer. On the final day to indicate a new cycle of life and the vanishing of our misery, we take the clay patima to the stream

and we wash them away letting the divine energy from the patima seep into our hearts.]

I tried to be true to the goddess Durga and not let Mohan Lal's cruel words and actions penetrate my soul. I also attempted to think compassionate thoughts and feel joy but, in truth, I was so angry I could barely sleep at night. I was too busy scheming up ways of paying Mohan Lal back. My mind kept coming back to fire, setting fire to his home, burning him, throwing fire on his fields but I knew I would never go so far.

When the sixth day of the puja arrived, the pandal provided by Mohan Lal was erected out of bamboo and wood, decorated with floral garlands and filled with the beautiful clay patima. Everyone in Kamalgazi was in a state of excitement. The village was decorated with freshly picked flowers, hair was brushed, faces scrubbed and painted and plates of rice distributed to the patima. Everyone was so busy and so happy and so full of festival fever that nobody noticed me removing one of the patima and placing it underneath my freshly laundered sari. I had been eyeing this one for the three days it had been sitting there and I knew in my heart of hearts that this was the patima handpicked for me. Of course, now I realize that Mohan Lal was lying when he said he had had a patima carved specifically for me but an eight-year-old brain does not yet understand a wily nature.

I did not want my patima being washed away the next day. I wanted to keep her and have my own festival when my heart was ready to be cleansed.

I took the patima to my home. Our house was one of five mud homes clustered together in a higgledy line. When you live in such a small home most of life is spent outside in the shade of the trees, praying and eating together, sharing the communal well and the washing line and the outside toilet. The patima was not for sharing, though it was mine. I knew I *had done something wrong by stealing it but at the same time I justified it to myself saying that it was the one Mohan Lal had chosen specifically for me.*

I took my patima around the back of the houses along the edge of the paddy field up a path to the clump of trees, which we called the big forest, but it was just a few trees tightly packed together. At the edge of the forest was a banyan tree. There were other banyan trees in the clump but the one on the edge of the forest was my favorite because it had a hole half way up its trunk where I used to hide anything shiny that I found, like the golden bangle, which was not real gold because the gold chipped off, the metal hair clip and a brown button. I had planned to hide the brown book here before Gita made me return it. Wrapped in leaves and grass, I hid my patima. I patted it three times for luck and walking away, ate a piece of grass picked from the ground, for forgiveness.

Maya smiled at her grandmother's pluckiness. *May I too have this.* And then she laughed, Oh yes, I have it. Look at me sitting here under this tree with all I have to do. She was unfolding the third letter, shaking her head. It's always good to read about a rebel, she laughed. I must be relaxing, she thought.

-3-

To continue, Maya, when I look back on my childhood hunting around for a time of inner peace, it is to this, my eighth Durga puja, that my mind transports me, for however bad my life seemed at the time, it was a mere blemish compared to the devastation that lay ahead.

My dear, you will not have heard of the event that ruined Bengalis in the year 1943 for, by the time you are born, it will be all but forgotten. It has almost disappeared from the minds of us who lived through it, such is the adaptable nature of the brain.

It is an event, of which I must enlighten you about, to explain what happened next to our family.

When referring to the nature of men, we could look at the very big picture. It is men who start wars, men who sit in comfortable government chairs and tell us what to do, men who lead our religious institutions, men who head households, men who hold the purse strings. This is how it is in my lifetime, my dear. I pray that when it is your time, women will be in their rightful place.

At first I was elated having hidden the patima in the tree. In such a shared community I relished a secret but, when the tidal waves and the cyclone tore through Kamalgazi, wrecking homes and crops, I did wonder whether this might be retribution from the goddess Durga for having not released her divine energy into the stream.

The cyclone announced its arrival long before you could see it, roaring across the plain like an army of tanks. As I lay on my straw bed watching the wind rip the thatching off our rooftop, I half considered stepping outside into the eye of the storm, retrieving the patima and throwing it into the flooded rice paddies.

"What kind of idiot are you? Lie back down," Leela said, yanking me onto my bed.

Mohan Lal lost three-quarters of his rice crops to salt water from the storm surges, which put him into a stinking mood, going from house to house sacking his laborers, kicking his sodden crops and yelling obscenities into the sky. He came to visit our house.

"Where is Gita?"

"I am here, Sahaab," said Gita, appearing from behind the house where she had been washing at the well.

"Times are hard for me now," said Mohan Lal after clearing his throat. "So I have no choice but to give you two options. Option one," sticking a fat finger in the air, "you clean my house and I pay you nothing. Option two, you take your belongings and get off my land because you are worthless to me."

"Those are the options?"

"Yes, one or two?"

"I- I will have to consider," said Gita.

"Considering is not an option."

"In that case, we must be gone." Gita glanced across at Shakti, who was too nervous to step forward. "I cannot feed a family on air."

"Leave tomorrow morning," Mohan Lal turned, leaving us only the waft of curried cauliflower and sweet tobacco.

Two of my sisters, I can't remember which ones, burst into tears. Gita stood rooted to the spot. I whispered unrepeatable words, learned from Shakti, under my breath while Shakti suddenly sprang to life, shouting unrepeatable words interspersed with, "This is all your fault, woman. Can't even hold down a job," all the while punching the flimsy front door with his fist.

"We better pack," Gita said calmly, as the lines deepened around her eyes.

There is only one thought that occupies the brains of the poor and that is a full belly. As we packed all of our possessions into two small straw bags, we were thinking only of our next full belly. Nothing else mattered.

With no work and therefore no income, we would have a hungry season but the next season and the season to follow, *our bellies would be full. We had faith, we were people of the land and the land would always provide.*

As we traipsed from field to field and farm to farm we saw nothing but uprooted crops, withered and dead stiff cattle, landowners wringing their hands. What we had not realized, because our lives were so small, was that the greater world was at war and beyond the Bay of Bengal, Burma (one of our main rice suppliers when our crops failed) had fallen to the Japanese who were now on their way to invade Bengal. Our colonial rulers were commanding all crops that survived the natural disasters be destroyed to ensure an absence of food for the invaders. There was nothing growing to fill our bellies and, due to administrative errors and the rich hoarding surplus supplies, food shortages existed throughout all of east India. So, as is the way of the world, as the rich gorged, the poor were left to starve.

Welcome to the Bengali Famine.

All we could do was head to the city away from the dormant land. Vultures circled overhead as we marched, we were sinews to snack on, organs to hollow out, bones to suck dry.

I walked with my eyes fixed to the ground for a banana skin, coconut husk or a nutshell—anything that would make an imprint in my belly. How evil we were, for should we see such a treasure, we would dive for it in a collective mass, bones clashing with bones, elbowing loved ones out of the way in order to seize the meagre prize.

I am embarrassed when I think back to my primal behavior. That there is such a need existing in me that I can cast those I love aside so mindlessly for my own good.

Hunger makes people mean and desperate.

We were trudging forward in a line, heads down, using all our strength to stay upright. Ahead was the family of one of my best friends, Janya. Her father carried Janya's baby brother on his back. He was a good father who did not drink and wanted only the best for his family. If he had any tears he would have let his thirsty children lick them as they ran down his cheeks. That was his nature. Instead he sobbed quietly from dehydrated eyes, as he turned off the main road and onto the train track that ran diagonally opposite. He did not change paths when the train approached. We tried to call him, "Get off the tracks," but our dry throats produced only whispers. The train attempted to stop, jammed on its brakes, hammered on its horn but its speed was too great as it rode into Janya's father and the baby on his back. It flew them sky high so they resembled little more than plastic bags caught up in a storm.

Janya's mother threw herself to the ground with grief, yet we trampled onwards, stepping over her, flattening her withered form.

"Stop," cried Janya, "please help us." But we didn't stop because we knew if we did, we would never get up again.

"Leave her, Janya," Gita said, "come with us or you too will be meat for the jackals." But Janya stayed with her mother, burying her head into her shriveled chest.

There was only one hope for us in Calcutta and that was Shakti's cousin, a rickshaw wallah named Jagat. We found him on Central Avenue and he offered Shakti the nightshift. He also gave us rice and made space for us to sleep alongside the sprawled out bodies of other homeless people clogging up the roadside, kicking arms and legs out of the way to make room for us. We used our scarves to make shade and stuck out our scrawny hands to well-to-do passersby begging for money or food or drink. As a beggar you are so desperate, you have no pride. You are grateful if people clean orange peel off the bottom of their shoes and hand it over.

Over the days that we begged, my family grew unrecognizable, their cheeks so sunken it was as if they were inverted, eyes wide and scared, hair thin, skin yellow. It seemed only I stayed bonny. I did not shrink in the same way that the rest of my family shrunk. Esha shrunk the most after getting a gastric flu and died one evening. After Esha it was Bijal who succumbed to starvation. We found her one morning, a dead bag of bones curled up alongside a dog's skeleton. We had no means for creating the ritual of fire or any kumbhas or clay pot to bless their passing or oils to rub on their foreheads or even any strength for mantras, we simply bowed our heads as my sisters, along with every other corpse on the street, were collected up and burned in a heap.

Shakti, once he had money in his pocket, kept it for himself and spent it on liquor. He would come swaying in mid-morning after a night on the rickshaw and dawn at a drinking den, urine stains across the front of his trousers, and collapse stinking and drunk wherever his legs gave way. He was mistaken once by the street cleaner for a corpse and would have been swept into the cart of the dead had I not, on a foolish impulse, called out.

I went through the pockets of his trousers when he was out cold, looking for coins and occasionally came across half a paise, which I used to buy whatever was available, sharing it with Leela or one of the women or girl beggars next-door but, even in the city, food was sparse. Everywhere was starving.

How desperate we were for the slightest morsel. One night I woke up from one of those half wake, half sleep dreams and found my mother locked in silent combat with another woman over a pea-sized pile of cat excrement. There were tiny chunks of meat in the excrement and to my mother they must have appeared enticing. I dragged myself across to my mother and pushed the other lady out of the way so that she toppled backwards and collapsed in a heap. There were maggots in the excrement.

"Stop, if we eat that we die," I said, pulling Gita away.

"If we don't eat it, we die," said Gita, trying weakly to poke the excrement with her fingertip.

"Perhaps," I replied. "But it is better to die of hunger than disease."

My mother collapsed on the floor and pulled her thin scarf across her emaciated body.

I was expecting her to be next in the line of death but we were blessed. A few days later, Jagat found work for Gita washing plates in a hospital.

After a couple of weeks of Gita's income, we were able to afford to come off the roadside and into bustees built on stilts along the flat swampy marshland on the east bank of the River Hooghley. The bustees were overcrowded and damp and the smell from the river, used as an open sewer, was repellent but at least we had privacy.

It was only a couple of weeks after moving into the bustees that Leela became ill with a high fever. I tried to look after her, find water for her and food, and bathe her head but she too died in my arms. I held her close to me for the whole afternoon until Gita came home and carried her away.

I was the only child left in my family, but I do not think Shakti realized this. The occasional times he came to the hut, he referred to me as Esha or Bijal or Leela and only sometimes Kamla. Cousin Jagat, however, did not have that problem. He was a small man with a hooked nose and straight, straggly hair. He started coming not long after Leela died.

"Gita thought you might be lonely, Kamla." Or, "I was just passing and thought I might drop in."

At first this was once a week but after a while it increased to twice a week and then every day. He always bought something for me like a feather or a stone.

"Do you like your gift?" he would ask with insistence. I always thought of him as a restless man because he never sat, just paced the room like a trapped lion. I realize now that this was because he wanted me.

"Do you know, Kamla," he said one day. "When someone gives you precious things you have to say thank you."

"Thank you," I said.

"Do you want to keep getting precious things?"

I nodded.

"Then you must do something for me."

I nodded.

"You must let me feel inside your panties. Just a little touch to say thank you."

"Will it hurt?"

"Of course not."

I didn't believe him because I had seen Mohan Lal do similar things to Gita and it had hurt her.

It did hurt because he was rough. I hit his hand away and he hit me back.

"No," I shouted.

He slapped me around the face.

"Just a little feel. That is all, Kamla."

"No." He pushed me onto the floor and pinned my arms up behind my head before sticking his fingers into my knickers and up inside me. I screamed and kicked him away but, the more I kicked, the harder he stabbed me.

"You are being very naughty," said Jagat. "No more treats for you."

"I don't want treats," I shouted.

"Good," said Jagat. "Then we are square."

He removed his fingers, pulled up my panties and released my arms.

"I know you want this coin I have here," he said flashing half a paise before me. "Because I know you are hungry and want to buy something, don't you, Kamla? If you don't tell anybody about what just happened you can have this now and another coin tomorrow and the next day."

I could have said that I didn't want a coin but, truth is, I did. Being hungry deadens the senses.

"I thought so," said Jagat. "Then say nothing and I will be back tomorrow to bring you another coin."

He came back the next day and the next, each time with a coin and each time feeling in my panties. I stopped making a fuss, which lulled Jagat into thinking I was happy with what he was doing. He even started laughing and chatting with me as he was doing it telling me how beautiful my eyes and hair was. Really, what I was doing was directing every bit of negative energy I could muster into hatred for him. The anger I felt was so immense I found it hard to walk along the street without kicking or punching. In my anger for Jagat I also felt anger at Gita because, what Jagat had done to me, Mohan Lal had done to her, except that she had accepted it. She had kept going back for more even though she hated every moment of it. Both she and I had had to endure pain and indignity in order to satisfy the sexual greed of men.

A few days later there were job cuts at the hospital and Gita was without work. We had to leave the hut and head back onto living on the street, which came as a relief to me as it meant I would no longer be left alone with Jagat.

The streets of Calcutta resembled a funeral pyre, bodies piled on top of each other, animals prowling. Four million bodies in one year died in the Bengali famine. I ask you, how can one ever get used to the sight of dead people? Is it normal to stop seeing the dead in all their helpless naked form like it is normal to stop minding flies?

Gita and I were not alone in begging on the street. Everywhere we turned there were women and children like us. Men were few and far between. It was women having to go without, for their children. Whenever Shakti turned up wasted, Gita made him comfortable. It never seemed to cross her mind that his greed had deprived her and me and my dead siblings of sustenance. One time, as she gently dabbed the spittle of Shakti's chin, I asked her why.

"How can you still care for that man when he doesn't care about you?"

"He is my husband, your father."

"But he is letting us die so that he can drink."

"It is my duty as his wife, that is all."

I never pressed her further because I was too weak and she was too weak. It is a miracle that both my mother and I survived the famine. It is also a miracle that, when left alone with my thieving father, I did not kill him.

The sun was now a bit lower but still warm, still relaxing, as Maya read. But she also wondered about these men. Kamla had grown up with such terrible men. Thank God we as women are not so dependent anymore. Thank God her Ronnie is not like Shakti or Jagat. Thank God Kamla's handwriting is so legible, she smiled, but poor poor little girl, she thought, as she picked up the next letter. No wonder she was so strong.

-4-

1951

You know, Maya, I never planned to marry. Ever since seeing that animal Mohan Lal molesting Gita, I planned never even to be with a man. This in turn, was reinforced by Shakti's pitifulness and Jagat's abuse.

The person I married though was not like these men. I shall tell you about him.

After the famine I discovered I had a gift of caring for people, or rather caring for women. Men did not feature in my life. Perhaps I was lonely after the death of my sisters because I craved women's company. I found voluntary work preparing beds, cleaning toilets at a women's refuge close to the busy Chittaranjan Avenue in the middle of the city. The refuge was a series of small, white bungalows with dormitories inside, positioned around an outdoor dining area with palm trees and sweet smelling magnolia.

Funded by international philanthropists, it did not offer a wage but it gave me food and a simple room of my own and I was keen to move away from Gita and Shakti who, thanks to Gita working back at the hospital, were able to rent a small room ten minutes away, across the avenue.

I should just say that you cannot suffer the loss of three of your four daughters like Gita did without enduring severe grief. Gita never recovered. She lived her life like a ghost, floating through the days, cold and lifeless. She was driven by only one thing and that was the thought of finding me a husband. For me the idea was detestable, I had no desire to be married off and it was partly for this reason that I moved away.

The women in the refuge had suffered abuse, homelessness, shame and neglect. Many had turned to prostitution during the famine and been subsequently rejected by their families. They were all women like me, peasant girls of a lowly caste, the only difference between us was that I could read and write and they were blind to such pleasures. The women became my friends. I made up stories for them not dissimilar to the ones I had read under the table from the brown book at Mohan Lal's.

I was not afraid to stand up for what I believed in. Perhaps because I had no desire to marry and was outspoken in my disdain for men, I became something of a role model to the young women, showing them that it was acceptable to be alone. This was all modern thinking for these times, my dear. Already as I write this in the 1980s there are fewer women marrying and the divorce rate is rising, but Hindu marriage is sacred and, in the 1950s, a woman's place was most definitely in the care of a man.

Unfortunately the freedom I proclaimed for myself at the refuge did not match my real life. All the time I was belittling men and extolling the virtues of a single life, Gita was frantically trying to find me a perfect match or perhaps simply a match.

She found one in the form of a boy called Anish Gill. I say boy, he was 19, a little older than me. Anish, the son of a shopkeeper, worked in his father's hardware shop. Gita and I were invited to his parent's home for a pre-marriage meeting above the shop.

The moment I saw Anish I did not trust him. He had in his eyes the same craving I saw in the eyes of the men I hated. Craving for control, for sex, for power.

The purpose of the meeting was for everyone to meet and agree on the marriage. I was expected to be the shy bride-in-waiting, eyes lowered, modestly giggling behind my hand but this was not the approach I opted for. In the few moments I had to speak, I informed the gathering of my love for education, of how one day I wished to be manager of the women's refuge, that I did not care for children and, best of all, I announced that I was born on the day of the Durga puja and had been blessed with the spirit of the goddess.

"That is all, thank you, Kamla," said Gita. "And now, tell us about yourself, Anish?"

"Enough of this talk about yourself, Kamla," said Gita as we departed the modest home off the Bangur Avenue and walked the uneven path back into central Calcutta.

"Marriage is your dharma."

It was dharma—my duty—that I most feared.

After this, I waited to hear that the wedding had been called off because I was not the right match for Anish. This did not happen. Instead a date was set for the marriage on the 6th June.

"But how could they want a daughter-in-law like me?" I asked Gita in desperation. "I will never adapt to my duty."

"Anish's family believe your free spirit is simply a phase that you will pass through as you mature into womanhood. They are looking forward to you moving into their home and caring for them and their son."

"I won't," I cried.

As the day loomed, I had to inform the women at the refuge that, despite my contempt for it, I too was succumbing to marriage. I felt like I was letting my friends down. I felt also like I was letting myself down, giving in to Gita's expectations. There were many tears that evening as I shattered the bubble I had created in these women's dreams.

The goddess moves in mysterious and compassionate ways and she was indeed moving in such a manner throughout the 4.5 million inhabitants of Calcutta on the morning of 27th May, ten days before my wedding day. A girl named Anika was brought into the refuge with half of her face missing after the cousin of one of her friends threw household chemicals at her. The hospital had done little to help because there is not *much that can be done to mend a face that is burned through. She was fifteen and was soon to be matched up with a husband. After the attack her family rejected her, such was the shame of having an ugly, unmarriageable daughter.*

Like with all the women at the refuge, we took her in and listened to her side of the story. Her friend's cousin had attacked her because she refused to succumb to his sexual demands. The story was not a new one for women in the refuge. Men do not like women who refuse but, at the same time, they expect women to be pure. The man who did this to Anika was a 19-year old called Anish who worked in a hardware store off Bangar Avenue.

"Describe him please," I said to Anika, my skin prickling.

"His family name?"

It just so happened that the Anish who burned off half of Anika's face was the same Anish with whom in ten days' time I was to consummate a lifetime union.

It was wonderful news.

"We will not cancel the wedding, Kamla," said Gita. "Anish will be full of remorse for his actions. Men err, it is what they do. Our role is to offer forgiveness."

"Either we cancel or I will not turn up."

"Yah, Kamla, when did you become such a difficult daughter?"

"The day my sisters died in my arms because my father starved them to death. I believe it was sometime around then."

"Enough Kamla! How can you make light of my grief?"

Gita eventually offered to speak with the parents of Anish who refused to believe that their son had been involved in the attack and stated that Kamla must simply be suffering pre-wedding nerves.

"The marriage will go ahead, Kamla," said Gita. "More shame will come to you for being too old to marry, than from marrying a less than perfect man."

The marriage did not go ahead. I do not know of the events that occurred behind the closed doors of the Gill family home but Gita came to the refuge (a place she was wary of due to its "modern attitudes") and whispered to me over the hissing of the steam iron that the Gill family had called off the marriage.
"Anish said he did not want to marry a girl of such spirit. See Kamla, I told you your spirit would be the end of you."

As it happened something far greater happened to me anyway on the 6th of June. I was offered a position at the medical dispensary compound across a narrow lane from the refuge, helping with receiving patients, applying dressings and dispensing medicines. I was earning a salary of three rupees a day. I was also permitted to keep my room at the refuge if I volunteered to keep cleaning at weekends, which of course I was happy to do because the refuge was the center of my world. This position brought me great pleasure.
Gita was very upset indeed at the abandoning of the marriage. She felt she had not only failed in the upbringing of her one remaining daughter but she had lost the only focus that kept her mind off her grief. To make it up to her I suggested with my newly acquired income, that we go for a day trip together back to Kamalgazi to get away from the city. We both had our fears at such a trip, as it would of course be a reminder of all we had lost but I was hopeful it might also be of some comfort to Gita and give her some respite from my father.

We were to travel by tram, meeting at 7.30 am at the stop in between both of our homes. I was there on time and waited for Gita but she did not come. After 8 o'clock passed I decided to go and fetch Gita who must have been held up.

It was at least a month since I had been to my parent's home, a tiny room on the third floor of a dilapidated apartment block with shutters rotting off the windows and a central winding staircase draped with laundry. Everywhere smelled of incense and sweat. I tried to avoid visiting my parents, as I did not like to come face to face with Shakti, which Gita was aware of and that was why she always came to me.

There was no answer when I knocked but the door was unlocked.

"Mam-mi," I called, walking in and almost tripping over Shakti, face down on the floor, lungee gathered up around his buttocks. He was snoring long and deep.

"Mam-mi?" stepping over Shakti into the room, I saw Gita sprawled backwards over the room's one solitary chair, hair clotted with blood, eyes half open. I had seen enough corpses to know she was dead. There was a bottle smashed on the floor beside her and cuts up and down her arm. I guessed she had bled to death after being hit over the head with a bottle of cheap Indian wine.

I kicked Shakti awake with all the force I could muster, hammering into his scrawny rib cage causing him to cough and splutter.

"What have you done?" I cried. "What have you done?" I was screaming as I kicked and punched, slamming his stupid thick skull against the stone floor. I wanted him dead, god how I wanted that man's blood to spill. I really think I might have killed him there and then except that I was grabbed by two women and pinned back against the wall.

"Stop or you will go to prison," they shouted as I tried to free myself from their hold. "You will be the one to go to prison if you kill him."

They were wise women, a mother and her daughter, Gita's next-door neighbors. They understood the way of the justice system in India and I am eternally grateful they made me stop. Killing my father would have made me the villain.

Shakti had no memory of killing Gita although his fingerprints were on the smashed bottle and also around Gita's neck where he had previously tried to strangle her.

Shakti went to prison for killing Gita and I never saw him again. I heard some years later that he died in prison but I never attended his cremation—perhaps nobody did.

I went back alone to Kamalgazi a few weeks later with a neem tree sapling, you might know it as an Indian lilac, to plant in my mother and sisters' memory, the neem tree being a sacred manifestation of Durga.

It was with a heavy heart that I arrived alone at the paddy fields of my birth. They were lush and the neighborhood was alive with cooking and washing and half-dressed children scampering around. I felt like a ghost visiting a past life as I slipped into the scene, wanting to observe but not be seen. My purpose there would have required too much explaining. The big house still loomed over the fields but Mohan Lal was no longer the owner. He had sold the house, fearful that it would be overrun by Japanese during the war, and moved to Bombay. I wondered if he had taken the brown book with him. I doubted it. He had no love for books. It most probably ended up on a fire.

The banyan tree on the edge of the forest was still standing, of course, and I made my way along the edge of the field, watched by one solitary child with thick shiny short hair, brushing her teeth with a twig.

"What are you doing?" she asked, as I stuck my arm into the hole mid-way up the trunk. My arm was longer now that I was not a child; I did not have to dig so deep.

"Just looking for something that I hid here when I was about your age."

"Is it a frog?"

"No, it is.... this," I said, as my hand closed over a bunch of leaves.

As I unwrapped the leaf nest I had made all those years ago I saw the clay figurine lying there perfect, not a crack or a blemish on her. How could she have remained so complete when my world was broken?

"May I touch her?" the girl asked.

"You can hold her..." I said, handing the patima over.

The girl hugged the goddess up to her chest.

"Just promise you will leave her here, wrapped up in the leaves in the tree and don't tell anyone," I said. "Keep it a secret yah?"

Together the girl and I dug a hole for the Neem Tree just out of the shade of the Banyan Tree.

"In 150 years' time, this tree will be one of the tallest in the big forest," I said.

"Cool," said the girl. "Maybe it can protect our statue."

"Or maybe she can protect you."

Her mother was murdered, Maya thought. I had not known that. They kept it from me. Kamla must have hated men, deep down. Now the sky showed a brilliant sun beginning its descent. She felt, sitting there against the tree, like she was the sun traveling through a century. I'll go on reading. There is much I did not know. But she had to have married eventually ...

-5-

1953

I believe I am telling you how my marriage came about.

I was working at the medical dispensary, which I enjoyed—not only because I was caring for the patients but also because of the company of the medical dispenser, Rajeev. It was a small dispensary consisting only of an elderly nurse, a doctor, Rajeev and me.

This medical dispenser, Rajeev, was a quiet, studious man in his mid-twenties with thick curly hair, small round glasses and a wide smile that lit up his face. He loved reading like I loved reading although we did not share the same tastes. I preferred books about travel and adventures whereas he liked reading about history and politics. We spent our lunchtime breaks sitting side by side reading our books and eating our rice, occasionally sharing facts from our books or comments on the morning.

Rajeev was not like any of the other men I had known. He was gentle and funny, thinking nothing of teasing me if I tied my long hair up in a new style or pronounced one of the patient's names wrong, which occasionally I did because, remember, I had never learned to read out loud, which is when one corrects one's pronunciation errors. He always asked me how I was each day and whether I had any questions from the morning's session that I would like him to answer.

What I liked best was when he asked me my opinion on important matters.

"Which country do you think the West favors most, India or Pakistan?"

"Who is a better leader? Gandhi or Nehru?"

"Where would you rather live -- in the mountains or by the sea?"

Or my favorite sort of questions:

"What medicine would you recommend for somebody suffering from earache?"

"What is the role of the pancreas?"

I suppose you could say it was the first time a man had taken any interest in me. I don't mean interest in me as a face or a shape, I mean interest in me as a person. Rajeev knew that I had no interest in marrying or having children. I told him this not more than twenty minutes after we met because I did not want complications in our working relationship. He understood and said that he was engaged to be married to a girl called Anita in Delhi and would marry her as soon as her family returned to Calcutta.

As we were both unobtainable, we were able to form a friendship without pressure.

Rajeev was an educated man with a pharmacy diploma. His father was a history teacher and always pushed Rajeev to study hard. It was his mother, a nurse who had encouraged him to go into the medical profession, because she saw that he had a caring nature, and he had listened to his mother. The girl Rajeev was matched to marry was the daughter of a doctor. When I was with my friends at the refuge I felt educated, they turned to me with questions or for advice. Around Rajeev, however, I knew so little.

"Don't put yourself down," Rajeev would say when I told him I was nothing more than a peasant girl. "Where would this country be without people of the land?"

He knew the story of my family and made no judgment when I told him that I hated Shakti and hoped he would soon die in prison.

Our working day was meant to finish at 5 pm, which is when the doctor and nurse left but often we worked late, preparing for the day ahead or ordering in new medicines. We worked as a team, he would read out what needed ordering and I would write it down because I loved the way my writing flowed when I used his ink pen. It started to be a habit that I would go to the refuge next-door to collect my evening meal, sneak it out and share it with him in the dispensary just so we could extend the evening longer. He said he never thought overcooked vegetables could taste so good.

When Rajeev went away for a week to celebrate his cousin's wedding he was replaced by a fat, middle-aged man with yellow teeth and bad breath, who only spoke to me in snapped commands. It was a long, miserable week. When Rajeev came back I was so relieved I punched the air, which made Rajeev laugh and made me realize that I was in love with him.

It was a shocking discovery for I had no wish to ever be beholden to a man but Rajeev was so much more than a man. He was everything and I wanted him. I went from being carefree and frivolous in his presence to being serious and intense. When he teased me, I took it to heart and the questions he casually threw my way almost caused my brain to explode, I was so intent on giving the right answers.

Worst of all, I was jealous.

"Anita's brother is in Calcutta this weekend, I am going with him to the cricket."

"Yah, why are you telling me this, Rajeev? I have no interest in cricket."

"Nor does Anita," replied Rajeev. "She says it sends her to sleep."

"Well, I don't dislike it that much. Most probably Anita doesn't understand the rules."

"Yah, Kamla, and I suppose you are an expert?"

"I am sure I know more than Anita."

"I am sure you do, too. Anita has no interest in bats and balls."

"Well, she should, if she is to be your wife. She should care for everything that you care for."

"Ah, so you are an expert on marriage now are you, Kamla?"

"I believe I know what makes a good one."

"And you have learned this from all your many husbands, I suppose?"

"I have learned it because I know about life, Rajeev, something all women should know about before they become dependent on a man. That is, if you want a happy wife."

"I will let you know how happy Anita is with me."

"Well, for one thing, she should care about cricket."

And so I went on like this, sulky, creating mountains out of molehills simply to prove a point. It continued on like this for a couple of weeks until the night of the storm. As usual, Rajeev and I were working past 5 pm. I had collected my food from the refuge and we had eaten together arguing about the best way to cook rice or peel jackfruit or something as trivial as this. We spent a lot of our time playfully bickering nowadays. Well, Rajeev was playful, I was more often irritable.

We knew there was a storm coming because it made no attempt to disguise itself, wind speeds were increasing, doors and windows rattling. There were lightning and thunderbolts far in the distance. As we came to leave, I went to open the dispensary door but the power of the wind pulled it out of my hand and slammed it back into my face smashing into my nose and jamming my fingers in the door hinges.

"Kamla, are you OK?" cried Rajeev throwing down his briefcase and running over. There was blood pouring out of my nostrils and my fingers were turning black.

He directed me to a chair and padded around gathering up tissues and creams and dressings.

"Come, put your head back, let me check nothing is broken. Can you move your fingers?"

Gently yet with such expertise he stemmed the blood and rubbed cream into the cut on the bridge of my nose.

"Let me see your hands," he said taking my hands into his own.

"Bruised but not broken," he softly stroked my nails. "Your fingers are so long and slender, Kamla," he said continuing to stroke them. "And your hands too." I went to pull them away but he held fast.

"In fact, so are your arms Kamla, so smooth, I don't believe you grew up in the countryside. I think you were brought up in a palace and pampered every day."

"I wish."

"I bet you had servants who bathed your hands in oils and massaged your knuckles before breakfast. Am I right?"

I said nothing. I was unable to speak. Fireworks were exploding through every inch of me. He pulled up a chair and sat before me.

"You just lay there in a silky night dress, didn't you, smelling of jasmine while your handmaids buffed and polished. Correct?" Taking my hand he laid it across his stubbly cheek and over to his lips and kissed it with moist, firm lips. Then he kissed my arm, my elbow and, pushing up the sleeve of my blouse, he kissed the top of my arm. Pulling me towards him both gently and deftly, he kissed my shoulder up to my neck and across my collarbone to the shoulder. He continued to the other side, beneath the blouse on my other arm, down the arm onto my other hand. When he had completed this circuit he looked up at me, eyes sparkling.

"I've loved you forever, Kamla."

"Is forever seven months, twenty-two days and 11 hours?" I whispered.

There was a flash of lightning.

"Add another thirty-four days because that is when I first spotted you the day you came in here to pick up some medicine for the refuge."

"You saw me then?"

"I saw you and I loved you all at the same time." He was taking my fingers one by one and stroking them.

"But I was only in here for thirty seconds."

"I knew it after fifteen. You spoke, you smiled, you laughed, you walked with that bounce in your step and I was in love."

"And then you got to know me?"

"And I loved you even more. Why else would I endure evening after evening eating cold, soggy dinners from the refuge?"

"But you love Anita?"

"No. I feel no love for her," he kissed my fingers again.

"Because she doesn't understand cricket as well as me?"

"Only for that reason."

"This is going to get complicated," I said.

"Life is always complicated if you complicate it."

"What about your marriage?"

"I have been engaged to Anita for three years and in this time I have only seen her four times. A lot can happen in three years."

"Your parents will hate me. I am a peasant."

"They will grow to love you."

"And if they don't?"

"They will. Leave my parents to me."

Life did, of course, get complicated. Rajeev broke off his engagement to Anita and there was upset in his family. He came into work on a couple of occasions looking drawn and tired like he had endured an emotional evening but he always shielded me from this, saying only that "everyone will come around." At work he was just like he had always been: teasing, joking, patient. In the evenings we stayed late and kept eating the soggy tasteless refuge food because I didn't want any of the women at the refuge, who had been so beaten and battered, to get any hint of a change in our blooming relationship.

It was during these hours, though, that we were intimate. We might have known each other better than many young couples prior to marriage but there was still a lot we wanted to know.

It was over the occasion of the refuge's unusually tasteful creamy beetroot curry that Rajeev chose the moment. We were sitting at his desk in the back of the dispensary surrounded by glass medicine jars, stethoscope, blood pressure monitors and bandages. We had long ago become oblivious to the permanent smell of disinfectant but it was everywhere.

"This has to be one of the most delicious dishes that the refuge has ever served up," Rajeev announced positively relishing every mouthful. "There is only one thing that must take place in order to ensure this becomes the happiest meal of my life."

"Salt?" I asked.

Throwing his earthenware plate into a pile of papers on his desk, Rajeev stood up and clasped hold of me around my waist, pulling me up.

"Kamla, please would you marry me?" he asked, twirling me around.

"So, no salt then?"

"Kamla?"

"Of course I would love to marry you even though I intend never to get married," I replied, letting him pull me close to him.

"Pretend marriage where we have a wedding, consummate our vows and stay together and in love until we die."

"Yes, I can definitely do one of those marriages."

"Sounds perfect to me, pretend-wife."
"I love how you say that, make-believe-husband."

*I could tell you about the first time I met Rajeev's family at
his home, a smart townhouse in the center of Calcutta. Of how
his Baap greeted me politely but his Maa stayed back only
becoming animated when I told her of my interest in
medicines and administering to patients. I could tell you of
our wedding, which was happy but also sad because I had no
family of my own to look after me, give me away, to grow
excited with, no one to tell of my love for Rajeev.*

*The purpose of my letter to you, however, is to provide you
with insight into the men of my generation, so I will push on
with the story of our married life.*

*After the wedding we bought a small house together close
to the refuge and the medical dispensary. Rajeev got a better
paying job working at Calcutta Medical College and Hospital
and I received a promotion at the medical dispensary which
enabled me to order and log medicines as well as to
administer dressings and provide basic wound care. I was also
given a paid evening job at the refuge once a week offering
therapy to women who had suffered abuse. I loved this job
passionately as I realized I had a gift for listening and offering
support. I still volunteered as a cleaner at the refuge but only
on two Saturdays a month in order to ensure Rajeev and I had
time to spend together.*

We were happy.

*Rajeev taught me how to cook curries, saag and pakora,
something his mother had taught him. I showed Rajeev how to
care for our tiny garden. We planted a lemon tree and a peach
tree.*

He was keen to start a family and, because I was so secure in my love with Rajeev, it was something I was happy to consider even if it meant me having to curb my work.

At first we tried for a baby casually, "If it happens, it happens, but it would be good to have a bit longer as just the two of us."

Rajeev was an inquisitive lover. He cared greatly about discovering what it was that I wanted.

"Do you like it when I touch this?"

"What does it feel like if I feel you there?"

In turn, he liked me to be inquisitive too. "Here, put your hand here," he would say steering my fingers onto his penis. "I love it when you touch me here" he would gaze at me with hunger in his eyes, his breath hot.

When no pregnancy came, we became philosophical. "It will happen but things just take time." Our lovemaking got a little more rigid, less playful. After eight months of trying there became a subtle urgency about the situation. Rajeev mixed herbs and lotions for me to rub on my belly or consume at certain times of the month. He was always tender and reassuring but there was an edge of concern. Having no family of my own, I had none of the pressure that Rajeev had to endure from his family who asked constantly when a baby was coming.

"What are you waiting for, Rajeev? Wrinkles?"

Rajeev made an appointment for us to visit a doctor from the hospital, a school friend of his who examined me and asked me questions about my diet and my childhood. I didn't tell him about Jagat and what he did to me in the privacy of my house in the bustees. It didn't seem relevant. Jagat had never penetrated me. I was to all intents and purposes a virgin when Rajeev and I married. Why complicate issues?

The doctor claimed to find nothing wrong.

"Everything is where it should be doing what it is meant to do, Rajeev, your wife is just a little emotionally exhausted. Make sure she rests a lot and eats well. Things will happen, my friend."

But nothing did.

We tried to behave like life between us was normal, laughing, teasing and chatting like we always had, but Rajeev was sad. He became quieter like his mind was forever churning, although whenever I asked him what he was thinking he would simply reply, "About us," or "About work."

As his brothers and sisters started having babies, he became an uncle time and time again and the bitterness showed.

"Oh, another boy. Surely two is enough?" he said to his sister as she brought around her third to show us.

When word slipped out from his sister, that his Maa blamed his inability to have a baby on his breaking up the engagement with Anita, Rajeev became livid and stormed to his family home.

"I am only saying, Rajeev," his mother said, "we made the perfect match and you chose a gandharva marriage. If you marry for love, it comes with risk."

"This has nothing to do with my falling in love with Kamla."

"Hmm, maybe...maybe not," his Maa said, "but what do we know of her heritage?"

"Stop it, Maa, I love Kamla and that is all that matters."

At least, this was how he translated the conversation back to me and yes, I am sure this was how the conversation went, after all any agreement with his mother would have reflected badly on the decisions Rajeev took. I cannot say, however, that his mother did not plant a seed in his mind because that is what mothers do. They have a way of unearthing deep underlying concerns in their offspring and casually airing them. That was the only explanation I could find for Rajeev's sudden change. Almost overnight he became a critic.

"Kamla, why do you sit like that all sprawled on the chair, you should be more ladylike."

"Yah, Kamla, look at how you grip your fork rather than balance it like this, maybe you're a caveman, ha-ha."

At first I laughed his comments off. "Hush yourself, Rajeev, I didn't know the Queen was coming to visit." But when the reproaches became increasingly consistent, they began to hurt.

"Enough, Rajeev, if you have nothing kind to say, please don't speak."

"But if something is bothering me I should say it, Kamla. That is what you always tell me."

"Well, my new advice to you is, think before you speak."

"Why so uptight, Kamla? Can't I even tease you anymore?"

Of course, there were still moments of tenderness between us, when we cuddled and laughed and when Rajeev tended to me but it seemed they were fewer and far between. I began to work longer hours at the refuge undertaking training courses in counseling and spending more time with the women listening and offering advice. This, in turn, began to annoy Rajeev who wanted ample opportunity to make love to me in the hope that one of our lovemaking sessions would yield a child.

And one day it did. I realized I was pregnant when the smell and taste of my beloved chai turned me nauseous.

"Nauseous you say, like hot and dizzy?" said Rajeev looking up from the Times of India.

"Yes, too hot and dizzy to go to work and I think...." I cried leaping up from my chair, "I am going to be..."

Sickness was a big part of my pregnancy but the happiness and pride that my being pregnant bought to Rajeev cancelled out all of the ill effects. I am not sure if there has ever been a man more attentive to the needs of his fat, bloated wife. He transformed from ratty to loyal, affectionate puppy almost instantly. I wanted for nothing, I did nothing except grow fatter and, on October 2, 1959, when I was 22 years old, I gave birth to our beloved daughter, Rajika.

For someone who had never wanted a family or husband, I was in bliss. And that love for my child and then you, no matter what life has brought, has never changed.

-6-

There could have been issues between Rajeev and myself in bringing up a daughter. What I wanted for my daughter, Rajika, was for her to be independent, strong, educated and, of course, kind. Every person needs to have kindness. Fortunately, Rajeev wanted the same. He could cope with strong women in his life and was in full support of a fair and equal marriage. He encouraged Rajika to take an interest in history and medicine and would give her quizzes on the names of worldwide politicians.

"Name the Prime Minister of Great Britain?"

"And the President of the USA?"

"Which countries belonged to the Mughal Empire?"

Of course, he dreamed of having a son, what Indian man didn't in those times but, despite all of our education and interest in health, bearing children did not come naturally to us. We kept trying and hoping but we bore no results. We were a small but happy family.

As soon as Rajika began school I went back to work at the refuge as a counselor, healing victims of domestic abuse and violence. I advised them on becoming independent, finding paths of their own, on feeling empowered and promoting self-preservation in themselves. Little did I know that the information I was imparting to these women would one day become highly relevant to me.

1969

I did not see it coming. Rajika was ten years old. The Friday began as it always began, with Rajeev reading the Times of India over a cup of tea and a plate of bread and vegetables. He was dressed in his blue suit with the faint stripes and wore his red and purple tie to add flair to an otherwise dull attire. His hair was combed to the side, the curls flattened with a Brylcreem shine. He wasn't one of those men who opened the paper wide and hid behind it, preferring instead to read it folded in two so as to be accessible should I or Rajika address him. He routinely read every single word printed in the newspaper, which meant it lasted the whole day. Breakfast incorporated Indian and World news while Sport, Finance and Comment were reserved for throughout the day. Rajika sat beside him, as she did each morning, with her glass of milk, banana and chunk of bread, as absorbed in Louisa May Alcott's Little Women as he was in the inauguration of Richard Nixon. I was busy preparing for my day, which ironically included giving a lecture at the refuge to workers in the healthcare industry on "early signs of abuse." A normal day by all accounts except, looking back, there was one major exception.

Normally, Rajika left the house first on the dot at 7.45am with her satchel hooked over her shoulder, followed by Rajeev at 8am with his briefcase in his hand and his sunglasses on his head and finally me at 8.15 with my stack of papers and packed lunch. Today, however, Rajeev was still lingering as I prepared to go.

"Aren't you going to be late?" I asked him.

"That's OK, my meeting has been postponed until 8.45 so I don't need to be at work until then. You go on ahead."

I kissed Rajeev goodbye, like I always did. Affection was a big part of our marriage. Every day there was a kiss or a hug between us, which might have been unusual for long term married couples in those days. Rajeev kissed me back, his lips still warm from his milky tea.

I went to work and gave my lecture, counseled a pregnant woman new to the refuge who had been raped by her father-in-law, had my lunch sitting on a rickety wooden chair in the refuge dining area. After lunch I had a meeting with staff in the refuge about upcoming budget cuts, said goodbye to the refuge inmates and made my way home. It should have been a ten-minute walk from the refuge to home but it never was, as there was invariably a commotion involving a cow and a hand-pulled rickshaw, or goats blocking the tramway. So many unwieldy vehicles veered and weaved along the roads in those days. On this occasion it was a labor strike that held me up, not uncommon in the city, hundreds of angry campaigners spilling off the pavements onto the edge of the road holding up double decker buses. The streets were alive with car horns and shouting and bicycle bells. By the time I reached my house my ears were ringing, I was dusty and longing for a tall, cool drink.

The note was lying on the kitchen table next to Rajeev's empty teacup. It was folded over with my name across the front written in black ink in Rajeev's typically medical illegible scrawl. After my name there was a full stop. It was not unusual for Rajeev, Rajika or I to write each other notes, "Will be late tonight" or "Just popped out"' style exchanges. We rarely folded the notes over or addressed them to anyone in particular.

I picked the note up and opened it.

Dear Kamla,
I am leaving you. I have loved you but that love is gone. Do not
    try to change my mind. It is made up.
Sincerely,
Rajeev

I sat down, slowly re-reading the note and reading it again.
My hand growing shakier with each read. "Leaving you." "Love
is gone." What did Rajeev mean? My Rajeev? He wouldn't
play games like this. Gone. The love can't have gone. How
gone? Where gone? Why gone? I hastened out of the chair and
went to the front door. The obvious thing was to go to Rajeev
and ask him what the note meant. I stopped. No, I will wait
for him to come home. He can explain. It must be a mistake.
"Rajeev... are you here?" I called into the house. "Rajeev?"

Leaving you?
Love is gone?

The words were going around and around in my head.
Love is gone. Not our love, our love was never going to leave.
We were going to love each other forever. It was real love,
proper love.

"Rajeev..." I called into the house again, growing angry.
"What is the meaning of this?" I stomped across the rug in the
hall into our tiny bedroom. Our clothes were in a heavy oak
wardrobe that was already in place when we moved in. It was
the main feature of the room, a wedding present Rajeev had
called it jokingly when he saw my excitement at being able to
hang my clothes up for the first time in my life. The wardrobe
had round metal handles as big as bracelets. Heart racing, I
stuck my fingers in the handles and pulled open the doors and
came face to face with a line of empty coat hangers. I sobbed
and collapsed onto the floor. Every pair of socks, pants,
trousers, every handkerchief, shirt, tie and jacket had been

removed. *Only in my side of the wardrobe were there clothes neatly folded, blouses hanging, not quite taking up half the wardrobe as, by choice, I never had as much to wear as Rajeev.*

I stood staring into the yawning void. "Rajeev, what have you done?"

It was the same in the bathroom, shaving brush, foam, razor, tooth brush and nostril clippers gone from the bathroom cabinet, three empty shelves in the living room where he had removed his hardbacks as well as his trophy for lightweight boxing and athletics. I felt like I was waking from a dream where Rajeev existed, back into a reality where he had never stepped foot.

"Rajeev, what have you done?" That was all I could say as I breathlessly checked and re-checked the house flying from room to room for something left behind. Something to indicate he had not really gone. Something so necessary he couldn't live without it. But the house was swept clean of everything Rajeev related. He had even emptied the drawer of miscellaneous items in his bedside table. The one with the leaflets and plugs, dried up pens, old notebooks empty jars, and letters from his relatives.

I did not hear Rajika come into the house although she told me she called out when she arrived. She walked into the bedroom and found me sitting on Rajeev's side of the bed, head in my hands. She had seen the note on the table.

"What does it mean Mam-mi?"

"I'm not sure ..." I answered attempting to straighten up but slumping straight back down.

"It says he doesn't love you anymore but what does that mean?"

"I don't know. I am trying to understand."

"Where has he gone?"

"I don't know, Rajika. I know nothing more than you."

"But why would he go?"

Rajika sat down on the bed beside me, trying to nestle in under my arm but I barely noticed her. She had to lift my arm up and climb beneath it before I even registered she was there.

"He will come back, Mam-mi. I know he will."

"Yes, Rajika."

"He loves us."

I said nothing but my mind was turning and churning. Did he love us? When did he last tell us he loved us? Was it that morning? Did I miss the clues? Some sign of something wrong? Was he unhappy?

"He does, doesn't he Mam-mi? He does love us?"

"He does love us, Rajika. He's just confused."

"Shall we go and collect him, surprise him at his work?"

This was something Rajika and I had done once or twice when he was working late. We would take a tram across the city to the hospital and sneak up behind Rajeev in his office except we rarely took him by surprise because Rajika had never mastered the art of whispering. He always feigned surprise and would chase Rajika around the room pretending to be the policeman catching a burglar. Rajika loved it at the hospital where she got to sniff and poke in all of the medicine jars, trying on Rajeev's white coat.

"Come meet the loves of my life," he used to say about us to any passing colleague, beaming proudly at Rajika and me.

I felt sick.

"Yes, perhaps we should go," I said not moving.

"Come on then," said Rajika jumping up and pulling my hand.

Do not try to change my mind.

"I can't, we mustn't. Let's wait. I am sure he will come home. He can't just walk away from his life."

We waited all weekend for Rajeev to return, a weekend that seemed to last for weeks with so many possible scenarios rushing around our heads.

"All a joke, early April fools." Or "My loves, I made a mistake." Or "I must be mad, what was I thinking?" Or "I got a promotion at work and have bought us a new house. Shut your eyes, let me lead you to it."

None of our scenarios showed Rajeev never coming back. That just wasn't possible. Except by Sunday evening the reality hit. Perhaps he was gone.

"What did we do wrong?" asked Rajika.

"We did nothing wrong, my love. It is your father who is wrong."

We were lying on Rajika's bed where we had been for much of the weekend. I had no desire to sleep in my bed, not without Rajeev. As we lay there lost in our own thoughts the anger began to surge. It was the anger that spurred me into successfully undertaking my work at the refuge, anger that enabled me to speak of words like "liberation," "emancipation," succeeding in life without a man," "pride," "respect."

On Monday, Rajika went to school, bread and banana in her school bag to eat in her classroom. She could not face breakfast without Rajeev beside her at the table. When she was gone, I went into work at the refuge.

Up until this point in my life, all of my words, my training and my counseling were theoretical. I spoke of heartbreak and shame all the time, while being reassured that I was loved and cared for. How easy it is to comfort others when you are secure in yourself.

"Hi Kamla, good weekend?" asked Sammy, a therapist like me, half looking up from her clipboard as I walked into the dining area.

"Er, yes... you?"

"You look ill, everything alright?" she said eyeing me up and down.

"Just um ate something, churned up a bit."

"You sure?"

"No, not sure. If you really want to know, Rajeev left me." Sammy's jaw dropped.

"I was not expecting that. Rajeev?"

"Yes. Left a note on Friday."

"The bastard."

"I know." I tried not to cry but failed.

"I'm sorry, Kamla," Sammy hugged me. "I always thought Rajeev was one of the rare gems."

"He was," I said, "until his heart turned to stone."

"Be strong," Sammy said to me squeezing my wrist and heading off to the other countless women in the refuge to whom she would give the same advice, "Be strong." The refuge mantra: Be strong, stand on your own two feet, develop self-worth. It was advice given out daily to beaten, battered, desperate women like me.

It was the only way women were going to survive in a world where men had the upper hand and could just one day turn around and walk away, leaving their wives to pick up the pieces. That was how life was in my generation.

I found out eventually, Rajeev had fallen in love with a teenage nurse at the hospital, a smiley, submissive thing who laughed at his jokes and was there for him whenever he wanted her. I heard later on that his nurse had given birth to a baby son. He always wanted a boy. He simply stepped out of the life he had created for himself and straight into a new one. Meanwhile, my heart was broken and my world shattered.

Maya put the letter down. How sad. Poor Kamla. She always seemed so brave. Poor mammi, losing her father like that. What a terrible thing to happen to them. God, women's lives are so full of heartbreak. Maybe men's too, she didn't know. She picked up the letter again:

Darling Maya, you might be wondering why I have told you all this, involved you in the secrets of my heart. It is because I want you to know and to understand the hardships that women endure by being always subservient to men. Why do you think I have always gone on at you like a record that is stuck, to be independent, think for yourself, rely on nobody?

Getting over Rajeev, the man, did not take long, a few months perhaps. Dealing with the loss of my dreams, the grief of my daughter, the anger and the bitterness, that took a lot longer and, to be honest, I do not believe even now, as I write about this period of my life twenty years later, that I have fully got over it.

Rajeev wanted to sell our house so we were forced to move into a tiny apartment where my income barely covered the rent but it did have a small garden with a verandah. Perhaps to spite Rajeev, although he wouldn't have cared a drop for the sentimentality, I dug up the lemon and peach tree I had planted ten years before with Rajeev and replanted them in a sunny patch of my new garden.

I needed to work more hours at the refuge and ideally have another job in the evenings but Rajika needed me and I was not prepared to sacrifice my time with her. What I did do was throw myself into every aspect of my job advancing my knowledge of women's rights, of women's mental and sexual health, of caring for women as victims. I threw so much of my anger and misery into protecting and strengthening women that I grew hard-hearted to all men.

1975

I wonder, Maya, if you know your mother, Rajika, did not stay on the rails. The years following Rajeev's departure we were inseparable, spending every moment of our free time together. You could say it was intense, a woman approaching middle age and her pubescent daughter day in, day out but while we were recovering from the shock we wanted no one else and, with my relatives gone, there really was nobody else. With Rajeev we had been a family; now we were simply a unit. Rajika would accompany me to the refuge and spend time with the women. She grew up hearing stories of men killing women, women being abused and attacked and she came to understand that her story was no different to the millions circulating around Calcutta at any one time. I hoped this would make her stronger, less vulnerable but I do not believe she has ever got over Rajeev's rejection. Why do you think she married so wrong with your father? She sought a father figure in boys older than her, boys with motorbikes and flashy cars. She was hungry for love, dressing in short skirts, low tops. I am sorry to write to you about your mother like this but everything she did was "normal" behavior for girls who are rejected by their fathers. I do not know how much of herself she gave to these relationships. What I can tell you is, that for the two years this "playfulness" lasted, I was a nervous wreck expecting any day to receive the news that my beloved daughter was pregnant or attacked or, worst of all, emotionally damaged. The only blessing was that Rajika kept her head for her studies. We argued about her going out, the time she came in, the way she dressed, whom she spent time with but I never had to say to her, "Do your homework" or "Study for your exams." This gave me hope. Deep down, despite all of her mutiny and soul searching, my daughter knew that the best way forward for any woman was education. Something that was also instilled in you, as you have proven time and again with all your business success.

I suppose what I am trying to say to you is, don't rush into love. Men are not the key to happiness. You are young and headstrong and modern and you know so much more about life than I ever knew at your age but happiness comes from within, not without. Choose your path carefully. That is all.

God bless you

Nani-ji.

MAYA

July 2014

> *My dear Maya, you will notice that there are two other envelopes in the package I have left for you. They are addressed to Rebecca and Tanya. These are two women I have never met but I do know their grandmothers. Please find Rebecca and Tanya and give them the letters their grandmothers, like I did, have written.*
>
> *I have attached last known addresses and telephone numbers. Perhaps taking the time to find these two women will allow you pause for reflection on your own life. After all, one needs time to reassess before embarking on life changing pathways, and it is always good to embark on life changing pathways that will bring you closer to what you want.*

What could she mean, Maya wondered. The phone line to London was bad, which was not surprising considering Maya had once again chosen to WhatsApp Ronnie from the back of a taxi, on her way to the Netaji Subhash Chandra Bose International Airport in West Bengal.

"I said she wants me to go to New York," shouted Maya. "New York."

"But why there?"

"I have to deliver a letter to someone called Rebecca. The granddaughter of one of Nani-ji's friends."

"Can't you just FedEx it?"

"No, I sort of need to meet her face to face. It's personal."

"What about you FedEx it then Skype her from London? That's personal enough." Ronnie's voice was fading in and out as the signal wavered.

"It's not the same. The letter may be life changing and I would like to be there for Rebecca if she needs me."

"But you don't even know who this Rebecca person is, how do you know she is going to want you there?"

"I don't, Ronnie, but she might."

"Well I want you here," said Ronnie. "It's been bloody ages. I feel like a single man."

"Well don't behave like a single man," said Maya.

"Don't be too sure. I have needs you know."

"We all have needs, Ronnie, and this is my need. To honor my grandmother's request. If you love me, you will unders.... Ronnie?"

The phone beeped "reconnect.' Shit, thought Maya, hanging up. She glanced nervously at the time on her phone. She was running late for the plane and the taxi was managing little more than a crawl through a chaotic single lane of traffic. If I miss my flight to New York, it's fate, she thought, relaxing into the back seat. It is a mad decision to go to New York, she thought. Maya had still not quite figured out how it even came about. One minute she is booking a flight back to London, emailing Andy the good news that she would be back at her desk on Monday, the next, she is on the American Airways website reserving a next day seat for JFK. No wonder Ronnie is annoyed. He is not by his own admission, good at being on his own, which Maya always considered one of his endearing features. "I am a people person, I feed off people," is how he always described himself.

Maya, being more solitary, rather envied his sociable nature. Days could go by without her seeing anyone and she would barely notice. This was one of the many differences between Ronnie and Maya. Another one that came to mind as they were crawling to the airport was that she liked to go to bed early, 11 pm was her ideal but he would be up all hours and then impossible to wake in the morning. She likes spicy food, him, bland. She loves reading; he doesn't even own any books. She cares about her career; he cares about her caring for him. These are minor differences, though, she told herself. The fact that they get on well, he is generous, fun to be with and he makes her laugh, that is the basis of the relationship and, in this day and age, having someone who can make you laugh is a bonus.

Anyway, it was Rajika who had instigated this flight to New York.

"She needs to know the truth. Poor girl," she'd said clutching the letter from Helga.

"Mam-mi, you're not meant to be reading that? It's not addressed to you."

"I don't believe the other two letters were addressed to you either, Maya, but I am not sure that's stopped you reading them?"

"Do you think Nani-ji would mind?"

"Well she didn't tell us not to read them, did she? And anyway, if she is expecting you to go half way around the world delivering them, she could at least let you know why."

"Yah mam-mi, I do believe your rebellious side is beginning to come out again," Maya laughed.

"I am not a rebel, Maya."

"That's not what I read in Nani-ji's letter."

"Maya, stop it. You can't hark back to something that happened twenty years ago like it was only yesterday."

Maya had been surprised to see Rajika blushing at the reference to her past.

"Nani-ji has told you too much," she said.

"She wants to protect me, that's all mam-mi. Not that I need protecting. No man nowadays would dare treat me like they treated women in her time. Life moves on. I know that Ronnie loves me through and through and is not the type to up sticks and leave. He is so far the other extreme from Shakti or Jagat or even your father."

Rajika stood up. "OK.. So um, now, if I were you, I would just book that flight to New York." She picked up an empty plate and a half full cup of tea and wiped invisible crumbs from her T-shirt, generally busying herself doing anything, Maya noted, to avoid having to look her in the eye.

Maya asked, "Is there something you want to say?"

Rajika turned around. "I have this odd feeling that everyone is about to learn new things about themselves."

"What do you mean?"

"Your grandmother seems to be sending messages from the grave. She wants us to be clear eyed, I think."

"We are."

Rajika turned back to the sink. "One never really knows what one is seeing. One just has to be open to it."

"Do you not like Ronnie?" Maya asked.

"I don't know him well and the real question is, Do you?"

KAMLA MEETS HELGA

1970

In the days when Kamla was working at the women's shelter, she was certain that the gods were working with her the day her auto rickshaw ran into the little foreign lady with the big suitcase. And when the auto rickshaw driver melted into a fit of hysteria that the front tire might be punctured, it was left to Kamla to disembark and check on the health of the victim. She was sitting upright on her suitcase dusting down the front of her jacket, blonde hair spilling across her face. Judging by her shaking hand, she was in a state of minor shock but fully functional and didn't hesitate when it came to taking the hand that Kamla offered to pull her up to standing.

Kamla might have thought nothing of the incident and resumed her journey to work if the woman had not produced out of her bag an envelope and pointed to a hand-written address. The address was for a road three blocks up from the refuge. She smiled hopefully at Kamla, showing a small, neat line of teeth.

"Come," said Kamla hailing another auto rickshaw and beckoning for the woman to join her. It was the least she could do having been a culprit in her collision. They squeezed side by side on the worn leather seat, the woman's canvas suitcase resting on their sandalled feet.

After years of working with needy women, Kamla was quick to assess that the foreign woman was anxious. Her nails were bitten to the wick and she had heavy dark bags beneath her eyes ageing her face beyond its middle years.

"Dirty dress," said the woman in English, spotting Kamla eyeing her up. She patted her lap and, half-heartedly, brushed away specks of black dust.

Kamla smiled, only half understanding. She was revered at the refuge for her prowess at deciphering English words in medical textbooks but that was about the extent of her abilities.

"Abrasion," she said suddenly noticing a small graze on the palm of the woman's hand.

"Oh it's nothing," said the woman rubbing her hands together.

"Surgical spirit for clean and dress with bandage," Kamla said. "I take you to my hospital."

"No need for that," said the woman her sky blue eyes softening. "I need to…" she paused. "I need to find my daughter."

Kamla knew "daughter."

"Daughter here?" she asked.

"Hopefully she is here," said the woman patting the address on the envelope. "If not here then," her eyes welled with tears, which she blinked away. "Then, lost, vanished… pff … disappeared." She threw her hands into the air like a miming juggler.

"Daughter discomfort? Injured? Wounded?" Kamla was working her way through the medical dictionary.

"Just gone," the woman replied, allowing a tear to fall down her cheek. "And it's all my fault."

Kamla instinctively laid her hand over the woman's hand and stroked the soft, pale skin. "Find cure for your daughter," she said not entirely sure what condition the daughter might have.

"Look, this, my hospital," Kamla said as the auto rickshaw drove past a compound of low, white buildings. "Lots of women cure," she said. They drove on, turning left into a road with a barber's shop on the corner. Kamla shouted out the address to the driver who jammed on his brakes outside a dilapidated, two-story building with remnants of old posters stuck to the wall, the contents of which were long washed away by seasons of grey Calcutta rain.

"Here, daughter?" asked Kamla. The first floor windows of the buildings were wide open with windchimes hanging from the curtain rail and empty bottles lined up on the narrow balcony. "She married?" Kamla asked.

"No," said the woman. "It's a retreat, I think, sort of religious."

"Hmm," said Kamla. This was not a place she would like to find her Rajika. There was a crowd of blond-haired foreign men gathered around the entrance to the building smoking rolled up cigarettes and staring vacantly at passers-by.

"You come my hospital. Find me, I Kamla," Kamla said feeling suddenly concerned for the wellbeing of this small foreign woman currently sliding out of the rickshaw pulling her suitcase behind her.

"You Kamla, me, Helga," said the woman. "Thank you." She gave Kamla a small wave and nervous smile.

Kamla waved back. "Come hospital find Kamla," she said again, as the auto rickshaw pulled away.

"OK," said Helga.

This was Kamla's first interaction with a foreign person. A strange one by all accounts but the womanly bond was there. *For women in need, there are no boundaries,* she thought as the auto rickshaw pulled into the refuge. *We are at our strongest when we are at our weakest.*

When Kamla got to the hospital, she was a bit late. Her assistant looked up at her. "Everything okay?"

"I hope so. Anyway I practiced some English words on a foreigner. I don't think they were okay." And they laughed.

MAYA MEETS REBECCA

July 2014

Rebecca Gunzburg was easy to track down because of Google and Facebook, and a phone call to the New York number provided by Kamla, which took Maya straight to Rebecca's voicemail. This and also the fact that Rebecca Gunzberg turned out to be a well-known NY Jewish journalist and feminist who had recently taken to the stage to air her views through stand-up comedy. A stalker would have a field day with Rebecca, thought Maya, alighting from the subway and following Google Maps to locate the Portobell Station Bar where, according to Rebecca's Twitter page, she was playing that night.

She thought it wise not to bring Helga's letter with her. She could hardly prance up after the show and say, "My name is Maya. Thanks for making *me* laugh, now here is a letter that is going to make *you* cry." She needed to meet her first.

The show was funny, which came as no surprise. Everything Maya had read written by Rebecca was witty from, the "10 Reasons Why I Wear A Boiler Suit" to "Stereotypical Parenting." She had great insight into NY society, which made Maya feel a bit awkward. But from reading Helga's letter, Maya had some insights into Rebecca, insights, which Rebecca knew nothing about. Rebecca, most likely, knew nothing about her grandmother's past and how it had affected Rebecca's life. Maya held the key.

Maya was browsing her phone, sitting up at the bar when Rebecca came across, changed from her stage boiler suit into a stylish pair of skinny jeans and cashmere sweater. Maya noticed a certain pretty delicacy to her looks, long dark hair, small features, quick eyes, that matched her Viennese background.

"Hey," she said sitting down on a barstool. "You're Maya, right?" Her actual voice was far gentler than her stage one and Maya hadn't noticed she had the slightest hint of a lisp.

"Hi Rebecca," said Maya. "That was a great show."

"Do you think? I'm so pleased. I was trying out some new material so you never know how it's going to go down." She sipped a drink. "I love getting a compliment. Unfortunately, I need all the encouragement I can get," she added. "It's a tough gig in a man's world, not to mention stand up is a tough gig in any world."

"I could never do it,.." said Maya. "I'm not nearly brave enough." She paused, quickly taking a sip of her red wine.

"So, the reason I'm here," Maya continued placing her glass slowly back on the bar, "is because I have something for you from your grandmother, Helga."

Rebecca froze.

"My grandmother? That, I have to admit, I was not expecting ...." she said, looking intently at Mira. "When you called, I thought it was to ask for an interview or get some tips on, I don't know, home baking or something."

"Our grandmothers were friends," said Maya repeating the line she had practiced earlier.

"Really?" said Rebecca. "How interesting. And?"

"And your grandmother wrote you a letter, which my grandmother kept and, as a parting wish, requested me to hand onto you."

"But, my grandmother died when I was a baby," said Rebecca. "In the early 1970's. I never met her. Cancer, I heard."

"Ah, OK," said Maya getting up from the stool and pottering in her bag to avoid Rebecca spotting her blushing cheeks. "Just tell me where we can meet tomorrow and I will bring the letter."

"It's so strange," said Rebecca. "A letter written to an unknown granddaughter?" she paused. "It's sort of sweet but a bit scary. Maybe she was a creative too. Although I hope it's not all like, "Marry well, fulfil your duty as a wife." If so, you will have carried a letter for no reason."

Rebecca stared off and added, "Well maybe I can use the contents as creative material. You never know."

Maya smiled. "I guess you'll have to read it. I'll meet you back here tomorrow and hand it over. I got a letter too, from my grandmother. It's kind of special...getting to know them. And when you've read it, give me a call if you'd like to, you know, discuss stuff." Maya hoisted her bag over her shoulder. "No rush, just when you feel ready."

HELGA MEETS KAMLA AGAIN

1970

Kamla did not notice the little foreign lady with the thick blonde hair entering the gates of the refuge. Nor was she paying attention to the sound of the suitcase wheels dragging along the garden path. The doorbell was always ringing with deliveries or staff or women entering, so she barely registered the front door opening. She still could get lost in her own thoughts about Rajeev, which confused her. He had left her, he was gone from her world yet he continued to inhabit a fulltime position in her brain. How could this be? Why is the brain so savage it would not let her forget? She found that strange things she would do would remind her in some way of Rajeev right down to the way she curled the stem of her *f*'s like she had done just now. Rajeev always laughed at her *f*'s, calling them affected. "Why not do the lines straight, yah?" he used to say. "What is it? F for fancy?" Kamla was in the midst of a deep sigh, one that she hoped might rid her of the dull pain that had lodged itself above her diaphragm, when Ajeele, one of the nursing assistants, knocked on her office door.

"Kamla, you have a visitor."

Kamla looked up from her desk and the report she was writing. Before her was the lady from the rickshaw. Helga's eyes were red and, in her hand, she clutched a tissue.

"Helga." Kamla stood up motioning for the little foreign lady to sit down on a spare plastic chair.

"You OK?"

HELGA nodded smoothing out her dress before sitting down.

"You daughter? She OK?"

At this, Helga buried her head in her hands and sobbed a deep, heart wrenching sob.

"She injured? Need er bandage? Er crutches? Er appendicectomy?"

"She wants nothing, nothing from me. She hates me, she is ashamed of me."

"She sick," said Kamla.

"Yes, she's sick," Helga replied.

"We find medicine," said Kamla.

"The wounds are too deep for medicine."

"You wait here," said Kamla disappearing out of the room to return a few moments later with a glass of hot chai. "Medicine for heart," Kamla said handing the glass to Helga. Sitting down beside her, she allowed her own mind to drift momentarily to the subject of her own heart and how it could still ache but dragged it back again to Helga. Here we are, two women, she mused, from different sides of the world yet both weighed down by sadness.

She wished that she could converse with Helga, understand her. Grasp what she was saying. She sensed such weight in the woman's soul. Perhaps because she could not understand her in words, she had to read into her with much more depth.

Kamla had devoted her life to womens' afflictions, Indian women, women who shared her past and culture. Helga was so foreign, with her light skin, light-colored hair, her formality, so different, yet she wore her sadness like all the women Kamla knew. It had never occurred before to Kamla that women were afflicted the world over. She thought it just an Indian woman's lot to suffer, as only Indian women have to endure Indian men. She patted Helga's hand and smiled a kind, empathic smile.

It was Rajika bursting into Kamla's office from school in her blue tunic and white socks that ripped apart the melancholic reverie. Barely noticing the small foreign woman with the blonde hair curled up on the chair, she threw herself across Kamla's desk and let forth an irate torrent.

"I am still a child am I not, mam-mi?"

"Yes, you are, my dear."

"Then why is Mrs. Rajaputee asking me to write my childhood memories for an English essay? What is she thinking?"

"Indeed. And what memories did you write?"

"About Pap-pi of course."

"Of course."

"How he left us for a pretty woman and we dug up his peach tree."

Kamla winced. "I see…"

"Although I wrote how I would rather have Pap-pi living in our garden than his scrawny little peach tree."

"Did you finish your essay?"

"Yes, I wrote three pages but here's what's funny, I feel much better about my childhood."

"That's good."

"Mrs. Rajaputee said that whenever you are sad, you should write down your sadness on paper."

"She speaks so fast," said Helga suddenly interrupting Rajika's chat.

"What did she say?" Kamla asked Rajika.

"She said I talk fast."

"Yes fast fast," Kamla said back to Helga, "And much much."

They all laughed.

"Rajika, this is Helga. She too is sad. Perhaps she should write down her sadness."

"And so should you mam-mi."

"Yes, perhaps you are right."

Kamla put Rajika under instruction to find out what it was that was upsetting Helga. They were able to spend most of the afternoon talking in English, and Kamla was so impressed at how good Rajika was with the language.

It was not until after dusk that Helga made signs of leaving the refuge. She got up from her chair and, walking across to Kamla, gave her a hug.

"Thank you," she said. "I lose one daughter and I gain a new one," she said turning then to hug Rajika.

"Write it down," Kamla said as the lady left, dragging her suitcase behind her.

"She said, to write it down," translated Rajika. "Write your sadness."

"I will," Helga replied. "I will write to you. There is much to say."

And then she went off to a pension that Rajika and Kamla recommended for her. She seemed cheerier as she left.

Kamla said, "You were wonderful, Rajika, you lifted her heart."

Rajika, "Sometimes I think you and I have our problems but compared to them, we are like lovers."

Kamla laughed. "Yes I love you."

And it was true, they had the love of each other and this was a wealth unto itself.

REBECCA

July 2014

Rebecca left work the next evening with the letter in her bag. It was a thick envelope with her name on it. She smelt it like she always smelt new objects. It had an earthy aroma, a little like damp soil interspersed with Maya's bamboo scented perfume. Rebecca had a sharp nose for smells even believing she could smell the good or the bad in people. A strange skill to have but one she relied upon some said a little too much. She had always blamed her ability to smell unpleasant smells for her dislike of men. Men smelt different from women and Rebecca never got on with the smell. The only man she could abide the smell of was her father, which she put down to being used to him. All other men smelt sour, which is why she had vowed when barely into her teenage years, never to be with a man. A decision not based on sexual preference just smell.

"Don't ask me to explain it," she used to say to her friends. "It is a purely carnal instinct."

Twitching just to plonk down on the sofa and read the letter straight off, Rebecca forced herself to change into a light T-shirt, make herself a cup of chamomile tea and brush her teeth, her bedtime ritual. It was her third late night in a row at the club and, with four more nights to go, she had to conserve her energy.

She considered waking up Matty to tell her she had the envelope but Matty was not good at 1 am. She wasn't particularly good at 7 am but *1 am*—forget it! and, anyway, Matty hadn't been that interested in hearing that she had a letter from her long dead grandmother. She had enough family issues of her own.

It was pushing 1:30 am by the time Rebecca was set. Tearing the seam along the back off the envelope, she settled her head on a cushion and began to read.

October 2008

Dear Rebecca,

Please let me introduce myself. I am your grandmother. I doubt you will forgive me for never introducing myself until now and for what I have done but I hope that this letter, at least, goes some way towards explaining why I did what I did and why I behaved as I have. Shame is a debilitating condition but it is also a selfish condition and, by bathing for so long in my own misery, I have neglected the world around me. I failed your mother and I have failed you and you deserve at least to know why.

I know all about you and your life. I have followed you through school and university and read every article you have ever written. You could say I am your greatest fan.

It is time now for you to know about me.

Once upon a time, a very wise lady told me I should write my sadness down. I have been writing it down ever since but I have never before shared it with the people who matter most. Your mother could never understand most probably because, to her, I could never explain it. I want to share it with you, my granddaughter.

It is unlikely we will ever meet as I have requested this letter be kept until I am no longer in this world. Cowardly perhaps but I never want you to feel you have to find me or forgive me. I have inflicted enough upon you already.

I will keep loving you and admiring you from afar.

Your devoted grandmother,
Helga

Rebecca saw there were many more pages. A lot. She could already smell the sadness in this letter and did she have the energy for that just now? Just then Matty came in.

"What are you doing up?" Rebecca asked.

Matty was wearing a flowery nightgown. Rebecca could never get over that Matty, an arch feminist, liked to look like she was in a 30s movie.

"I missed you. Are you reading the letter?"

"I just started. I just read the prologue. It looks heavy."

"Family stuff only looks good on comedy shows."

They both smiled.

"How was the show?"

"Pretty good. Maya, the letter postmistress, is lovely. Indian. British sounding. Truly kind. She even likes the show."

"Lots of people do, come on."

"Never enough, you know that. I chose a business of rejection. My mother wasn't enough."

Rebecca and her mother barely spoke. Her mother was always angry, terse, hidden. Everything that would constitute the opposite of nurturing. Rebecca needed audiences to provide that.

"It's late, Rebecca. Read the letter later. It might stop you from sleeping."

"I guess you're right. Okay."

And they went off to bed, the letter sitting demurely on the table by the couch.

KAMLA MEETS LYNETTE

1981

Kamla nearly cried with joy the day Rajika came running in from school bursting with news, a teenage girl, grown up, grown out of her boy-mad phase, blooming with youth and vigor.

"Mam-mi, I have chosen my path in life."

"You have?" Just to hear the words "chosen" in connection with her path in life caused Kamla to inwardly glow. *My daughter has a choice.*

"I am going to be a physiotherapist."

"That is the perfect job for you."

"I will study for it at university." It was no surprise to Kamla that Rajika would go into a medical profession. It was a world she knew so well. It was the only world she knew.

As she hugged her daughter close, letting her long, shiny hair envelop her face, she couldn't help but think back to her own youth. How would her parents have reacted to such news? "What about marriage, Kamla? You are 20 now? You have a duty." That would have been her mother. Shakti wouldn't have cared. But here was Rajika, the daughter of a peasant attending a university. It was for Kamla, a dream come true.

The only downside to Rajika's life ambition was that it incorporated cricket. She was given a placement attached to the

Indian women's cricket team. That women even had a cricket team was an eye opener for Kamla.

"I have a ticket for you to come to a game," Rajika said a couple of weeks in, excitedly flashing a white card under her nose. "India versus West Indies, a friendly match but hopefully not too friendly. I would like a few juicy injuries to treat."

"Wonderful news," said Kamla, her heart sinking.

The women's cricket match was at the Brigage Parade Ground on one of the vast open fields. There were other cricket games on that day at the ground and also a football match, schoolboys no older than ten or eleven, Kamla deduced, on the field next-door, cheered on by parents on the sidelines. There was no denying that the football match was far more exciting to watch than the cricket. It was fast and there was yelling and clapping. Kamla was not even certain whether or not the cricket match had started.

Not sure of spectator etiquette, Kamla surreptitiously produced a medical journal out of her handbag and turned to the center spread to continue with an article she had been reading that morning on a new disease being unearthed in Africa. Glancing up at the sound of shouting she noticed that one of the football players was injured. He was lying on the floor clutching his leg and crying. The referee was calling for medical support from the cricket game, while the shouting was coming from two fathers arguing and pointing fingers at each other. Pleased to be well out of it, Kamla watched as Rajika and another physio walked across to the football game and knelt down beside the young boy. One of the men, who had just been shouting, knelt down too causing Rajika suddenly to recoil, stand up and walk away. The man, after a short pause, then stood up and followed

Rajika, calling her name "Rajika," which was when Kamla realized with a sickening jolt, that it was Rajeev.

"Oh no," Kamla said out loud. Barely thinking what she was doing, she flung her journal into her handbag and ran down the steps to the field.

She was blind to everything but the view of Rajeev and her daughter in the same space. The two of them together, it didn't look right. Rajika was crouching behind a row of benches on the edge of the cricket pitch, her back to the game, pretending to frantically search inside a bag.

"Rajika," Rajeev removed his sunglasses and placed them in the top pocket of his stripy blue blazer.

Rajika said nothing.

"Rajika, do you recognize me. I'm your pap-pi." He held out his hands like he was expecting her to run into them.

Nothing.

"I don't think the girl want to see you," said a West Indian woman in English, sitting on one of the benches right by where Rajeev was standing. She was middle-aged with hair slightly greying around the fringe line.

"Rajika, it's been a long time. You're grown up," Rajeev continued ignoring the woman. "I barely recognized you."

"I said, she don't look like she want to see you," said the West Indian woman, this time more loudly.

"None of your bloody business," Rajeev snapped back in English. "This is between me and my daughter."

The West Indian woman shrugged. "Just saying, she don't look like she want to see you at all."

"It's OK, Rajika…" said Kamla coming up behind Rajeev causing him to jump.

"Kamla?"

"I believe it is your son who is injured," Kamla said in a toneless voice. "You should go to him. I will deal with my daughter."

Rajeev stared at Kamla, mouth half open, half shut.

"He's broken his leg," said Rajika suddenly. Rajeev turned around again caught between the two women like a piggy in the middle.

"Rajika.. Kamla… you, I.." Rajeev was spinning around on his shiny leather shoes from one to the other. "Wow. You watching cricket, Kamla?"

"Just go," said Kamla. Rajeev rubbed the designer stubble around his chin and ran his fingers through hair that he had greased back from his forehead. He was fatter around the face and had a second chin resting on the collar of his shirt.

"Broken?" he said to Rajika.

"His fibia, yes," said Rajika adopting her professional voice. "He must be in a lot of pain."

"You've chosen a medical career." Rajeev gave a nod. "That's good."

Neither Rajika nor Kamla spoke. A silent agreement borne out of years of solidarity had kicked in, a wall they had built up, which nothing and no one could knock down.

"Well, I suppose I better go to him then," said Rajeev giving a little laugh. A stupid laugh. "Take him to the hospital."

Still neither woman spoke.

"Nice seeing you." He gave a weak little wave that made him look effete.

Kamla walked past him to the bench and sat down fixing her eyes on the cricket. Rajeev lingered a few moments then walked away.

"Jeeesus," said the West Indian woman under her breath watching Rajeev's retreating figure. "That was awkward." She patted Kamla on the arm. "You done good, girl."

"Come, sit over here Rajika," Kamla said beckoning across to her daughter. Rajika got up and joined them sitting between Kamla and the West Indian woman. Both women hugged her. "We always thought that day would come, didn't we?" said Kamla.

"Men are pigs," said the West Indian woman. "Ain't never known a good man me whole life."

"He looked so normal," said Rajika. "I had kind of built him up in my mind to look like a rat or a criminal or something."

"He looked fat," said Kamla. "And weak."

"That's the spirit," said the West Indian woman with a laugh.

"What's strange is he didn't look like a man I ever could have loved."

"They never do," said the West Indian woman. She spoke with all the worldly wisdom of a woman double her age.

"Mam-mi, meet Lynette," said Rajika, smiling. "She's Alicia's mam-mi. Alicia's the West Indian bowler. Lynette's joining her on tour."

"Good to meet you, girl," said Lynette, with a big smile that flashed her white teeth. "I don't understand any of that Hindu or

Muslim or whatever it was you was speaking wid dat man but I understand body language and that made me sad."

"It was certainly unexpected," said Kamla drained. She dropped her head into her hands. "I have thought about bumping into that man so many times over the last ten years but I never expected it to be here at cricket." Kamla spoke English for the benefit of Lynette. Years of study and practice had left her stilted but fluent.

"That was my half-brother lying on the floor," said Rajika dreamily. "I'm sorry to say it mam-mi, but he was cute."

"All little boys cute, girl," said Lynette. "It's when dey grow up you got de problems."

"I so agree, Lynette," said Kamla laughing. "It sounds like we could be friends."

No one noticed that there was a lull in the cricket match until Alicia came over throwing down her gloves. Rajika introduced Alicia to Kamla, and told Alicia the story of how they met and how Lynette sided with them, without knowing who they were.

"Sounds like you and Kamla got a lot in common, Mam," said Alicia, when she sat down next to her mother. "You should write to her when you get back home. Like a pen pal, share your stories of men."

"Don't sound like it going to be no cheery letter," said Lynette.

"I would like that," said Kamla, laughing. "I always thought it was only Indian men but it appears it is men the world over."

"Men like pigs everywhere," said Lynette. "Big babies. Don't know the meaning of the word responsibility."

"Don't get her started," said Alicia.

"We should compare notes," said Kamla. "I work with many women who feel the same as you."

"There you go then, friends," said Lynette playfully shaking Kamla's hand. "Us women need to stick together, you know that, Kamla?"

"I can't thank you enough, Lynette," said Kamla. "You brought some humor and support to a very horrible experience and made it almost enjoyable."

"I'm gonna write you girl. A problem shared is a problem halved."

"And I'll write back."

Turning to Rajika, Kamla said, "I think I'm going to head home now. But thank you. I've loved watching the cricket. And I made a new friend."

"Liar about the cricket."

"Well it's been quite a day."

Alicia was pretty and athletic. "It's funny how our mums became instant friends," she said to Rajika, as they walked off together. "It's moving."

"You'll see," Kamla called out, hearing them, "how important it is that women are friends. We tell each other the truth. Work things out together. It's the only way you can know anything."

Alicia started running in place as she turned to listen. "I better go back to the field. I'm glad all of you are alright. Especially Rajika."

"I am."

And all the females smiled, knowing that they all were there, ready to back each other up.

-1-

Rebecca chose the next morning to go to a local New York coffeeshop. The Polish waitress she always saw brought fruit and coffee for her without her asking. They knew her well. She hardly looked up at the grandmotherly waitress when she brought the food, because she had begun reading the letter from her own grandmother:

April 21st 1926, my birth date, a Wednesday. A Wednesday's child is full of woe, isn't that the English rhyme? Woe, grief, sadness, despair.

It was my father's dread that I should be born on a Wednesday in April. Not because he knew about this nursery rhyme, I am sure of that, but because it was a Wednesday in April, that he lost my two brothers. Lost? Why do people say the word lost when referring to death? He didn't lose my two brothers. He knew where they were when they died. My first brother, he died in my mother's womb. She gave birth to a corpse. That was a Wednesday in April 1922 and my second brother, he died in my mother's arms, two breaths into life, that was all he managed, a huff and a puff and... nothing. That was a Wednesday in April 1924.

When I came into the world, on a Wednesday, in April 1926, my father was nowhere to be found. He chose to vanish, which is understandable after all, how much grief must a man bear in childbirth?

His cousin found him and spread the joyous news. He was lying low in the synagogue library. This was not a customary place for him to visit, well, the library at the top of our street, that was not unusual, but the synagogue was. My father acted no more Jewish than a bratwurst. Vienna was his race and creed...long live Austria.

"Cruel world," that is what my father said on hearing of my birth, "Cruel, cruel world." He needed a son, an heir, somebody to continue the prospering Schleff family leather business. "What point with a girl?" I was daughter number three, "fodder.' Good only for marriage, children and polishing leather.

In my father's eyes, I was a dead end.

Fortunately, my father was not one to live with regret for long. When I grew up with the blonde curly locks and the pale skin of my mother, my father's deep brown eyes melted beneath his heavy set brow. "How can one as ugly as I create such a work of beauty?" That's what he used to say to me, rubbing my soft cheek with his long, smooth knuckles. My father was not an ugly man. I know many people think the Jewish look is all hooked noses and weak chins but my father was distinguished and dashing. Appearance was very important to my father. He was what I believe Americans call "dapper." He wore only the finest lounge suits styled on the latest from Saville Row, double breasted with a narrow cut lapel. His neck forever adorned with a silk bowtie and his upper lip with a pencil moustache, waxed and groomed. It was only in such attire that my father would grace the Strasse and Platz of Vienna.

My mother, I will not mention her, not yet, many decades have passed but still, I find I cannot talk about my mother. My time with her on earth was severed and, much like when one's leg is amputated, a limb remains in phantom form. This is how my mother remains to me, a phantom presence, I am not yet able to acknowledge she is gone let alone reveal what she meant to me, in words. All I can say about my mother, for now, is that you would have respected her, everybody who knew her, respected her.

I could tell you about my sisters, Lizzie the eldest, Edith the next. They were born in the odd years, 1923 and 1925. I know family is very important but really, as a child, they were not a big part of my life, they were a twosome and I a one and rarely did we make a three except for when my father insisted on a family portrait. For this, we had to dress up in our laciest lace and huddle together, hair in ringlets, arms around one another. I was always thrust to the forefront like the prize doll. The rest of the time, though, my big sisters were more attentive to carrots on their dinner plates than to me.

Maybe if my sisters had noticed me a little, my bond with my mother might not have been so strong. I might have played childish games, fairy tales, make-believe, dressing up. As it was, I played mother-daughter games, cooking, sewing, crosswords.

"Look at my Doppelgängers," my father would say when he came in to find my mother and I wrapped up together on the sofa, my mother reading, me cuddled up as close as I could get.

We both had the same sky blue eyes. Oh yes, and the same shaped mouth, heart shaped, my father called it kissing my mother's lips, then mine.

My sisters found my attachment to my mother difficult to stomach. Siblings are always rivaling in some form or other, playing mind games, seeking superiority. The three of us were no different. We all wanted a slice of mummy but it seemed, because I was the baby, I got the biggest.

Rebecca looked up from the letter, and sipped her coffee. It seems narcissism isn't only the illness of my age, she thought. This letter just seems "Wasn't I beautiful?" And worse, I didn't get the blue eyes and blonde hair. Too bad. Of course, I already know it's going to come in handy. Jewish and Vienna. I know what's going to happen. Well she was alive to write this. Rebecca took a spoonful of her fruit salad and went back to reading.

-2-

For the first eleven years and five months of my life, I loved our home, our family home. After this time, though, it haunted me.

Do you know Vienna at all, I wonder? Not many people do it seems, nowadays, beyond Mozart and schnitzels and strudels. Our house was not far from the cathedral, down a narrow street of four-story townhouses with a church at one end and our local synagogue at the other.

That the church was adorned with a white and gold façade and the synagogue, near invisible with a grey door set back from the street, has some relevance to Jewish history in the city but very little of our mental energy was spent deliberating religion.

We were Jewish, you know that by now, but really we were more "ish" than Jew, fair weather Jews you might say. We took all the best bits of the Jewish faith, like the present exchanges at Hanukah and the roasted lamb and egg dinner parties on the eve of Passover. My parents fasted for 25 hours at Yom Kippur and we all attended the invisible synagogue up the road on this day to pray for God's forgiveness of our sins but really that was about all we did to acknowledge our faith. And when it came to the praying, I am not sure any of us even did that particularly devoutly. I know I did not. My brain was like a butterfly, never staying on one thought for longer than a few seconds, which isn't how you pray. Praying is all about meditation, focus and stillness. My father was as restless a character as me. He could never sit still even on Saturday afternoons for his nap in his green velvet chair when we all had to creep around the house, but even then, his leg would twitch like it had better places to be. Praying was not a Schleff family skill.

Growing up, my favorite time of year was Christmas. Oh, how I loved the Christmas markets of Vienna. Perhaps you can picture them? The cinnamon scented stalls lit up with brightly colored fairy lights and gingerbread houses, snowmen with knitted scarves, embroidered baubles, Glühwein, that's our Christmas beverage with oranges and lemons and spices, how I loved all those smells.

Rebecca stopped reading. She loved smells? Rebecca felt a stab of connection with this phantom woman, then continued:

It was at Christmas that I regretted most of all that I was Jewish, Rebecca read. Oh, it was not so much a regret, more a pang because it was when I most stood out from the rest of my classmates.

"Why are you joining in the carols?" my friend, Katrina used to say to me. "How can you sing about baby Jesus being born when you don't know the same Jesus as us?"

Every year, I was asked the same questions about baby Jesus and Christmas trees. "Why are you singing about Christmas trees when you haven't even got one?"

Every year I gave the same answer, "Oh, I don't really pay attention to the words, I just like to sing the melodies," which was partially true as I did love singing, I still do except now when I sing I sound like a lame horse. Really, I mustn't complain. I am lucky I can talk at all as throttling can cause permanent damage to the vocal chords.

There were two others in my class at school who were Jewish. Daniella Wildenstein, who was not a good friend of mine as she was very bossy and always liked to go first in every game. And Max Knox. He was a kind boy, quiet, always reading or deep in conversation about space, the universe. I don't know, as I told you, I was far too skittish to move in his circles.

My group consisted of Katrina, Angelina and Gertrude. They were all non-Jewish. I think the reason I liked these three girls the best is because they looked like me. I know that sounds shallow but schoolgirls are shallow. We were called the Bombshells.

"So what do your family do on Christmas day?" my friends would ask me, standing just a little too close together.

"Well, we treat it like any other day, my father sings, my mother tells him to be quiet, my sisters avoid me and my dog lies on his back waiting for somebody to scratch his tummy."

This was not entirely true. It was a stock phrase, something I had up my sleeve for when conversations made me uneasy. I was often the clown within the group and I suppose this was because I needed just that little bit more than the others to ensure I fitted in.

We always had very happy Christmas days in my family, ignoring Christmas. Yes, my father did sing but we all sang with him. Thanks to my father's passion for opera, we were almost word perfect on Mozart's Le Nozze di Figaro, ll barbiere di Siviglia. *I will never forget my father's version of Figaro's* Aria. *He had a voice that carried such gravitas, such depth and he loved to do all the actions, pretending to brush the waves out of my mother's hair, powder puff Edith's already very rosy cheeks.*

He was a born actor, my father. The world he inhabited was a fantasy where there were no sad endings and everybody, however angry, always ended up in an embrace. Friends and colleagues and butchers and bakers, were liebchen, *which means "darling." My mother, his* verliebte—*beloved and my sisters and I, his* Bärchen, *I don't know how you translate this, perhaps, it means teddy bear or little bear. Everybody was referred to with a term of endearment mainly because he had the most terrible memory for names.*

In retrospect, oh how fortunate I am to live to experience retrospect, I believe my father was a snob, a snob against the Jewish faith. Yes, this sounds harsh but he was much more enamored by arts and culture than by religion. I once heard him announce that the synagogue atmosphere made him depressed because it was so gloomy and cold.

My father would read to us from the December book, a book that he brought out on the first day of Advent and read every evening until Christmas day. The December book I remember most was Mary Shelley's Frankenstein. *I was 10 years old when he read it to us and even though I had sleepless nights and stormy dreams, I insisted he read on until it was finished. I don't think it was the horror of this story that got to me, it was the sadness of the monster, the loneliness and the way the book questioned what it is to be human. There have been times in my life when I have felt like Frankenstein's monster. Still now, when I am lost in my thoughts, it is to Frankenstein's story that I return.*

Perhaps because he inhabited a world of make-believe, my father, unlike so many in Vienna at the time, had no fear of war or of Hitler. He rarely read newspapers preferring instead works of literature or simply to become lost in music.

My father, who normally had a story to tell for every incident of his life, rarely spoke about the expectation that rested upon him to continue in Schleff family leather. "Business is business, home is home." That was his motto were anyone ever to bring up a subject pertaining to the factory, once the pointy leather slippers were on his feet.

We lived a life of relative opulence so the business must have been successful. I don't recall wanting for anything. My first bike, a bright red tricycle, was the finest tricycle money could buy. It shone on the flagstones in our hall on the morning of my fifth birthday with a fluffy blue bow tied across the handlebars.

When I was seven years old, I had seen that I was my father's favorite child. I don't say this with any hint of a boast. In fact, it was burdensome having to be so loved. It was not that my father didn't care for my sisters, he did I am sure, but he cared for me more.

I am not sure why I feel the need to impart this to you. It is not as if my story will be any different for you knowing this but it is a guilt, one of the many I have carried with me all my life.

Perhaps being the favorite would have been manageable if it had not been so obvious to my sisters but my father, because he lived his life lit up like a firework, made few attempts to hide it. He was always cuddling me or ruffling my hair or tickling my cheek, it was like he had eyes only for me and of course my mother. Maybe it was because he did love my mother so much that he treated me as a miniature version. I do not believe my sisters ever forgave me for the extra hugs I received. And I, in turn, began to not trust my father for this favoritism.

I have one child, your mother. Perhaps having a favorite child is normal when you have multiple children, but sadly, I never even favored the one child I had. I was, what I suppose psychologists would call, a neglectful mother. Nobody knew this, not from the outside because I hid it well just like I have hidden so much in my life.

Your mother does not love me now and I cannot expect her to. Perhaps one day, I will be able to make it up to her, explain everything. Apologize for the lies, no, not lies, silence.

It was my silence that killed our love.

So you see, life has its ups and downs. Bad years, regrets, these are what we carry with us as fresh wounds or healing

scars. My family, my people, me, we, had no control over our
destinies. We were told what to do and where to go and it was
simply luck that dictated if we would live or die.

Perhaps if my parents read newspapers or used the wireless
to listen to more than Mahler or Schubert we might have
known what was about to hit us. My father might have had
time to accept what was happening, made changes, been
prepared.

Ach, my mother, she was wise, she knew that life had an
underbelly but because she loved my father she was swept
along in his optimism, his day dreams, his fundamental belief
in happy endings.

How wrong she was.

Rebecca put the letter down. So many more pages. Should I
finish this tomorrow? Yes. This is enough. Okay my
grandmother wants to talk about the war. Those survivors never
did speak in real life so it makes sense she wrote a letter. She's
guilty for being a bad mother. Everyone in New York is in
therapy for being or having a bad mother. Her grandmother
should have just moved here. I'll try again tomorrow. Whatever
is next, I am sure, can't be pretty.

Or maybe she got away. She must have got away somehow.

The next morning Rebecca, back at the coffeeshop, with her
fruit salad and coffee, began again.

-3-

It is easy to say, now, why didn't people do more, fight
more, read the signs, but how could we predict?

Perhaps you already know that übel is the German word
for evil. My father did not permit this word to be uttered in
our house. "Love, peace, spirit, beauty and kindness, only these

words matter, my Bärchen. Use these words and you will always be safe."

"You are to come straight home from school," my mother commanded each day as we left the house, after my sister was spat on. "Heads down, no singing, no drawing attention to yourself, Lizzie do you hear me? No stopping off to spend your pocket money. Edith and Helga, stick with your sisters, you do not need to race ahead, there are no prizes for getting home first. Yes? Do you all hear me? Now go."

I was eleven years and eleven months old when my father was taken from us. The day he left us was the day after I announced that I hated him. I know, "announced my hate' sounds like I stood on the balcony, hand on heart and called out to a passing world.

It began with Gertrude. Out of the four of us in my friendship group at school, she was the quiet one, rarely letting on about what she thought. A closed book you might say. It is because of her nature, of course, that I did not see it coming.

At first it was so subtle. Gertrude brought a handkerchief into school. It was a pretty handkerchief with her initials GS embroidered in a corner next to a little white and green daisy. She kept the handkerchief in the pocket of her dress, occasionally bringing it out to ostentatiously pat her brow. At playtime, as normal, we came to play amongst other games, the clapping game. You might have played clapping games yourself when you were at school:

Under the bram bushes
Under the sea
True love for you my darling
True love for me
When we get married
We'll have a family
A boy for you
A girl for me

Living on an island
Very happily

Do you know this? I am sure we had other rhymes but only this one sticks in my mind. I began to notice that at the end of every game with me, Gertrude took out her handkerchief and wiped her hands. She did not do this with anybody else after a game, just me.

The following week, both Katrina and Angelina also had handkerchiefs, equally pretty ones like Gertrude's.

"Why have you brought handkerchiefs?" I asked genuinely surprised to see my friends behaving like pansies. "You can't all have colds."

Katrina and Angelina were a little embarrassed and thrust theirs back into their pockets.

Gertrude looked me straight in the eye and said, "No, we haven't got colds; this is to stop us from catching germs."

"Why, is there something going around?" I asked. I was innocent, so innocent.

"Yes, haven't you heard it is a disease carried only by pigs," except of course, she didn't say "pigs" she said "schwein", which sounds so much more derogatory and she said it in such a way that the "w" caught in her lip, for better effect.

"But there aren't any schwein *around here," I said, going to push Gertrude's arm as you do playfully with friends. Gertrude leapt back like I was carrying a red-hot poker. The speed she moved at...*

"Don't touch me," there was a look of what was it -- disgust, horror, confusion in her eyes?

"What are you talking about?"

I looked across at Katrina and Angelina both of whom had retrieved their handkerchiefs and were covering their noses, eyes pinned on me like I was a savage animal.

"You are the schwein," *said Gertrude. "The* Judenschwein."

"The what?" I asked. This was the first time I had ever heard this word.

"The Judenschwein, the Judenschwein," chanted Gertrude. "The stinking, stinking Judenschwein."

"I am not a Judenschwein," I yelled all of a sudden registering what she was saying.

"Judenschwein, Judenschwein, Judenschwein."

My classmates milling around, started to form a crowd, close but not too close, fingers jabbing my way.

"Judenschwein, Judenschwein, Judenschwein."

"But Gertrude....?" How pitiful I must have sounded but nothing like this had ever happened to me in my life. I was lost for what to do.

"Judenschwein, Judenschwein, Judenschwein." I was surrounded on all sides.

Katrina and Angelina, my two other best friends stood still, neither joining in with the taunts nor making any attempt to come to my aid, just there set apart from the others with their handkerchiefs in their hands.

"Judenschwein, Judenschwein, Judenschwein." Everyone chanted.

"Katrina?" I mouthed. "Angelina..... please?"

They didn't move. We held our stares, me looking from one to the other, them at me, their eyes clear and bright, mine, probably round and red and filling with tears.

I was half expecting any second for the crowd to disperse, slap me on the shoulder and cry. Only joking, or even better, "Tag," and go running off for me to catch them but the crowd was getting angry now, their voices jeers and sneers.

"Please Katrina, Angelina... Gertrude?"

And then, it happened.

With a motion so subtle yet so powerful, Katrina gave a miniscule shake of her head, turned up her nose and broke our stare.

In those three simple actions, the extinguishing of all my childhood friendships, every birthday present exchanged, every book or bracelet swapped, every leapfrog, every skip, every sweet shared. Vanished.

Looking across to the crowd, Katrina took Angelina's arm. As one, they turned their backs on me and as one they walked across to Gertrude. When they turned to face me again they were like strangers, cold, unfamiliar, übel.

"Judenschwein, Judenschwein, Judenschwein."

I suppose I wondered where the teachers were. Why were they not stepping in, breaking up the bullies? Commotions were not allowed in school.

They were there of course, they were there, present but in the background, aware but doing nothing.

Now of course I know why.

After what felt like three lunchtimes rolled into one, someone did step in to rescue me. It was Max—quiet, profound, deep Max, small and pale and Jewish. Like a lifeboat, Max swept through the amassed bodies and took a hold of my hand.

"Let's go." It was all he said and we went, him pulling my hand, keeping his head down, determined.

Too terrified to touch the Judenschwein, the friends, classmates, people who just the day before I had thrown balls to and shared jokes with, cleared a path for us to leave, not daring to touch the germ ridden pigs, scurrying for shelter.

Max steered me out of the school gates with no fuss and no bother and no regard for the rules prohibiting children from leaving school in the middle of the afternoon. Brave Max. Slipping momentarily from my panic, I noticed the hint of a quiver in his hand as he wiped a band of sweat from his top lip. How scared he must have been, going against all those children just to save me?

I could tell you how Max walked me home sticking close by but giving me the space I needed to stagger along in a daze or how after depositing me at my front door, he turned and said, "You might be a juden, *Helga, but you are certainly not a* schwein."

Or I could tell you how even though my path did not cross with Max's very much after this, when it did, my heart fluttered just a little bit.

But, really the purpose of this letter is to tell you how it came about that I told my father I hated him and also, I suppose it is to highlight to you quite how naïve I was to everything going on around me. I had barely even registered I was Juden.

Ach, looking back, it is all so silly. My father insisted on me returning to school that very same afternoon. That was all it was. I told him, red faced, foot stamping that I hated him for not understanding me, for not listening to me and he just stood there letting a smile dance upon his lips and said, like he was wise and understood,

"Ah Helga, girls will be girls, this is what girls do my Bärchen, *they quarrel and they make it up. You will see. Go now, back to school." And I was dispatched tear-stained and petrified, accompanied by Ingrid our housekeeper who insisted on comparing my plight as a* schwein *to the plight of her fellow sopranos in the church choir who were being picked on by the altos, tenor and bass. "Never before," she exclaimed, "have the bass ganged up."*

Of course, my father was incorrect. Going back to school was an utter catastrophe. Fraulein Amalie made me stand at the front of the class for the entire afternoon as an example of what happens to truants. I was not, of course, the first person in my class ever to have left the school grounds without seeking permission but I was the first to be publicly punished. A small gripe really, compared to what came next but often it is what comes first that most sticks in our mind.

The next day my father disappeared.

Rebecca wanted to go right to the next letter. She looked up, ordered another coffee, (after all, aren't I of Viennese descent? Coffee, coffee, coffee), and opened the next one.

-4-

This was a Saturday morning. Normally, I could hear very little of family life on the floors below but at that moment, my mother's voice traveled my way, crying and pleading on the street outside, as loud as a chiming clock.

I flew out of bed and strained to see down onto the street from my small triangular window. There was a truck parked up, hogging the narrow road with its passenger door swinging open. I could see the top of my mother's hair, unraveled from a night's sleep, arms waving frantically as two men, dressed in blue uniforms with polished black boots, shoved my father, silk, green dressing gown hanging off his shoulders, across the pavement into the back of the truck where they continued to poke him with long sticks like he was a rabid maniac.

"Papa!" I yelled, frantically knocking on the window like it might actually do any good. I was torn, fists clenched, between rushing downstairs to my mother's side and staying put, not daring to take my eyes off the truck. Clutching her flimsy nightdress, my favorite one, black with gold ripples, my mother in her thinly soled velvet slippers raced up to the truck doors shouting at the soldiers to "Bring him back," pursued by my sisters in their less elegant nighties attempting to grab hold of my mother and return her to the house. The soldiers cast my mothers and sisters aside like they were nasty smells, climbed back into the front of the truck and looked like they

were about to drive away and god I wish they had. Instead, almost on a whim, the passenger door reopened, the soldier came out, stick in hand, strode across to my mother and began beating her like a dog, across her legs, her back, her shoulders. I was frantic, screaming, scratching the windowpane with my half chewed fingertips, helpless to make them stop.

By the time I arrived downstairs, the truck was gone, my father was gone and my mother was slumped on the pavement, a disheveled heap. Her milky white skin gashed and torn. We tried to disentangle her limbs, my sisters and I, but she would not unfold so we lifted her up and carried her inside gnarled like a tree root, Edith supporting her underneath as if she might spill open. She was shaking and whimpering, blood dribbling down the side of her temple on to her cheek along the side of her nose, and edge of her mouth. We took her to a walnut chair at the kitchen table and placed her onto the cushioned seat to make sense of the damage. She sat hunched on the chair, fingers clutched together like she was fervently in prayer, head hanging on her chest.
"Mummy?" I whispered, my fingers flickering across her kneecap.

"Helga, go fetch Moritz and Marta," said Lizzie quietly, calmly, like she was practiced at treating the wounded. I shook my head. Moritz and Marta lived only two doors up, they were my parent's good friends but I was too scared to leave my mother's side not until she said something. I was so worried that the soldiers had damaged her brain, left her helpless.

"Helga, now," Lizzie said more forcefully. "We need some help here." She paused and then added, "Help with Papa."
"Papa?"

"He's been arrested. We have to find out where they have taken him. Moritz will help us. Helga, please go."

Lizzie had never spoken to me like this, like an adult speaking to a young child, like an older sister. She was forceful, in control, kind. And all the while she was speaking to me, she was gently stroking my mother's back while Edith rinsed towels in the kitchen sink ready to administer to my mother's wounds. They were pale and their faces stricken with panic but, because they were calm, I too needed to be calm.

I stood up brushing down my nightie. I was, of course, not yet dressed.

"Can I go like this?" I asked.

Edith was now washing along my mother's arms and around the top of her chest.

"Just put your coat on top," said Lizzie.

"Is she going to be alright?" I whispered motioning towards my mother.

"I will be fine, Helga," my mother said suddenly, putting on a strong voice.

I ran across to my mother and crouched down. She stroked my forehead with her bruised fingers.

I stood up and backed away to the door barely daring to take my eyes off my mother. In the hallway, I threw my heavy duffle coat over my nightie and crept out into the street expecting it to be silent and empty like it was minutes before except now it was busy, there were families strolling, young children bouncing beside their parents, couples arm in arm, car horns hooting and in the distance, cheering and clapping. I could not figure out whether the carnival-like atmosphere was simply everyday life magnified because I was in shock, or whether a carnival was actually in full swing.

Keeping close to the walls, I arrived at Moritz and Marta's house and knocked gently on the door. When nobody answered, I knocked again, louder. I could hear footsteps just inside the hallway.

"Marta, Moritz, it's me, Helga," I called putting my mouth as close to the door as possible, "I need your help."

After several seconds, the door opened, just a crack. It was Moritz. He looked up and down the road before fixing his eyes on me.

"Yes, what is it Helga?"

"It's Papa, he's been arrested and Mama's been beaten and I don't know why... please come."

"I am sorry, Helga," Moritz's voice was stern, schoolmasterly, "But Marta and I cannot help your parents. We can no longer be associated with you, it is, too..." he stopped here, hunting around for the next word....
"Dangerous. Good day."

He closed the door leaving me standing there, shivering. Good day?

"Oy, Juden..."

I spun around, a boy I recognized from school, Edith's year, or Lizzie's perhaps was standing less than a meter away. "Been playing in the mud, have we?"

"What?" I asked.

"You're filthy."

"What are you talking about?" I said, glancing down at my duffle coat, perhaps I had missed something putting it on in the hall.

"I'm not," I replied.

"Are now," said the boy sticking his hand into a bag and removing a handful of tomatoes. He swung back his arm and threw tomatoes first, then eggs, then flour. Protecting my head, I scampered back to my house and banged on the front door, more frantically than I perhaps intended. Behind me people, my neighbors, were laughing and jeering, "Don't waste your groceries, Stefan, I'd piss on her if I were you."

My mother was upright when I raced into the kitchen, a trail of detritus in my wake. She was holding a wet towel across the side of her face where a laceration was refusing to clot. Somebody had lit the stove in the kitchen so the whole room was boiling.

Edith and Lizzie entered quickly behind me firmly shutting the kitchen door. Shutting the world out.

"Oh my poor darling," said my mother helping me slip into the day coat. "I knew we should have gone," she cried. "I told him we had to leave."

"It's Hitler, mummy," said Lizzie quietly. I hadn't noticed the wireless on in the corner. I don't know how I had missed such exuberance from the commentator. Lizzie was sitting beside it, face flushed, eyes brimming with tears. "The Third Reich has entered Austria, Mama, we are now German. Austria has gone." Lizzie burst into tears clasping her hands to her face. To say we were filled with emotion is a desperate understatement.

"What does this mean?" asked Edith softly.

"Hitler hates Jews. That is why Papa is gone," Lizzie said.

"Did you speak to Moritz, Helga?" asked my mother.

I had completely forgotten about Moritz. I shook my head. "Sorry, mummy, he is too scared to help us."

My mother just nodded like she understood.

Sleepless, scared and shocked, none of us were expecting Monday morning when it arrived and with the blinds down in the kitchen, the only way we knew it was here was when Ingrid stepped in to the kitchen and gasped.

"Holy heavens, you have a problem with the stove? The electricity? There is a flood, what is going on here?" Considering she was brought up a cowgirl in the Alps, Ingrid was an archetypal drama queen. Perhaps that was why my father hired her. Suddenly spotting my mother's bruised, battered face, she threw her hands to her mouth and muffled a scream.

"Frau Helene? ... Quick, your mother," she shouted to us girls like the emergency was just unfolding. Padding across the

kitchen to where my mother was propped up against a series of pillows, she began fluffing each pillow, requested towels and water and creams and dressings and bandages. So frantic was she in her desire to provide first aid that it was hard not to laugh, which led her to reprimanding us that this was no time for laughter.

When she was done with her fussing, she took my mother's hand and patted it. In return, I saw my mother clasp Ingrid's wrist. "Thank you," she mouthed.

Ingrid was a strict Catholic attending church three times a week, singing in the church choir and performing the grace before every meal. It was perhaps due to her being a religious presence for most of our lives that I knew Christian prayers better than my own.

"I am not a bad person," she said looking at all of us. "You are my Viennese family and I will not let you down." That was all she said, that is until my sisters and I pinned her into a corner and asked for a blow-by-blow account of what was happening out on the streets.

"It is a horrible sight. How can our people just roll over and let the Germans tickle their tummies. Have we no pride, where is our patriotism? I am today, embarrassed to call myself an Austrian."

It was clear that my mother wanted a quiet word with Ingrid and so my sisters and I vacated the kitchen for the first time in what felt much longer than two days.

It was Ingrid, who helped us. Remarkable Ingrid.

Rebecca swallowed and felt ill. In fact, she felt like she had been beaten, too. She immediately went to the next letter.

-5-

That Monday, of course, we didn't go to school but Ingrid made sure we left the house. "If you fall off a horse you must get straight back on the saddle," she said. Always with an eye on God, she insisted we visit the synagogue to see if we could obtain any information about our father.

"Stand tall," she told my sisters and I as we walked out of our front door into traces of the flour and eggshell from my pelting two days before. The air outside was sour and alien, like the Germans had filled it with a scent of hatred and prejudice.

A tank was parked up outside the church, opposite the synagogue. It was straddling the pavement, surrounded by a crowd of German soldiers crouching down for young children to present them with handfuls of flowers. There were squeals of laughter as the soldiers removed their helmets for the little blond heads to try on.

It was not so much me because remember I did not look Jewish, it was my sisters who drew the eye of the soldiers. My sisters with their black hair, long noses and pale skin were unmistakably Juden and, not only that, they were tall and pretty and at the age where men notice girls. It is almost disgusting that in front of so many innocent children, the soldiers could become, I don't know how to describe it, like jackals.

It sounds absurd but it was at this moment walking towards the German tank when I first discovered men. Of course I do not mean in a pubescent way or indeed men like my father or Opa or the Rabbi, I mean men as testosterone-fueled creatures controlled by physical impulses.

I knew it was going to be trouble the moment I saw one of the soldiers look at another of the soldiers and wink. Batting off the children they stood up, nudging one another and three of them swaggered over.

"Off to pray are we, nice little Jewish girls? Yes? Want to pray for this?" a dark haired soldier whispered sidling up to Lizzie and rubbing his hand up and down his crotch.

Placing her hand firmly on the small of my back, Lizzie attempted to steer us out of the path of the soldiers.

"I was talking to you, Hündin," said the same soldier, grabbing hold of Lizzie's arm. Hündin, if you don't know, is the German word for female dog. Lizzie and Edith stopped but one of them pushed me forward to carry on walking, which I could because I was not the feature.

"Nothing to say for yourselves? Even dogs have tongues, Jewish girls." Neither Lizzie nor Edith moved but their shoulders stooped and their faces reddened.

"You, come here," said another of the soldiers with a red face and bulging eyes, grabbing hold of Edith and pulling her towards him like a rag doll. "Didn't your mama teach you how to get dressed?" He yanked at her creamy silk blouse so that the pearl grey buttons flew off in all directions.

"Look at this, white underwear, look everyone, so clean," said the soldier holding Edith's shirt wide open. As Edith tried to seize back her dignity, the soldier slapped her hands. "Dogs don't like clean, do they Jew? Dogs like to roll in the mud." Digging his hand into the curb, the soldier got a handful of gravel and dust and cigarette butts and massaged them into Edith's white cottons, running his fingers slowly over her breasts. "Do you like that, bitch? Muddy little bitch?"

"Anyone else got any mud for the dog?" the soldier called. "Doggies like to eat shit."

"Stop it," said Lizzie grabbing Edith's arm.

"Ha, the Jew speaks," said the other soldier, the dark haired one. "Jealous, are we?"

I noticed, blending as I did into the crowd, that there was a mix of humor and discomfort among my fellow Austrians. Some people were outwardly laughing, others shuffling their feet like they wanted to leave but most were captivated by every humiliating second.

"Leave my sister," said brave Lizzie, teeth clenched, lips barely moving.

"Why would I listen to you?" said the red faced bulgy-eyed solider. ""Who are you to give me commands?" Picking up a handful of gravel from the curb, he threw it into Lizzie's face so that it filled her eyes, her mouth. "Nobody listens to you, Jew, and you better learn that."

I cannot tell you how difficult it was for me, standing there witnessing this, but so helpless. Yes, of course, I wanted to step in to pull the soldiers off my sisters but how? I was scared. I crept away, around the back of the crowd and raced down my street back home.

"Ingrid, please, you have to come and help Edith and Lizzie," I cried as Ingrid opened the door.

"What is it?" asked my mother clutching her poor, bruised chest.

"You stay there," Ingrid said to my mother and me. She grabbed her hat and coat and exited the house.

I explained to my mother about the humiliation, bursting into tears as I watched her crumple into a chair. "I should go with Ingrid," she said but we both knew this was the wrong idea. Years later it struck me how not being able to rescue her own daughters from terror must have mortified my mother.

Twenty minutes later, Ingrid returned along with both my sisters. She was splattered in mud and gravel and she was shaking although I was not sure if this was with fear or with anger at being called a "Jew lover," a "hypocrite," a "traitor."

There were many more incidents to come, when Ingrid stepped in on behalf of my sisters, my mother and I, often having to bear the brunt of abuse. I lived with endless guilt that she put herself through so much on our behalf, more guilt for her than sadness at the way my family was treated. Perhaps this was because Ingrid was protecting us out of choice, whereas we had no choice, we were victims.

I still do not understand why she sacrificed so much for us. The one time I asked her, she simply replied, "We are all people, dear Helga."

Rebecca put the letter down. Yes, she knew these stories but that it happened to her great aunts made it a bit different. It went into her own body. Would she have been as brave as Ingrid? What would she have done? Did she go into comedy because there was so much tragedy in her DNA? This was enough reading for today. Maybe they all got out.

-6-

My mother was the type to make decisions while simultaneously coming up with the plan. That is why one evening, with fire in her eyes, my mother announced that we were leaving Vienna for America in five days' time.

"It is all arranged. We must pack sparingly, one suitcase each. That is all. Only pack what you can carry." She spoke without emotion, which was rare for my mother although I imagine that she spoke like this simply to keep us calm.

My first reaction, I am ashamed to say, was to burst into sobs, which was promptly followed up with a nosebleed, an ailment I am prone to. It was a common occurrence for me to cry on the processing of breaking news. I was reluctant to change. I still am. Vienna was my home. I wanted to stay. Nowhere else in the world, I was certain, however bad it got, matched Vienna.

"But what about Papa?" I sobbed.

"We will correspond with Ingrid so that when Papa returns," here her voice gave a slight quiver, "she can keep Papa informed."

"And Palomina? Who will look after Palomina?"

I have barely mentioned to you our sweet Palomina, an Alpine Dachsbracke, a typical Austrian breed. She had eyes like melted chocolate and brown, silky fur and she loved us, particularly my mother so much that she and I often had to compete for my mother's lap.

"Ingrid is going to take her home to her village. Her family will care for her. She will love it in the countryside. Imagine all that hunting she will do. Now, you must be brave, Helga."

I nodded and hiccupped and stuffed handkerchiefs up my nose and sniffed and wiped blood-stained fingers across my tears. This was all too sudden.

It was the day before we were due to leave that my father returned home to us. It was almost like he knew. He rang the doorbell like a stranger and looked, at first, like a stranger, woolly grey hair in place of his neatly coiffured side parting, thick moustache, stubble on his chin and brown clothing. It was the brown clothing that shocked me most, my father hated brown.

"NO, my verliebte, we are not leaving Vienna," is what he said to my mother. "This is our country, NO ONE can force us to leave."

There was something different about my father on his return. Of course, one would expect certain differences. He had, of course been locked up and treated like vermin. There were other differences too, though, changes in his personality. He was terse, stressed and irritable.

"What have you done to your hair?" he asked my mother one day during breakfast. "I don't like it like that."

And the next day, "Why are you slouching, Helene? Stand tall, woman, stand tall." I might not have mentioned that my mother, when she was attacked, was inflicted with a blow to her shoulder, which left her neck too sore to straighten. My father knew this but he constantly demanded she "stand tall."

He sometimes made comments to me like, "You need to eat more, Helga your cheeks are sinking." But most of the time, he just stared at me without any of the affection I was used to. Of course, these were terrifying times we were living through and I am sure my father's mind was on bigger things than kisses and cuddles. At least that is what I told myself, until the day my mother's cheek turned black.

She hid it behind thick make up, which is what gave it away as my mother never wore make up. She didn't need to, her coloring was full of contrasts without it.

"What happened, Mama?" Lizzie asked

"Oh, I hit it on the edge of the bannister, that is all. Please don't fuss."

And then there was the split lip and the shouting and the muffled screams.

There is no other way to describe it than to say my father had become a monster. My gentle, thoughtful, eccentric father had transformed.

The five of us were living at this time in the closest proximity day in, day out within the confines of our home. My father's factory was gone, "discrepancies" they said, in his paperwork causing it to be "taken into new management" and my father barred from entry. My sisters and I were "removed" from our school and Ingrid did most of our food shopping. That is if you could call it food. We were living off vegetable broths and potatoes while my father's bank account was frozen.

My mother inhabited her bedroom, only coming down for meals during which time she picked at the contents of her plate, only speaking if she was spoken to. My father spent his days in the drawing room playing music so dark that I still shiver at the very sound of Verdi's Requiem, *Mozart's* Funeral March, *Berlioz's* March to the Scaffold- *ach these songs etched onto my brain to equal misery.*

122

*My sisters retreated into the comfort of each other. They
shared the same taste in books and magazines while I spent
my days sitting outside my mother's bedroom door longing for
her to come out. From breakfast to lunch, lunch to dinner I sat
there picking, picking, picking at the thread of the Oriental
rug, wrapping it tight around my fingers until the tips turned
blue. I neither dared to enter my mother's room or to leave the
door for fear she might come out and be gone.*

*This must have gone on for over a week until one occasion
when I left my post to go to the lavatory. I must have been
gone no more than a few moments, but when I returned my
mother's door was pushed a little way open and there were
voices coming from inside. I pushed the door further and
positioned myself just inside the doorway shielded by the door.
My mother was sitting on her bed with her back to me. Beside
her barely a centimeter apart, was Ingrid. Palomina was
curled up on the floor at the foot of the bed, one sleepy eye on
me.*

*My mother and Ingrid were speaking softly and my
mother's shoulders, how thin they had become, were shaking.*

*"You have to leave now, take the girls," Ingrid was saying.
"I have seen what is happening to Jews and it will happen to
you too. Please go, Frau Helene."*

*I am not sure how he managed it as my father had feet
flatter than a slab of butter but he crept up behind me and
pushed open the bedroom door so hard that it banged into the
bedside table behind it. It made me jump while my mother
and Ingrid flew off the bed clutching their chests.*

*"Helga…. Go," he said looking straight over my head onto
the wall in front. He was breathing deeply but there was a
quiver in his hands, which I did not trust.*

*I moved out of the doorway and resumed my position on
the hallway rug.*

"Whatever conspiracy you two are hatching," he said to my mother and Ingrid, entering the bedroom, fists clenched, "you can forget it. My family stays here... do you hear me Ingrid?"

"But Herr Schleff I implore you..." said Ingrid with a sob.

"My fa-m-ily ... stays ... here...," my father replied slowly through clenched teeth. "We are not refugees, we do not beg for asylum. We are Viennese citizens. This is our home. Do you understand me, Ingrid?"

"I do but the danger, Herr Schleff, you are in such danger..."

"OUT!" cried my father pointing his finger at the bedroom door. His face was scarlet, the pulse in his neck throbbing.

Grabbing a handkerchief from her pocket and stifling a sob, Ingrid ran out of the room, my father close on her heels. Paying no attention to me, he slammed the door shut.

"Is that what you want my verliebte?" I heard him say to my mother. His voice was tender. "We do not run to America at the first sign of trouble. Why pack up our lives and leave. We have committed no sin."

"That is arrogant, Freder. What makes you think our lives are any more cherished than the thousands of Jews who have left Vienna already? Must we be sitting ducks letting others decide our fate?"

"Show me the danger. I see no guns, no daggers. What is to fear?"

"Our lives, Freder, the lives of our daughters. Does the humiliation we have suffered already mean nothing to you?" My mother was shouting now.

"Don't speak to me of humiliation, Helene," there was a sneer in my father's voice, I could not see his face but I knew he was up close to my mother, pointing his finger in her face. "You have no idea about humiliation. To run to America away from here like a coward. To lose my family business, get thrown in jail in only my bare feet, my wife attacked and left

ugly, my daughters publicly disgraced, my housekeeper staying at my home out of charity. Do not speak to me of humiliation."

"Then let's leave, Freder. Our country has turned against us. Mama and Papa, David, they are all leaving tonight but they do not want to go without us. Come Freder, see some sense."

"My family stays here, Helene. We are not leaving. Never." That is what he said, his once soft, melodic voice thick with fury. "This subject is closed." He treaded heavily towards the door. "Helga, go read a book," he said, stepping over me and pacing downstairs, his red and gold brocade dressing gown billowing out behind him.

Oma and Opa and Uncle David, Auntie Sara, Simon and Aerial, left Vienna that night on a train bound for France. They had an American visa. We also had an American visa and passports that were up to date. My mother had seen to that. We were as good as out of Vienna, except, that my father forbade it. I never understood why this was, until it was too late.

Early the next morning when the sky was still dusk, there was a rapping on our front door. We were all awake immediately, filling the hallways with a flurry. I do not believe anyone in my family had slept soundly since the day my father was jailed. Ingrid, who had taken to staying over nights with us, sleeping in a small cupboard off the kitchen, was the first to the door. Her hair was in curlers and she had a pair of thick stockings on her legs.

On the doorstep were three men wearing the brown shirt uniform of the Sturmabteilung, *the SA paramilitary Nazi storm troopers complete with the swastika armband and kepi hat, a look now so familiar to us, you might say, the enemy face of WW2.*

"Herr Schleff, you have orders to vacate your home in fifteen minutes," one of the men said, a young man with stubble on his chin.

"Don't speak nonsense, Hans," replied my father. "Fifteen minutes or three years, I refuse to budge."

"I am sorry, Herr Schleff," replied the soldier, "But orders are...."

"Ach, why are you bothering to speak to this Jew with respect?" asked one of the accompanying storm troopers barging his way past Ingrid and into our hallway.

"He used to be my boss," replied Hans.

"And, now you are his boss, so move it." The accompanying men shoved my father out of the way and opening up big sheets from their shoulder bags, spread them out on the floor for filling with objects from our home.

"What are you... No, stop!" cried my father as the men removed paintings from the wall, clocks from the mantelpiece, ornaments from the bookshelves.

"That's nine minutes...Jew."

Such greed, like wild creatures starved of prey, the men devoured our house cramming their sheets full of lifetimes of possessions, many valuable but most simply sentimental. Every drawer was opened, every cupboard meticulously ravaged. "Five minutes," they shouted.

We stood there helpless, my family and I not knowing what to take, where to begin. We often used to discuss, the five of us, what we would rescue if our house were to go up in flames.

For my sisters, it was their diaries, my father his music, me, my cuddly Schnorbert even though he was a little bit threadbare around the ears and the paws, oh and Madelaide, my white rabbit. For my mother, it was simply, her girls. So long as we were safe, that was all that mattered.

This, though, was not a fire. This was almost more terrifying. This was other people moving into our home, into our cupboards, our beds, our sheets, our clothes. What to bring?

At the three-minute time check my blasted nose began to bleed, globules of blood spilling onto the Persian rugs, the flagstone floor. I ran downstairs looking for Ingrid but she was too busy in the kitchen wrapping up bundles of bread and preserves for us to take on our way.

"Bleed away darling Helga," she said shoving me some handkerchiefs, tears pouring down her cheeks. "I will not be washing this floor again."

When the fifteen minutes were up and we were pushed out of our own house, all I had in my possession was a bundle of blood-stained handkerchiefs along with Squidge, the scrawniest of my teddy bears and my least favorite.

As we crossed our threshold onto the street, I turned back for one last look at our home. Ingrid stood on the doorstep with Palomina in her arms and tears rolling down her plump, red cheeks. Taking one of Palomina's dainty brown paws, she raised it and waved it, then hugged Palomina tightly to her as if she was hugging each of us in turn.

My grandmother was right to admire Ingrid, Rebecca thought, sitting in the coffeeshop. I admire Ingrid. What strength to maintain humanity in that brutal world. Rebecca looked around her, smiled at the Polish waitresses, what had their families gone through? The Poles hated the Germans and yet the Poles were terrible anti-Semites. And here I am safe in this New York coffeeshop. Free to be a Jew, free to make jokes in a club, free. What did Helga suffer so my mother and I could be here, free? Rebecca looked at the clock on the wall. She should be somewhere but she couldn't remember where. She was going to keep reading till someone, anyone in this story was as safe as she is.

-7-

We were not the only Jews walking heads down, clutching onto meagre handfuls of possessions, there was a crowd of us. The pavement was strewn with glass from Jewish-owned bakeries, toyshops, jewelry shops, all smashed up, their interiors looted and the walls covered with insulting graffiti. It seemed everybody in Vienna was a vandal.

Robins, blackbirds, larks were singing as we trudged our way to Leopoldstadt, the second district and the only district in Vienna where Jews were welcome. The air was so fresh that morning as it is before daybreak but how could it be that everywhere around us was inflicted with disease?

We took lodgings at the house of a Frau Kaleki, somebody my father vaguely knew. I cannot tell you too much about this time, my memory is vague, perhaps I forget it deliberately. I seem to recall we shared the third floor of Frau Kaleki's house with another family who had two young sons, maybe five and six. My mother took up sewing drapes and cushions so that we could afford our lodgings and my father found a simple job working as a bookkeeper for a small Aryan firm who still had sympathies for the Jews. The house was crowded and noisy, the toilets always full and nobody really liked each other except that, for solidarity, we all made attempts at getting on.

There was a Jewish school, which I have some memories of my sisters and I attending but as this was not enforced I just hung around the house, no doubt clinging alongside my mother's hemline. I became a shy child, I remember Frau Kaleki referring to me as sullen but really my role was to take on the protection of my mother from the abusing hands of my father. Yes, how absurd, all around us were enemy soldiers, vandals and thugs but it was my own flesh and blood that I feared the most. My mother had become helpless and my father, despite his words of love, peace and beauty, a monster, an Übel monster. My mother needed me.

Fortunately this task was not difficult to accomplish as all my family slept together in the same room with nothing but paper-thin walls between us and the other lodgers. There was very little chance for my father to whet his fists.

Sometimes my mother insisted my sisters take me to school with them. There were only three remaining schools open for Jewish children. I didn't know any of the ten other Jewish children in my class and I was reluctant to make friends, as I believed friends would distract me from my mission, but being standoffish was not an option. When your very existence is vulnerable you inevitably bond with those in a similar position. I made a friendship with a girl of my age called Lauren. She was blonde like me and we stood out in the class of brunettes. That we were blonde meant that we could get away with more in the city. Jews were barred from entering parks or cinemas and most shops so we did not break these rules but we traveled inconspicuously on public transport as we had our free student bus passes. I began to enjoy myself, to loosen up a bit, even relish being away from my mother as the intensity I created being pinned to her side was stifling.

I did, of course, still rush to my mother on returning and surreptitiously examine her for bruises and at times I found some. They were mostly hidden, on the top of her arms or her thighs, sometimes when she lifted her beautiful long, thick mane of hair they were there on the back of her neck—that hateful man.

It is a strange feeling, falling out of love with a father. Ach, as I have explained, the way I felt towards my father up until this time was always on the love-hate cusp. Love because he was clever and funny and so very much alive, hate because he spoiled me and put me on a pedestal I had no desire to mount.

I imagine that falling out of love with a father is a little like falling out of love with a lover. At first there is the childlike adoration, the sense of comfort and security that life is safe. How devastating it is, therefore, to realize that this world is only make-believe, an illusion. There are no sparks of life, just grey and gloom and the sense that you are completely on your own.

You might wonder how, when the whole of Vienna was hostile and Jews were being attacked and humiliated and synagogues burned down, I was able to fixate only on my hatred for my father. It is, indeed, odd but if you ask me to remember life between 1938 and 1941 when I was 12-15 years old, the only memories I really have are of my parents. Of course there are snippets. One such snippet being when Germany invaded Poland, causing all of the Polish Jews to be rounded up in Vienna for deportation out of the city. This included Frau Kaleki meaning we were forced to leave her lodgings and relocate to another house, a smaller, more crowded one where we shared a room with an old lady, Auntie Margarita, who had green and black toes and was permanently bed bound.

Mother and I used to bathe Auntie Margarita. She wore heavy stockings on her legs, which were cut off at the feet. Beneath the stockings her legs were red and crusty. She smelled sour, a bit like yoghurt smells when it has been left for too long and she had a very saggy bottom. Apologies for being coarse but, to a child, an elderly lady's bottom is intriguing. Together my mother and I used to turn Auntie Margarita onto her side to wash her back. Her bottom, which had several layers of flaking skin, would slop onto one side exposing a hip as skinny as a chicken thigh.

She was such a kind lady and she never complained.

"Cold hands," she used to say to me clutching my skinny fingers. "Warm heart."

I have since learned that you can judge the character of a person by the way they react to the disabled and infirm. My father, he never went close to Auntie Margarita or even acknowledged her. He carried with him a sachet of lavender to mask her overpowering smell, which he permanently dabbed his nose with. I don't think he ever addressed her, even with a word of greeting; cruelty in my father ran deep.

I also remember having to wear the yellow star handed out by our headmaster, "You must not wear these out of shame but out of pride," he told us. "Pride for your race and pride for your religion."

Now I was no longer a Jew in disguise but a Jew out in the open, laid bare for all to ridicule. The first day I wore the yellow star I was attacked, along with Lauren, by a bunch of teenage boys who threw mud in my eye and spat in my hair. They made Lauren and I crawl around the pavement picking up cigarette butts, pointing and laughing at us with any passersby.

Typically, it was my father who reacted the worst to the yellow star. My father for whom personal style was so important, positively relished his individuality. Apologies, you see, I am back on my father again. What kind of field day would a psychiatrist have with me? He was beaten on several occasions for hiding his star behind his lapel or beneath a scarf. The only reason he was not seized and thrown into prison was because the boss at his bookkeeping company was "well connected" and liked my father's "inventive" style with numbers.

That he had a secure job at a time of such insecurity was the only strand of positive feeling I had towards my father, although I am sure this was centered around the fact it meant he was out of the house for most of the day leaving my mother (and in turn, me) some peace. It did, unfortunately serve to validate my father's argument that he had made the correct decision staying in Vienna.

"Flash in the pan." That is how he referred to our plight.

My father knew that I hated him because I made no attempt to hide it. "My baby is growing up, no more time for Papa." It was only when he spotted me noticing the hand shaped bruise at the top of my mother's slim, pale arm that he realized I was on to him.

"So careless, Helene always bumping into things," he said attempting unsuccessfully to pull my mother into his arms. "You should rest, you do too much." This charade stopped when I sighed and narrowed my eyes. After this, he left me alone, skirting around me as much as I skirted around him. Only occasionally did he draw attention to the length of my hair or to my unpolished shoes, my father hated drab leather.

The letter requesting the deportation of my family came in 1942. It was not an unfamiliar letter, Auntie Margarita had received one a few months before and my mother and I helped her pack the only suitcase she was permitted to take. We aided her as she walked down the stairs, well it was more carrying than walking. She was so frail her, knotty elbow jutting into my spine as she draped one arm across my shoulder. We later heard that Auntie Margarita was shot in the back before she even got to where she was being dispatched. The SS had no tolerance for old age.

Our letter stated for us to pack a bag and report the following morning at 8am to the Sperlschule, where we were to await deportation transport. It was on receiving the letter that my father, for the first time, broke down and sobbed. Until this moment I do believe he thought he was above the law for Jews. I told you before, my father was a snob. He thought himself as Jewish as a racehorse might consider itself a Shetland pony.

*In the midst of his sobs, he grabbed my mother who was
standing close by and pulled her to him seeking, I imagine,
some form of comfort but my mother did not put out her arms
as she had done when Auntie Margarita sobbed at the same
news. She simply stood like a pillar, still and cold, but I could
see this was not easy for her.*

Rebecca decided to read the rest in her living room. It was
almost too much to read this in a coffeeshop where everything
was in abundance. *Maybe this next chapter will be how she got away.*
As she walked to her apartment in the sun, with the New York
city sirens somewhat unnerving her, Rebecca was all too aware
that this was no comedy. And this generational hatred of fathers.
Although in her mother's and her own case, the hatred was
because their fathers did not seem to bother to even exist.

She got home, took off her sneakers, plopped down on the
couch and began again.

-8-

*There were already hundreds of people at the Sperlschule
when we arrived early the next morning to register. Judging by
the stench of human sweat and stink of excrement, the snoring
and moaning, the sobs and shouts, it seemed many had been
there several days already. There were beige mattresses
scattered on the floor in each of the classrooms, and people
sitting on the edge of the mattresses, miserable, empty
expressions in their eyes. I had no idea, as I looked around the
dingy, crowded classrooms that compared to the place we
were going, this was deluxe.*

*Commissioned is what we were, this means that as we
crouched together like cows to the slaughter, Anton Brunner
(the war criminal hung in 1946 for crimes against Jews)
systematically tore up every ounce of evidence indicating that*

we ever existed. Birth certificates, identity cards, marriage certificates, diplomas, citizenship papers. He hated Jews, you could see it in his eyes; to him, we were simply as irritating as dog shit. This didn't stop him laughing at my father's sob the moment he tore up his papers.

"What's wrong with you? This never was your promised land, Abraham..." he said. "But I promise there will be land where you're going. Lots of it." He nudged his assistant and the two of them sniggered like schoolboys.

"Come, Freder," said my mother gently hauling my father to his feet. "We can visit the land together." Taking my mother's hand, my father stood up, faltered a little, straightened up and together my parents walked to the awaiting transport.

-9-

So many things happened in the next few weeks and months but these happenings are not the purpose of my letter to you.

Before I set forth on the next stage of my story, I must inform you that I will be going this part alone. My father, he was not put on the same transport as my mother, sisters and I. Men were herded one way, women another.

About my mother and my sisters, I will explain.

We were crammed together in the dark, crowded train carriage, no chairs to sit on, no water to drink and a bucket for our toilet, which, within moments of the train leaving the station, was knocked over so we had excrement seeping into our shoes. We traveled all day in an unheated goods train watching fellow passengers fall around us, icicles collected on their nostrils. We clung together so tightly my mother, sisters and I, eking out every iota of bodily warmth but still we were rigid. Disembarking the train, Edith slipped. She was so cold, her shinbone snapped like a pencil as she collapsed onto the icy ground.

Unable to walk, Lizzie and Mother took an arm each and heaved Edith up. The three of them hobbled onto the station platform.

"Is there anywhere for my daughter to sit?" my mother asked a German soldier with a long, lined face and a gun resting on his chest. "She's broken her leg."

"No chairs, it's a ten kilometer walk to the ghetto, I hope you are feeling strong Mama?" he said clearing his throat and spitting tobacco out in a straight squirt.

"She can't possibly walk that," my mother said. "Surely there is somewhere for her to sit just to rest it for a while."

"Take her to the truck," said the soldier pointing to a lorry parked adjacent to the train, "she can travel in there."

"Oh thank God," said Lizzie who was bearing Edith's full weight.

"Just you three go," said the soldier restraining me with the side of his gun. "She can walk."

"Please, we must stay together," said my mother.

"She won't be far behind. You can have her bed ready for her at the Ghetto Hotel."

"Go Mama," I said. "I can walk."

"See," said the soldier. "Let her walk," he looked me up and down. "She's strong. I can take care of her." The soldier pushed me one way and pointed his gun in the direction of the lorry.

I did not look back, I was steered into a line and commanded to walk and all I could do was dream about getting to the ghetto to a bed and a warm room. I had no idea what to expect but I knew it had to be better than trudging through the forest on slippery ice.

When we arrived an hour later, I was herded through metal gates and onto a wide street surrounded on both sides by barbed wire fences. Behind the fences were lines of two- and three- story houses. If it were not for the barbed wire and signs proclaiming, "Anyone Attempting Escape Will Be Shot,' the ghetto would not have looked that different from a typical European town with narrow lanes and lampposts.

I was steered into a house on the outskirts of the ghetto with back windows that overlooked a barbed wire fence. Crammed against the fence in a pyramid were the corpses of eight elderly victims, eyes staring in at me, piled on top of each other along with books and shoes strewn on the ground. I felt sick. I searched around frantically for my mother.

An elderly man with no teeth and sunken cheeks asked me my name and showed me to a grimy mattress in the corner of one of the small pokey rooms already occupied by a sleeping body. There were already at least twelve people in the room asleep in various arrays of clothing, some fully dressed, others in scarves, vests and hats. Everyone was dirty and skinny and pale.

"You get half the mattress," the old man said.

"Where will my mother and my sisters sleep?" I whispered.

"I don't see any mother or sisters?"

"They came on the truck, they should be here already."

The old man shrugged steering me to my bed, "I dunno, maybe they got assigned to another camp. It happens."

"No!" I cried, "I have to find them."

"Go outside and they will shoot you, young lady," said the man adding in a gentler voice. "Wait until the morning, you can find them then."

I slept fitfully, barely able to stretch out for fear of kicking my feet or arms into the girl at the other end of my mattress.

There was no sign of my mothers and sisters when I queued for my rations at the local food store. Feeling sick, I asked around if anyone had seen a teenage girl hobbling about with a broken leg but nobody engaged me in conversation. There was not time, mornings were when everyone had to go to work.

If you did not work you were shot. I was given the job of cleaning the SS offices, which according to the job assignment officer, a Jew like me, was a coveted job as it meant I could stock up on food by stealing scraps from the dustbins.

There was still no sign of my mother or sisters three days later when I came face to face with the SS officer from the train station responsible for dispatching them to the truck. I was inside the SS officer's toilet block where there were four tiny toilet cubicles and a small public area for washing hands.

"Oh, it's you again," the officer said regarding me on my hands and knees, scrubbing a toilet seat. He came into the tiny cubicle with me and closed the door. "You know you don't look Jewish. Maybe you were adopted," he laughed. "It happens you know, perhaps there was a mistake and you are actually a pure Aryan girl. Why else would I want to touch you?"

"Where did you send my mother and sisters?" I asked the officer, toilet brush in my hand, not looking up from the floor for fear he would see the desperation in my eyes.

"Oh, don't you know," he said. "I am surprised nobody told you. Well, you will find out soon enough."

"I'd like to know now," I said.

"Who cares about what you want to know, adoptee Jew." He took a step towards me, which made him too close, put his hand under my chin and jerked my head up.

"I don't give a damn."

Crouching down before me so that his watery blue eyes were level with my face, he began running his hand over my shoulder down to the front of my blouse and fondling my nipples with his fingertips. "I give you commands."

He let his hand travel lower, panting hot tobacco breath into my nostrils. I made to stand up but he shoved me back down onto my knees.

"Don't fuck with me, adoptee whore," he said. "Or I won't show you the letter I have here for you from your mama." He

patted his jacket pocket. "She asked me to give it to you and I said, of course but only if she lets me see her naked."

I did nothing but my heart was racing. I knew there was no letter from my mother but, at the same time, I didn't know, maybe there was.

"Get naked," the officer said, slapping me around the face.

I'd barely unbuttoned two buttons of my blouse when the officer threw me backwards so that my head hit the edge of the toilet. Mounting me he slid his penis out from his trousers and began masturbating on top of me, his knees rubbing against the narrow cubicle walls. He was grunting and moaning and all the while rubbing me up and down, pinching me and slapping me around my face. After ejaculating all over my blouse he stood up, buttoned his trousers and patted his pocket.

"You never got naked, whore, come back same time tomorrow. You only see the letter if you get naked."

Checking himself for orderliness, the Officer unlocked the cubicle door and left me lying on the floor, stinking of semen and covered in welts and bruises.

Did I go back the next day? I am ashamed to say yes I did. I wanted so much for there to be a letter and I believed that if I did what the officer asked and removed my clothes I might get to read it. You see how easily the young are lured into a trap. Of course, I was never quick enough removing my clothing, always the officer was onto me and mounting me and grunting before I had even begun.

On one of the days I was undressed before he arrived, I didn't care about revealing all to this animal, I was beyond such emotion. How shocking this sounds back in the real world but nothing about life then was real and I was so desperate for that letter. When the officer arrived and found I had anticipated him he simply spat at me and said. "I did not command you to get undressed, bitch," before turning on his heel and departing the toilet block.

It made no sense to me, the whereabouts of my mother and my sisters. I was frantic to find them but so limited in what I could do. If I got caught out after dark, I was shot. If I ventured into another section of the ghetto away from where my group was located, I got shot.

I got talking with some of the girls in my group. My favorite was Sally who was not Jewish but arrested for having Jewish sympathies. She called herself the "resistance' but she was so frail. We whispered together late into the night, which annoyed the elderly inmates in our room. She told me stories, terrifying stories of what happened to people who went missing, stories I refused to accept.

I was desperate to inform Sally about my daily humiliation in the SS offices but I was too nervous. What I was doing was shameful, if they knew they would want nothing to do with me. What I did not realize is that I was not the only one. Sally came to me one early morning in floods of tears telling me she was pregnant and showing me bruises up and down her inner thighs.

That there was a brothel in the ghetto was common knowledge. It was SS nightlife but I was naïve. I did not really understand what a brothel was and I certainly did not know that Sally was being used as fodder. "Don't let them drag you down there, Helga. It stinks of rat's urine and they beat you and throw you on the ground and spit on you while ramming you between your thighs."

I continued to meet with the SS officer in the toilet cubicle for several weeks, each time with him requesting me to get naked but never letting me get that far. Sometimes he was violent and punched me in the stomach or kicked me in the legs, other times moody and sullen where he just "got the job done,' and barely spoke but he never attempted to have *intercourse with me. I expected it every time we met but it never happened. I accommodated him and his moods for the tiny spark of hope that he might have something, anything from my mother.*

It shows, I suppose, how far I had stooped when I began questioning why I was not picked for the brothel. I was already so filled with anxiety for my mother and my sisters, that the thought of being dragged into a brothel and sexually abused was almost too much for my nerves. One day I stole a packet of cigarettes from a desk in the SS offices shoving them into the waistband of my skirt. It was a crime that would get me a public hanging but the only way to butter up the elder heading up my group was with cigarettes. It was the elder who handed out clothing chits and I wanted to obtain as many clothes as I could in order hide the curse of my womanliness from hungry eyes.

It was in the clothing store known as the Kleiderkammer *run by two inmates from the ghetto that I spotted my mother's red coat. It was staring out at me from a hanging rail complete with the missing button on the cuff. I stared at it for what must have been a minute, my mind racing as to all the possibilities of how it got there. There could be only one possibility, my heart leapt. She must be here.*

"That coat," I said to one of the two ladies running the shop, "it belongs to my mother."

The two inmates glanced at each other. Something told me they had been in similar scenarios before.

"And is your mother at the ghetto?"

"I think so but I haven't found her yet," I answered.

After a few questions from the lady in charge of the Kleiderkammer, *she took me aside and gently explained that the clothing was from people who had perished. She told me that the truck that I believed would transport my mother and sisters to the ghetto was in fact not a truck but a gas chamber* and that people entering the gas chambers never made it out alive. She told me in a direct manner, which I appreciated and then took the red coat off the shelf and said, "You have it for free. It belongs to you."

Apologies but I cannot linger on this bit of my letter, the greatest tragedy of my life. I must move on.

I did not attend work for the next couple of days choosing instead to sit on my half of the mattress and stare at the chipped brickwork walls. I might have stayed like this for days if all ghetto inmates had not been hauled onto the street on the third evening. This happened every so often when the ghetto got too overcrowded. The SS officers paraded up and down the lines of inmates shouting,

"Where do you work?"

Any inmate who was elderly or infirm was taken into the forest and shot.

"In the SS offices," I said in a voice so weak the officer hit me with the side of his gun and requested I speak up.

I was forced the next day to go back to work by Sally who said she needed me alive so that I could go with her to the doctors for an abortion.

The rage I felt having to face the lying officer who had no letter from my mother and never did was unbearable. When he entered the cubicle, his face was throbbing with anger. He was carrying a pair of scissors.

"I could kill you right here," he said pointing the scissors at my jugular.

"When I look for you, I expect you here." He was looming over me inside the narrow cubicle. "What do you think this is, some holiday camp, come and go as you please?"

I made no comment. I couldn't. My mouth was stuck fast. I had all the words I wanted to say, the abuse I wanted to throw his way, nails poised to tear out his eyes but I was too scared. Would a hedgehog attack a wolf? This man had sent my

*mother and my sisters to their deaths and lied to me. I was
sick with hatred but all I could do was stare straight ahead at
the bottom of his polished black boots. Without even bothering
to mount me the officer remained standing, undid his trousers
and worked his penis, juddering and gasping as the semen
spurted over my legs. When he was done and his trousers
buttoned up, he grabbed me by the neck and strangled me, his
hands like metal clamps. I kicked him and punched him
trying to bite his hand but this only made him squeeze harder.
It takes very little time to throttle the life out of someone.
Within seconds the world was grey and I was floating to the
floor, hands flapping helplessly by my side. I don't know why
he didn't kill me. It would have only taken a few more
squeezes and I would have ceased to exist. Instead, as I was
gasping for breath like a fish out of water, he took a hold of my
hair and dragged me out of the cubicle, out of the toilets, away
from the SS offices and onto the main street that ran through
the center of the ghetto. He threw me to my knees and here, for
all to see, he hacked off my hair taking handfuls of golden
locks and slashing them like he was threshing wheat. People
on their way back from work stopped to watch, SS officers
cheered and shouted out, "Whip her, strip her!"*

*My head was so light from the asphyxiation that I barely
registered what was happening. My focus was on obtaining
oxygen into my lungs. When I came around I saw only the
blade of the scissors, brutal in their attack, one or two
centimeters and they would have had my eye out.*

*When he was done, the officer threw me to the floor and
leant over me.*

"There was never a letter from your mama... Jew."

*I half expected him to shoot me but he didn't. He just spat
in my face and walked away shoving the scissors into the
pocket where the letter should have been.*

-10-

The doctor, an elderly Jewish man with a small beard and thinning grey hair looked Sally and I up and down when we entered his tiny office. I nervously clutched my shorn head and wrapped my mother's red coat tightly around me.

"Yes?"

"Abortion," said Sally in a low voice.

"Tut... how many weeks?"

"Six, maybe or five."

Sighing, the small, arrogant doctor led us to an adjacent room, and asked Sally to lie on a cold, metal table. Pulling back her several layers of skirts so that her thighs, still black and blue were revealed he said, "You should be more careful. Keep away from men."

I went to protest but Sally shook her head.

"Yes, doctor," she said.

I was sent to wait outside the medical block. As I stood there at least fifteen gentile women walked in, all young, all pretty beneath their tangled hair and dirty clothes. I found out later that the majority of operations the doctor undertook were abortions on the "Resistance." And with each abortion the doctor gave a tut and told the women to keep away from men.

"This is the only abortion the doctor will let me have," said Sally as she emerged from the medical block, pale and sore. "If I get pregnant again he will sterilize me like a dog."

I have to tell you, my friend Sally did get pregnant again but she was so fearful of being sterilized she remained pregnant, hiding her growing belly under heavy clothes. When she was around seven months pregnant, she was discovered. She was shot in the back making her way to work. It would not surprise me if the officer who shot her was the very same soldier who got her pregnant in the first place. These were desperate times. Any amount of cruelty was feasible.

I left the ghetto to be relocated to Auschwitz, sullied but not ruined. I still had my virginity and, pitiful as it might sound, that meant a lot to me. What it meant was that however many times I was spat on, beaten, humiliated, abused, I could inwardly hold my head high.

This did not mean that the SS ghetto officers were gentler than in other camps. Far from it, they were like animals the way they salivated and lusted after any woman with breasts bigger than golf balls, taunting us with sexual jibes, forcing us to undress and dance naked or perform like monkeys for their sexual thrills, but it was rare that Jewish women were violated. At the ghetto, SS officers stuck loosely to the rulebook dictating that any Aryan caught partaking in sexual intercourse with a Jew, would be convicted and charged with forced labor. Sex for SS officers was reserved for imprisoned gentiles like Sally.

But everything was different at Auschwitz. A day before my deportation, I caught a stomach bug. I am surprised I was not shot on the station platform, I was so pathetic, clutching at my guts as I boarded the train. I was a sorry mess, crouched in the corner of the carriage retching dark green bile into a metal plate I had found on the floor of the train. It is hard to describe to you how wretched a person can feel and I am not keen to hark on too much about my experience because what I was enduring was no different to that of the hundreds of thousands of other men, women and children during those times.

There was a selection process for Jews arriving at Auschwitz. Women with children, the elderly and the sick and pathetic like me, we were dispatched one way. Stronger women like I had been two days before, were dispatched elsewhere. I knew I was in the line for death. What good were the old, young or sick? We were shown into a white tiled room and commanded to remove all of our clothing, every single item. As I stood shivering with misery a stick hit me on the shoulder and I was shoved against the wall.

"You, stand over there."

I was made to stand alone as the crowd of naked bodies were led out of a door at the far end of the room, struck with sticks or fists if they paused. A tiny girl, no more than seven, glanced back at me and our eyes locked. As she exited the room, she gave a tiny wave, the kind royalty gives when they are riding in their carriages. I did not know, she did not know that the room she was filing into was a gas chamber. She would have been dead within seconds of that wave.

"This way," said an officer when everyone else was gone. I was shown through a door off to the side of the main room. Inside the matching white room was a line of women naked like me. Two inmates, men in striped pyjamas were shaving the women's bodily hair. There was no privacy. The SS officers were hanging around chatting and pointing at our exposed features like we were penguins at the zoo.

Bald and clad in a hand towel I was directed along with the other women to a stone block close to the main gate of the camp. It smelled of disinfectant. The officer pointed into a room barely bigger than a coffin with a narrow camp bed covered with a tartan blanket.

"You, in there," he said to me, "And put this on." He shoved a long blonde wig and some blusher my way.

I was to learn much later that non Jewish prisoners were "rewarded" for their work with coupling with non-Jewish female prisoners.

I never understood why they wanted to watch the Jewish men be with we Jewish women. Why they would want to watch this. But nothing was rational then, only cruel.

"Try and make yourself attractive." He shut the wooden door leaving me alone. The room was airless and windowless. I examined the wig. There were specs of blood on the lining and patches of bald fabric where it looked like it had been wrenched off.

"You ready?" came a voice knocking at the door.

"For what?" I asked in a weak voice.

"Sex," said the officer entering. "You've got two minutes per man. Be ready or I'll shoot you." He took his gun and aimed it at my breasts, circling the nozzle around my nipple.

What could I do? I was dead if I did what was commanded and dead if I did not. I slumped down heavily on the bed, barely able to find the strength to attach the wig to my skull.

"Man one," said the officer shoving in a bent corpse dressed in striped pyjamas.

"Two minutes, you on top," he said to the emaciated inmate.

"Whore, lie down on the bed."

I lay down on the lumpy hard mattress as the skeletal form removed his hat and fumbled with the front of his trousers.

There was white stubble on the inmate's chin, encrusted with a week's worth of food. As his face neared mine I could smell the stench of decay in his breath. He positioned his bony hips on my pelvis and jabbed at my vagina like a woodpecker.

"Like it, do you?" he said eventually entering me and feebly ramming.

"Stop," I cried weakly trying to push him off, but he paid no attention thrusting at me, and panting.

"Out," said the officer opening the door.

The man stood up, fumbled once more with his trousers, replaced his hat, gave me a slight nod and left me alone on the bed shivering with shock. I dragged myself up and clutching onto my stomach, retched into the corner trying to rid myself of my guts. Nothing came up.

"Don't do that again," the officer said, seizing my arm and throwing me back on the bed. "Whores don't say stop."

He looked down the corridor. "Next."

There was another man and another, six that day in total or maybe it was seven.

Sometime that night the queue of skeletal, fired up, hungry men drew to a close. I was told to sleep on the same, soft, lumpy mattress sticky with semen and sweat and given a watery bowl of broth.

What I became that day was a brothel whore. Day in, day out, scrawny, hungry men were sent to me to paw and salivate and, if they were lucky, ejaculate. Sometimes the men were too weak to mount me, so they wasted their two-minute slot simply lying beside me feeling my breasts. Sometimes they were angry and rough, other times sad and sobbing.

Then there were the soldiers turned on by observing through the spy hole in the door, unable to restrain their lust. They were the worst because they were well fed and full of energy demanding sexual positions that I could never summon up the energy to give.

It happened a few days later, a man was pushed into my room. I no longer paid attention to the men. I didn't even raise my eyes from the mattress as they groped for me, manhood bulging inside the droopy confines of their pyjamas. The man pushed into my room was no different to any of the other men, shaking with anticipation, wheezing and panting with gaunt frame, sallow cheeks, shaved head and eyes submerged behind overly pronounced cheekbones, a typical Auschwitz inmate. Mounting me the man began to hum the deep, low hum of Wagner's Ride of the Valkyries, a tune so familiar to me sung in the way only I knew it to be sung that I leapt up sending the man smashing to the floor. "Wagner," I cried bursting into tears, "Do not sing Wagner."

"Helga?" the man on the floor squirmed and wriggled, attempting to subdue his penis. "You, Helga?"

"Papa?" I cried. "Papa?"

The door burst open but not before I saw the look of utter disgust flickering across my father's worn out face.

"Two minutes of sex you pig shit, not choir practice," the soldiers yelled, hitting my father around the head.

"That is my daughter," my father's voice was quivering.

"Good, a bit of inbreeding that's what you Jews do isn't it, screw your cousins? Now get on with it."

"Do you not understand what you are asking me to do?" said my father.

"Do it or I'll shoot off your pecker. O whore, back on the bed!"

Sobbing, I dragged myself onto the mattress and my father directed by the end of the gun climbed on top of me. "You disgust me," he whispered as the officer jabbed him with the gun nozzle.

"Whip it out, time waster," the officer said, "If you want to keep it."

I felt my father's semi erect penis hovering around the entrance to my tired, bruised vagina.

"Put it in old man. This isn't romance."

"My daughter, a whore," said my father. "Cheap sex." I could feel his penis harden as it entered inside me.

I just silently cried. How could this be happening? And to see him also be humiliated like this, to act like an animal.

"Your mother was a slut too, did you know that?" he said starting to push against me. "How else do you think she got us our travel visas?"

"Mama is dead," I whispered, tears coming down my face.

"Dead?" he slumped momentarily.

"Your fault, Papa."

"How do you think she got us our visas? Helga?" he continued breathing harder, fingers squeezing my shoulders. "It was by getting in touch with that ex-lover of hers, why else do you think I was so angry with her, Helga? She would have gone to America and deserted me."

"Cum yet, pig breeder?" asked the officer entering into the room and pointing the gun into my father's ear.

"Nearly," replied my father.

"Don't leave it much longer," he said shutting the door. There was the sound of crude laughter in the corridor.

"You had to know the truth, Helga, in case we don't meet again. That was why I beat your mother, to help her understand, marriage is for life."

And this life was death. I don't know if I cared anymore about life.

He gave a judder, withdrew his penis and fell off me.

"I loved her, Helga, but I was never prepared to share her. Why else do you think I prevented us all leaving Vienna. It was for love, Helga, always for love."

"Get out," I spat, unable to see from too much grief.

"You Jews are sick," the officer said as my father left the room, coming in and undoing his trousers. "Screw anything that moves you would."

-11-

I was in the midst of a timeless sleep, hours later maybe weeks, when an officer dragged me by my hair, down the narrow corridor and out into the dazzling white snow. It was days since I'd seen light beyond a dim low bulb. I did not care where I was going. I barely noticed the ice seeping through the soles of my bare feet. I had no feeling in my body. I was thrown down, landing heavily on a pile of spiky limbs. Women and girls lying like rocks on the ground, held in check not so much by the guns directed our way as by the loss of a will to live. Two soldiers deep in conversation barely looked our way as they began to shoot. Bodies rolled and popped and squelched around me as cold hard metal punctured skin and cracked bone and ricocheted off skulls. I clenched every inch of my body and squeezed my eyes shut. Death did not scare me, just the pain of dying or perhaps the indelibility of human nature. I lay motionless for minutes before I dared to ease my tension. Bodies were on top of me, heavy like cement and there was blood to wipe from my eyeballs, my mouth, other people's blood, not my own. I could feel no pain. I was free of bullets, I was screaming inside from fear but instinct told me I would not survive the hour in the cold if I did not find warmth.

"Move Helga," I said to myself, "move." Using my elbows I freed myself from the solid heap almost fighting through the limbs in my desperation to be free.

Eventually I was able to push myself up onto my arms like a bloody corpse rising from the dead, which is how I must have looked to the terrified boy soldier standing over me who ran off shouting in an unfamiliar language. I had barely shifted when another solider appeared, not German but equally blond, and with thick, gloved hands, he lifted me out. He laughed at the sight of me naked and covered in blood but called to one of his compatriots for a clean, woolly blanket.

Ach so, it was the Soviets who liberated us, this you know. We were a line of starving terrified inmates marching out of the gates of the camp flanked by Soviet soldiers throwing bread for us like we were pigeons, many of us were so weak we fell and had to be lifted and propped up by fellow inmates. We were a sorry sight, as we exited our prison but we were free.

My father was rescued that day, too, but he was too ill to walk much further than the gates of the camp. I spotted him sitting against the trunk of a tree coughing into his knees, an emaciated bag of bones. His eyes were glazed and I do not think he saw me even when I stood before him.

"Papa," I said but he did not answer me. "Papa."

Truth is, I did not want my father to survive. I did not want to spend my days looking after his grieving, cruel heart so I did what no daughter should ever do: I walked away. I told nobody that I was his daughter and, standing a fair distance from him, I watched him cough and choke and fall sideways into the snow. When the soldier came to him he must have already been dead because no attempt was made to prop him back up.

Rebecca put the paper down, almost feeling numb herself. What more is she going to read? It was a horror that was unspeakable. She had to admire her grandmother's honesty and clarity. Her will. Her strength of mind. But even reading this, Rebecca felt broken. How could one survive this? She picked up the pages again. She had to go on, even if this was beyond terrible. Her grandmother, she could already see, was going somewhere that she wanted her, Rebecca, to know. *This horror is the prelude to something relevant to my life,* Rebecca thought. And it made her sick to think so.

-12-

I gave birth to Levana, seven months later. I was in a displaced person's camp in Poland. There were hundreds of us. We were fed and clothed and we were free except we were not free because we had nowhere to go. We were unwelcome everywhere and our homes were gone. I knew where I wanted to be. This was with my Opa and Oma in America and my

Uncle David. I wanted my cousins. I craved family but how could I go? How could I explain to my loved ones that I was a whore and that the child in my arms was born of a Nazi or a criminal or a Latvian, Pole, Czech, German or God forbid, born of my very own father? I was so full of shame and worse than that, full of remorse because I hated my daughter. I could not look her in the eye because I did not know into whose eyes I was looking. I could not feed her my breast milk, as I was too malnourished, at least that was what I said, really it was because I did not want any affection between us. They say that a mother's love conquers all but not this mother. You might ask why I did not give my daughter, your mother, away if I felt like this? So many women would have cried out for such a beautiful brown-eyed girl. I thought about this on many occasions but it was not feasible because selfishly, Levana kept me safe. I prayed men would think twice about laying their clammy hands on the mother of a baby.

There it is, Rebecca thought. There is the ice for my own heart.

Helga went on:

I found it hard to make friends in the displaced person's camp even though I was desperately lonely and unhappy. I trusted nobody, particularly not men. In fact, I avoided men at all costs because I knew what lay behind the smiles and chivalry. Men were panting, hungry, greedy animals. I had been with enough to know.

We were living in an army barracks, cold and noisy and too crowded even to dry a towel without it touching someone else's laundry. I rarely left to go outside the room, sharing a bottom bunk with Levana who was a twitchy, restless baby prone to projectile vomiting. As you can imagine, we did not endear ourselves to our roommates.

152

People were always asking if I intended to look for my family and I believe I shocked them when I said that I had no plans to do so. It was all anyone spoke about, plans for returning home or dreams of reuniting with loved ones and of course their grief. We were so many traumatized people tightly packed together, prone to sobbing and shouting and screaming and tearing at our skin with our nails, or staring into space rocking back and forth like we were in a demented state. That was for us, normal behavior.

I must have been more bitter and angry than most because after a while people avoided me. I spent hours sitting in silence on my bunk reading any books I could get my hands on while Levana slept or lay at my feet staring up at the bunk above, under stimulated and unkempt. I was hungry for fantasies or thrillers, whatever could separate me from my misery. The only genre of book I avoided and still avoid to this day is romance. This turns my heart to stone, happy couples kissing, holding hands and falling in love.

When I wasn't reading I listened to the radio, it was my lifeline to the outside world. I became fanatical about the BBC, the music, the poetry and the news. It was from the BBC that I learned to speak English. I am sure it is also the reason Levana speaks English so well, because that was the only voice that engaged with her as a baby.

I was at this camp for I suppose a year when a Jewish man approached me and asked if I wanted to begin a new life for myself in the homeland. Of course I knew of British-led Palestine and of the largely unsuccessful attempts of Jews to enter illegally into the country but it never occurred to me that I might be one of these settlers, able to start afresh.

He was called Julian and I cannot tell you too much about what he looked like because I never looked him in the eye but it was he who smuggled Levana and I out of Poland, across land by train and foot to the displaced person's camp in Italy where I was told to wait until a crossing became available. It was also he who made sure we had enough food and water and that I had sensible shoes. It was indeed also Julian who carried Levana on his back and made sure she was warmly dressed. Not me, her mother. Ach, it was also Julian who wanted repayment from me for his kindness when we arrived in Italy and who grew angry when I refused to service his desires.

I was rescued from Julian by Marina, a hotheaded Italian volunteer who reminded him in front of me, that he had a wife and a baby in Palestine, who were awaiting his return. Marina who seemed old to me, somewhere in her thirties, fell instantly in love with Levana, the bambina and spent many hours cuddling her and singing to her and doing everything maternal that I had never done.

It was with Marina that your mother spoke her first words, "Ma-Ma."

"See she is calling you," Marina said to me with tears of pride but of course I knew the Ma-Ma was for Marina, not me.

I changed my name when we arrived in Israel. I wanted no one to track me down, seek me out. I intended to start afresh, retell the story of my survival. To my new friends, I strove to provide Levana with a true father who tragically died in the camp. "The love of my life," I used to say, "Levana has his smile." I proclaimed this to everyone except Levana. I couldn't bring myself to lie to my own daughter. When she asked about her father I simply said, "Not now, Levana." Or "Why does it matter so much to you?" Heartless comments that were intended to make Levana hate me. I needed this, except she never did hate me. She grew up hating herself instead. By eight, Levana was bald from pulling out her hair, by ten she was cutting her arms and legs with kitchen knives and, by fourteen, she was as thin as an Auschwitz inmate from self-inflicted starvation.

Still I never gave your mother my love. I left her to wonder at her life, her past and, as before, I never looked her in the eye for fear of my father's eyes staring back.

When Levana was twenty-one years old and out of my care, she met a boy, well, a young man I suppose you could say, at a Tel Aviv nightclub. He was called Joseph. He proclaimed to be in love with my beautiful daughter, the first person in her life to truly love her. I cannot go into details of their love affair because Levana never let me in. All I can tell you is that I received a phone call from Levana at the start of 1967 telling me with great joy that she was pregnant with Joseph's baby.

Of course, I had mixed feelings, grief, joy, pain, anger but I pretended to Levana that I was happy for her. Pretending was something I did well.

Five months later, I had a phone call from Levana. Her voice was hollow, weak, quivering.

"What is it Levana?" I asked.

She told me that Joseph was dead. His plane was shot down undertaking military pursuits in the Six Day Arab – Israeli war. She told me she had miscarried and that her baby was gone. She told me she was going to travel to India on a retreat and that I was not to look for her.

"I need to be alone," she told me.

I wanted to tell her that she had always been alone but I didn't. To be truthful, it was something of a relief to have her gone. All her life, I had longed for her to be gone.

Two years later I started getting pains in my stomach, excruciating pains that left me writhing around on the floor

*screaming for help. Nobody responded to my screams, of
course, because I had nobody to hear me. I had purposefully
created a life with nobody in it. It was easiest this way. I didn't
deserve people in my life. How could it be right that I had
survived the war, a whore, when so many innocent people like
my mother, my sisters had died? Nobody in my life meant
there was nobody to ask me questions and no need for me to
lie.*

*I went to the hospital eventually. They told me I had
cancer of the stomach and operated on me two days later.
They asked if I had any family to take care of me and I told
them, Yes. I made up a family of care providers in order for
them to allow me home.*

*It was while I was recovering that I felt the need, no
stronger than that, the longing, to find Levana. The doctors
were not sure of my prognosis. A 50:50 chance of the cancer re-
occurring, they said. Perhaps it was the prospect of my
mortality or maybe I simply developed a heart, I don't know
what it was, but I bought myself a plane ticket to India. I had
received three letters from Levana in the two years she had
been gone, two of them birthday cards. She never forgot my
birthday. She was a sweet girl, a sweet unloved girl. The most
recent was a letter, just a few words telling me she was alive
and well. It had an address on the back in Calcutta and so it
was to there that I made my way.*

*I arrived at the address in the back of a rickshaw. I was not
a good traveler and found India a very overwhelming place.
Too hot, too dirty, too confusing. I had thought only of finding
Levana and not of my own comfort, such as accommodation
or indeed what I might do if I could not find my daughter.*

*The address was for a run-down house, it did not look to
me like a retreat but then again, I had no idea of what a
retreat should look like. There was a long rope that resembled*

a lavatory chain. I was informed by a young man loitering by the door it was the doorbell. It was opened almost immediately by a girl not dissimilar in age to Levana. She was French but spoke some English. Enough to inform me that Levana was no longer living there. She had moved on three months before.

"Did she leave an address of where she was going?" I asked. The girl shrugged and disappeared inside leaving me to stand on the doorstep.

"Er, come in," she said reappearing suddenly and holding the door wide.

I entered into a room thick with smoke that danced in the slit of sunlight peeking in between a pair of badly hung drapes. There were many people in the room, young people in all states of dress and undress, lounging on cushions on sofas, lying across rugs on the floor. I tried to avoid breathing in the scent of stale sweat. Out of place in the room, I was unsure of my purpose there and was considering leaving when the French girl appeared carrying an airmail envelope.

"For you," she said thrusting it at me.

The writing on the front was Levana's and it simply said, "Mum.'

"She told me to give it to you if you ever came here," said the girl with another shrug. I took the letter and backed out of the room, careful to avoid any low-lying limbs.

Dear Mum,

I told you never to come looking for me in Calcutta and if you are reading this it means you did not respect my wish. I do not want to upset you, as I know you are vulnerable and sensitive but I have my own life now. It is a life that makes me happy. I am happy. I want you to be happy too and I know the only way this will work is if we do not see each other again.

A lot happened in your life before I was born and I know it did
    something to you that I will never understand and you have
    not been able to share. That's OK, I have accepted this but
    being together is bad for both of us.
This is the best solution.
Yours,
Levana

*I deserved it, of course, but it broke my heart, which I was
not expecting. The years had really softened me. I intended to
respect my daughter's wish, however, and did not attempt to
see her again. For once, I would do what it was she wanted,
not what I wanted.*

*When I returned to Tel Aviv, I moved house and I left no
forwarding address. I do believe Levana heard from a friend
that I had cancer and I imagine that Levana drew her own
conclusion that I had not survived it. She thought me dead.
This letter to you, Rebecca, is most probably something of a
shock. I apologize.*

*Levana returned to Tel Aviv, I know that because although
she never knew it, I kept a secret eye on her. Not in a creepy
way, simply like an interested friend. That was how I heard
that she was getting married to Johnny and of your birth,
Rebecca.*

*Unseen by Levana, I attended some of your school plays
and netball matches. I traveled regularly to New York when
you moved there and watched you grow up. I took so much
more interest in your life than I ever did of your mother's.*

*I survived the cancer and I am an old lady now, an old
shriveled lady because I have over half my stomach missing.
Perhaps you will show this letter to your mother. I don't mind
if you do but I fear she will only feel anger towards me for*

what I did and what she had to endure. I completely understand how she feels. I am sad if her pain got forwarded onto you. You were a beautiful child to watch grow up. I hope you are thriving as you read this.

My sincerest apologies to you both.

Your loving grandmother,
Helga.

REBECCA TELLS LEVANA

2014

"She was alive, you realize, mom?"

"I know."

"You knew."

"Yes, I know she didn't die of cancer."

"Shit mom, why didn't you tell me?" It was 4am New York time and Rebecca was holding the phone, pacing around her apartment in her flimsy T-shirt, all hopes for a good night sleep dashed.

"It didn't feel right."

"It didn't feel right to tell me that my own grandmother was alive and well. Could you clarify which bit didn't feel right?"

"Look, Rebecca it was complicated." Levana's voice was hushed. There were phones ringing and muffled voices in the background. She was at work, it was mid-morning in Tel Aviv.

"No mom, it wasn't complicated. Not for me. I had a right to know."

"Look, Rebecca, can we not do this now?"

"If not now, when mom? When were you going to tell me?"

"I am not sure I was."

Rebecca felt the hair on the back of her neck prickle. "Oh, right, so you were going to make me believe my whole life that my grandmother died of cancer when I was born. Were you also going to keep it from me that she was raped by her father and that we are all inbred?"

Levana gave a sharp intake of breath.

Rebecca bit her hand. She hadn't meant to go so far.

"I'm not sure what..." said Levana.

"Sorry mom, I'm all over the place," Rebecca said. "Ignore what I just said."

"Where are you getting all this information from? All this stuff you're saying?"

"Helga left me a letter," Rebecca replied.

It was Levana's turn to sound angry. "Where? How?"

"She left it with a friend under instruction I only receive it after her death."

There was a silence down the other end of the phone. "I am sorry to hear that," said Levana.

"Which bit are you sorry about, mom?"

"All of it." She cleared her throat.

"Mom, I think we need to talk."

"If it is one of those talks, I don't think it is necessary."

"Mom, I know it now, the whole story. Helga's told me everything. Please mom, there's so much. You need to know it, too. None of it was your fault or her fault and she didn't hate you and...."

"Look Rebecca, I-I did a DNA test," said Levana louder than she most probably intended.

"You did."

"I wasn't going to tell you.....because, well we don't tell each other things in our family, do we?"

"Let's start now... It is so ridiculous. All this shut-downness. What did you find out?"

"Why don't you get on a plane and come over here. You know how much I hate doing stuff over the phone."

"You got it. I'll be right there."

It was a strange thing for Rebecca to hear, but she heard her mother laugh.

MAYA

July 2014

Once again, the phone line to London was bad, once again Maya had chosen to WhatsApp Ronnie from the back of a taxi heading into Manhattan. She'd delivered her letter to Rebecca, and now she could be back to her normal life. Well, almost.

"I'm coming back to England tomorrow," Maya said.

"About time," said Ronnie. "It's been bloody weeks."

"I know babe. I've missed you."

"Don't leave again yah. A woman's place is next to her man, Maya."

"Ha-ha, Ronnie. And where is a man's place?"

"That is none of your business."

"Look, Ronnie. I'm back in England tomorrow but I won't be in London until the day after."

"What, don't have a bloody laugh."

"I've got one more envelope to deliver. Someone called Tanya, she lives near Manchester so I'm flying into there."

"You are joking, right?"

"No, I'm totally serious."

"This is not funny anymore, Maya. You do realize you have a job here and a house and fiancé and you're just neglecting them all."

"My family is very important to me, Ronnie, just as you are, and Kamla was one of the most special people in my life. I am doing this for her."

"What?"

"I said… I'm doing this for…shit, hold on Ronnie, I have another call coming…Wait there. "

"Hello."

"Hi Maya. It's Rebecca."

"Rebecca. Hi. How are you?"

"To be honest with you, I'm in turmoil."

"The letter."

"Yes. Did you read it?"

"Yes." Maya felt herself blushing. "I'm sorry I just wanted to make sure my grandmother wasn't sending me on some goose chase all around the world."

"I understand. Don't worry. Then you can understand how I'm feeling."

"You have a lot to take in, I know."

Maya could hear the sirens of New York in the background.

Rebecca went on, "I just don't know who I am anymore. I mean, I never really knew but now I know more about my background, strangely I'm more confused than before. All I know is I want to start dealing in the truth. It makes things clear."

"Shall we meet tonight? I can come to the club."

"No, I'm at the airport on my way to Tel Aviv. I need to meet my mother and let her know and find out what else she's been hiding from me. I will call you when I get back though. I would like to talk with you. I feel our paths have been linked and that's, you know, important. For one thing, our pasts were linked through our grandmothers knowing each other."

"I would love that. Call me any time and good luck."

"Thanks Maya. You and your grandmother did a wonderful thing."

"Hello Ronnie, you still there? Hello. Hello?"

Damn, Maya felt, he's gone. It's probably not good to leave a fiancé, never mind a job, for so long. But sometimes you have responsibilities of the heart. It's only one more day for God's sake. And these letters, these letters, somehow are bringing people closer to their stories. And that can help guide people in their choices forward. God, she thought, I am beginning to sound like Kamla.

MAYA MEETS TANYA

July 2014

Tanya was "well pissed off" that she had to have some visitor come round to her house that afternoon, especially some pushy Indian who said she had a letter.

"What de fock? A "letter"? What's that?" she said to Jerome.

"Might be from some long lost uncle telling you you got an inheritance."

"Yeah right… you know there ain't no money in my world. That ain't why you stick with me, is it, Jerome?"

"I stick with you because you're so fucking happy to be with."

"Yeah, thought as much, ray of sunshine me. Get your sloppy ass off the sofa would ya and fix us a Coke."

Tanya was mainly pissed off because she was pregnant and feeling like shit. Morning was vomiting and afternoon was nausea and there wasn't much except humidity or rain going on in between.

"Another Coke? Shit, Tanya, you're going to make our baby diabetic."

"Yeah, well it ain't going to get no sugar coating from me."

"You got a point there, needs all the sweetness it can get." Jerome stood up and began pumping pillows, pulled back the curtains, cleared the coffee table of three-day old empty fast food packaging. "Don't want to look like we're slobs, do we?"

"You only care because you think there might be some money in this visit," Tanya replied, refusing to budge an inch from her sprawled out position on the sofa.

"I only care because if you have visitors you need to be hospitable and the way this room looks she ain't going to even be able to get in the door." Jerome opened the windows letting raindrops splatter across the window ledge.

"Er ... Coke?"

"Coming.. Jesus, how many more weeks have I got to put up with being your slave?"

"Twenty more weeks so you'd better get cracking with finding a job."

"I've got a job, Tanya."

"A real job."

"It's a regular salary, regular work."

"It's selling shoes."

"Yeah and people are always going to need shoes, Tanya. It's a job for life."

"Yeah, aim high, Jerome."

When the doorbell rang five minutes later, Tanya was up from the sofa and had her hair tied back from her face. Her tracksuit bottoms were replaced with maternity skinny jeans and she looked the part of an expectant mum.

"So good of you to see me at short notice," said Maya standing on the doorstep dripping raindrops off the end of the umbrella wrapped up under her arm.

"Come in," said Tanya standing right back.

"I'm sorry, I'm a little wet."

"Yeah, it's really raining. I haven't been out for a few days."

Tanya watched the graceful Indian girl, mid-twenties perhaps, in her long, elegant raincoat walk into the sitting room and felt shabby. She should have vacuumed.

"Tea, coffee?"

"No, it's OK, I just had a coffee before I got here."

"So, you knew my gran?" said Tanya sitting down on an armchair, indicating for the Indian girl to sit on the sofa.

"No, I didn't, but my grandmother did. They were friends, which is how I came by this letter. She wrote it as part of this project. My grandmother had what she called 'a granddaughter's project,' getting friends of hers to write letters to their future grandkids."

"Oh yeah, sweet," said Jerome coming into the room and sitting on the edge of Tanya's armchair. He introduced himself putting out his hand for Maya to shake.

"Yes, my grandmother, Kamla, she was an early day feminist and believed in women's rights. The letters are part of that."

"That don't sound like Tanya's gran, she didn't believe in rights for women just wrongs for men from what I've heard."

"Yeah, well you don't know anything about her," said Tanya defensively.

Maya unzipped her leather handbag and produced an envelope. "Here," she said reaching over and handing it to Tanya. It was heavier than Tanya expected, there were pages of the thing.

"I'm a bit busy at the moment so don't reckon I'm going to have much time for a while to read it," she said feeling suddenly shy. She couldn't remember the last time she read anything longer than the ingredients on a tin can.

"That's OK," said Maya. "I believe she wrote it around 15 years ago so what's a few extra weeks."

"That was around the time me mam died," said Tanya absently rolling the envelope in her hands. "She was Alicia, my mam."

"She most probably wrote it as a kind of therapy," Maya said. "That was the best time to write, according to my grandmother, Kamla."

"Yeah, well, thanks for this," said Tanya going as if to stand up but sitting down again. Perhaps she should wait for the Indian girl to stand up first.

Maya stood up. Her mission accomplished.

"Good luck with the baby," she said, eyeing Tanya's bump. " When you due?"

"November," said Tanya. "I think I'll wait until the baby's born then I'll read this. Just need to, you know, prepare myself. Look at how long it is. She must have really liked the pen."

"She had a lot to say," said Maya. "As I said, no hurry."

"Well thank you for coming all the way out here," Tanya said.

Maya had put her coat back on. "My pleasure. I loved my grandmother. She was very wise. By the way, I think she met your grandmother at a cricket game. They became instant friends."

Her grandmother at a cricket game?

"I think your mother played cricket, too," Maya added.

"Oh, she was good," Tanya said, finding herself smiling. "Maybe this bump will be too," she said, joking.

They laughed.

Jerome came in and said, "I'll get you a cab."

In the cab, Maya thought, This is all sort of fun. Now to see Ronnie, finally. I hope he'll be happy when I open the door.

LYNETTE, HELGA AND KAMLA

1998

It was an unlikely friendship, the one shared by Lynette, Kamla and Helga but they were three women drawn together by fate or the hands of the god, as Kamla's mother, Gita, would have called it. Men had torn their lives apart but they had also brought these women together, each inextricably linked.

It was dusk and the three of them, aged into their twilight years, were sitting on Kamla's tiny balcony on flimsy plastic chairs. Calcutta's busiest thoroughfare ran below them, the evening in full swing; ringing bells, tooting horns, barking dog shouts, cries, but they didn't hear any of these sounds, they were each lost in deep conversation, the type that women of emotion are most skilled at, conversation that emanates from the heart.

Kamla had been contemplating for a long time whether it was a good idea to invite her two friends from the opposite sides of the world to visit at the same time. She wanted very much for them to meet each other but would they get on?

It was the arrival of two letters each a day apart that spurred her forward.

The first, from Helga with the postmark Tel Aviv: She had not written for a while, she said, as she had been in New York secretly watching Levana and her granddaughter. This was, according to Kamla, a most peculiar affair, hiding from your own daughter but whom was she to judge Helga's reasoning? Sadly, informed Helga, things were not looking good for Levana who'd left her marriage and moved into a squat with unsavory characters. She was cutting up her skin and shoplifting. Rebecca, her granddaughter, appeared to be oblivious to this, thank goodness, very busy with her school work and Johnny, well he did not look like he was making many attempts to get her back. A very sorry little set up, said Helga. And as ever, I fear I am the cause of all the heartache. "Yours, 'The Sleuth'", she wrote, signing off her letter.

Lynette's letter arrived the next day. She too, apologized for the delay in writing, she had not been able to gather her thoughts or her mind for several months now ever since the loss of her beautiful daughter, Alicia, in a drunk driving road accident.

Kamla found herself gasping out loud and reading this line again, Alicia, the bright, bouncy cricket player. She sat down on her bed and read on. "My life is empty without her." Turned out Alicia's husband had been over the limit on whisky and hit the central reservation on the highway.

"Grief is so bewildering," Kamar found herself saying to Lynette that evening on the balcony as the small West Indian woman, tough as old boots but broken in the middle, retold the story. Alicia had fallen into a depression after retiring from cricket and, without any direction, fell in with a bad crowd of Rastafarian men smoking ganga, listening to reggae. It was a bad time but, with the birth of Tanya, she was attempting to pick up the pieces. She took Tanya to live away from the estate out into the suburbs but when you're black and single, life don't always treat you good and, well, she had it hard, kept falling in with the wrong men and see, it eventually killed her.

Kamla had seen it too with Rajika. "Find someone who treats you well," had been Kamla's advice over and over on learning that Rajika was insistent on marrying. Sanjay was so promising but proved to be so hopeless, nothing more than a lazy baby who could do nothing for himself. He had hidden it well until Maya was born and, then, he turned to jelly refusing to lift a finger. Thank goodness Rajika had the strength and a little financial support from Kamla, to walk away.

"I will never know of the grief you are feeling," Helga said to Lynette. "I lost my Levana years ago but I never felt for her the mother's love and this is why she is the way she is. A daughter who does not know a mother's love can never learn to love herself, for love and compassion is what we learn from our mothers."

It was sitting here amongst her friends that the phrase, a certain phrase kept appearing inside Kamla's head. "The past keeps repeating itself' was the phrase. It is a cycle, going round and round. "Our daughters are all the victims of our pasts," she said out loud to her friends. "We must put a stop to the cycle. Only by their daughters knowing of their pasts can any of them stand a chance at making a go of their futures."

Helga had her hand to her mouth. "Kamla, do you realize the damage I will do divulging my past history to Rebecca? It will break her."

"With all due respect, Helga, my dear, your family is already broken. Have you ever considered that your letter might, perhaps, patch things up?"

Helga nodded. Even Lynette nodded.

Lynette laughed, "Alright, I guess I better get myself a fine pen."

And then the women went onto discuss Lynette's job as a nurse for the NIH and Helga's freelance work translating German into English and Hebrew for various businesses and Kamla still was at the women's center and yes, these women did not have any men, but it was not a sadness for them, given what they all had been through. What they did have was enormous gratitude for being able to apply their minds to work that actually helped people.

LYNETTE'S LETTER TO TANYA

2000

Dear Tanya,

This is your grandmother's story. I hope it is of some use to you:

You know me and I have always loved you. But you never known my story. For one thing, me name Lynette Smith, maybe you know THAT. But you don't know I met a woman in India who said I should write my story for my granddaughter, you. Here it is. I hope it is of some use to you, dear. Gives you a sense of who we all are and what sometimes we have to go through to become who we are. So here goes, my sweet girl.

-1-

I was born in St James, west of Kingston in December 1944. It was World War Two raging in the motherland. Thomas, he my Dad, he grew up close by to Pam, my mam, and they was seeing each other off and on, nothing fixed. Just after she got pregnant with me, Thomas left me mam and went to join up with the war effort, boarding a ship full of fruits that sailed him to London.

You know, we was all patriotic them times for the Empire, when Great Britain called, we come running.

Me earliest memory must be that of my cousin, Malcolm Wood on the village green close by my house in St James. That was where the cricket pitch was. He was a pace bowler and hero of the village because he used to scare off every visiting cricket team far and wide. I must have been four or five. He lifted me up and swirled me about with everyone clapping. I don't know why he done that to me over any other kid but he did with his big, hot hands.

I loved the cricket pitch on a Saturday morning. It was like a party going on, fish n bammy, pinda cake, mango fresh off the tree, everyone dancing and shouting and singing. After the game us kids would run into the forest and climb trees. We would be out all day. No one ever knew where we was so long as we was home by dusk.

Yes, course, everybody love cricket. It was how Pam and Thomas got tight you know. He was a top batter, best hook stroke far and wide before he left for war.

I seen a photo of him in his cricket whites with matching teeth, all tall and trim standing outside the meat shop with a cow foot in his hand. That was Jamaica all over them times, cricket, meat and smiles. It was England what put the fat on Thomas.

They say Thomas come home from the war like a stallion strutting his war hero feet like he won the war singlehanded. The first time I met him, he picked me up and said, "Hello Angel, are you my baby?" giving me that Union Jack flag, the one hanging over there in the calendar.

He did not stick around long. There weren't no work and once you got a whiff of life out there, you want more, he wanted more, he was restless. Used to drive everyone mad me mam said with his stories of life in the motherland. Going to dances and the pubs, the underground stations and the lights of Piccadilly Circus.

He played the harmonica day in day out, Blackpool Rock, Blueberry Hill, I Got A Lovely Bunch of Coconuts. I never knew the names of them tunes at the time, learned them since. Everyone used to shoo him out of the house when he played. "Give us a bit of peace and quiet Thomas, would you?"

When word got round of the ship, Windrush, leaving the harbor bound for England, Thomas was all set although he didn't have enough of the £28 fare so you know what he done? He sold his harmonica, sold his trilby and he was the first in line on May 24th to walk the gangplank and step onboard.

There weren't no backward glance for the life he was leaving behind.

Men ain't never been worth much in Jamaica. It's the women what do the work. Truth is, with Thomas gone, my mam breathed a sigh of relief, as he weren't nothing but noise and testosterone.

Pam and me, we was poor like everyone else them times. I done haggling to make a living, selling fruits off the trees, eggs from me Grandmammi's chickens, milk from her goat. Pam was a fine seamstress, she could have made a fair mint from stitching suits and dresses but no one never had no money to pay her. She had an IOU longer than a woodpecker's tongue. Ended up sewing sheets and quilts, patching up clothes. That was what got us our bread and butter. Good days and bad days they was but however tough them times, they was nothing compared to uprooting and moving to England.

Arrived in England what must have been mid 1950's, I was about eleven. Me uncle, that's Thomas's brother William, he paid our way although me mam contributed all her hard-earned coins. She wanted everyone to know this, didn't want no one thinking she weren't able to fend for herself. She said we was going to make a better life for ourselves; better education, better place to live, job, clothes, the lot.

She made a whole ton of promises to her sisters and Mam that she would send money home. "Get ready to line your pockets pretty girls," she shouted, "I'm gonna make us rich."

"We gonna build a business in London town," is what William said to Pam just before he left for England, following

in his older brother Thomas's footsteps. "A tailor shop, you cutting the cloth, me selling the wares." He could see my mam had skills and he had a business brain. Where Thomas was the sportsman, William, he was the entrepreneur. He was always trying new schemes in Kingston but none of them took off as he was ahead of his time. "The world just isn't ready for me," he'd say.

Pam says to me, "Pack a bag with all de smells of Jamaica because de motherland don't smell like here." That I already knew because it was one of Thomas's favorite topics of chat, "In England, the air is so cold it numbs your nostrils. Deadens the senses."

I didn't know what Jamaica smelled like because I had nothing to compare it with so I just packed me bag with some sand, jasmine petals and a banana that stank out my bag so bad I had to throw away anything the banana touched including nearly all the grains of sand and the petals before we was a day away from home.

I was sick for most of the crossing, three weeks of rocking, rolling waves. Below-wow I have never felt so ill. Pam weren't much help to me because she felt the same—worse she said. Any bad language I'd not yet picked up hustling in the city, I learned now. She weren't ever a sweet-mouthed doll but raas she was spewing the words out faster than her dried crackers.

I never been on the sea since that day and I never want to. Where I come from you look at water, you don't ride it.

Don't remember nothing about first stepping foot in England because I didn't step, I tripped all the way down the gangplank and cut open my head. There was blood dripping on my forehead. What I did notice, which I was not expecting, was the ground I found myself laid out on, was warm. The sun was beating down and I was dressed in every item of clothing I owned because I had been told to dress up warm "cause England cold."

Two white faces was looking down at me.

"She alright? Are you alright?" they asked.

Pam pounced on me from behind and pressed hard on my head to stop the blood.

"Trust you to make an exhibition of yourself ya clumsy girl." She pulled me upright, peering around my head for any more serious wounds.

"She all right," she said publicly, tying her headscarf around my head.

A white man with a blue cap was there to pick up my bag. "You going to the train?" he said.

"We are." Pam was tidying her flattened hair after losing the headscarf, which was now wrapped around my head like a bandana. Never did I expect to see no white man carrying my bag and nor did she, we was all upside down. In Jamaica we carried the bags for white men. This was a big deal I remember that, white men selling newspapers, driving the train, checking tickets. They was none of them happy about it neither. Got no smiles or good day, just business.

Uncle William the bumbohole was meant to meet us from the train in Paddington, that what he said but he weren't there. Seemed everyone else was though, grey, and brown hats and suits, clutching black and white newspapers, shoving and pushing us to get places in a hurry. Anyone who took the time to stop was staring like we was fresh from another planet. I don't think many of them ever seen no Jamaican kid before let alone one with a blood-stained face. I tried to smile but I didn't feel like it. I needed the toilet but I weren't allowed to jiggle to stop the urge because it made Pam mad. I knew she weren't really mad with me for needing to pee but she was mad nonetheless. Mad because William was a bumpaclot and we had spent all our money coming on the boat and train fare and, without him, we didn't know how to get where we was going.

Pam could not take her eyes off the crowd even to look down at me in case she miss William. I wanted to tell her that I thought William would spot us easy as we was likely to spot him, we was like magpies in a flock of seagulls.

"The place called Notting Hill he tell me," said Pam. "Let's find a hill and climb it, see if anyone know the place from there."

As we left the station we had no idea if we was going to be walking north, south, east or west or for minutes or hours. Pam set off fast and in no particular direction.

"Ask someone," I said, trailing behind.

"We find it on our own," she said.

"But we don't know where we going."

"Can't be that many hills."

She was proud Pam was, proud and on this occasion stupid because we walked for half an hour without getting nowhere.

"Ask this lady coming here," I said when me feet was too tired to carry me. We was standing on a narrow road with manikins dressed in tweed, checking us out from behind shop windows. The lady coming towards us had yellow hair and was dressed in a deep green dress and blouse.

"Excuse me," Pam says when the lady gets to be in earshot, "Excuse me," she says twice.

You know what this lady done? She looked behind her like Pam might be speaking to somebody else and when she realizes Pam is addressing her, she sticks up her hand like you do when you don't want someone to take no photo and she walks away hidden behind her hand.

We was dumbfounded—I mean right proper jaws to the ground.

"Wah di russ?" Pam said shaking her head.

"It's OK," I said to Pam because I could see she is right upset almost wanting to cry.

"We'll ask someone else."

There was a greengrocer on the corner of the road and out of it like she was sent to guide us, was this woman same looking as us. She was dropping coins into her purse. I spotted her before Pam. "Ask her," I said nudging Pam into her direction.

Pam steps over to the woman who greets her with a smile like she wants to know her. Lady had her black hair tied up into a bun with long grey threads running through it. I stood back not able to hear what they was saying but I saw the lady pointing and nodding. Next thing I know we is all walking down the street together to take the red bus to Notting Hill. Turns out our new friend's auntie live in St James west of Kingston, Jamaica just like us. She got friends from our village. I was warm all over like the world suddenly shrunk and we know half of the people living in it.

Lady, her name was Grace-Ann, she paid our bus fare so long as we paid it back was the deal Pam made and we ride top deck front of the bus. Grace-Ann was laughing at us 'cause we was sure every building we passed was a palace or a castle. You don't get no normal homes built with golden frontage or stone balconies or front doors wide as highways. Pavement was wide and we could see the tops of people hats looked like they was floating.

I was all the while thanking the Lord that I had a bladder big as an ox's, as I never got to go pee. Instead I listened to Grace-Ann who talked and talked like she not spoken to no one all day, which according to her was the case as no one friendly in England, no one welcoming, no chatting with passersby. "Here, everybody got their own business."

Grace-Ann worked as a cleaner at St Thomas's hospital. National Health Service crying out for West Indian workers to fill them jobs the British never wanted. She didn't like the job but it paid enough for her to send money home to her Grandmammi who was looking after her three year old son in Jamaica. "Do what you got to do," she said, "and what I got to do is earn enough to get me boy, Tommy, to come here be by my side. Boy needs his mother."

As we approached Notting Hill, faces white and uptight merged into black and watchful. People on the streets slowed down, not moving so fast as they done back across the bridge. Looked more like Jamaica look on a Saturday night, men grouped together passing the time bantering, kids running up and down the pavements weaving in and around. Was getting to be dusk so I never saw all the dirt and dust worse than home but I saw houses no more than piles of rubble, other houses growing weeds out the windows or tumbling down. Weren't a pretty sight but I liked it better than them palaces back where we took the bus. Felt more like we might fit in here.

Really, it weren't that different in Notting Hill them times to what you got now, you got the same shoe shops and sweet sellers and the market although then you didn't have no West Indian food as you got now. You got sweet potato, okra and mango now, as well as peas, beans and white potatoes in the markets. Streets were quieter too. Now you got buskers and sound systems and them loud mouth motorbikes. Clothes, they was stylish, men in three piece single breasted wool lounge suits with their braces and hats and hair creamed back. Better than all these new fashions, zips, holes, flaps, tie-dye, leather, studs -- that style don't do nothing for me.

So we arrive and Grace-Ann needs to get back to her house, feed her husband but she don't want to go leaving us with no place to go, same time, she don't want us hanging around her as she got stuff to do.

"My house, it's up three roads on the left from here and the fourth house on the right number 18. If you don't find no place to stay you come knocking on my door." She pats Pam's arm, "Anytime. I'm happy to help."

We was left standing there on Ladbroke Road not knowing whether to go left or right, Pam fuming, "What sort of business William hoping to start if he can't even stick to his word?"

"Can't we just go with Grace-Ann?" I moaned.

"No, we cannot. She done enough for us already. We going figure this one out for ourselves, we've made our bed so we gonna lie in it."

I might have thought about having a cry for my bed back home, my friends likely all doing hopscotch in the yard, Grandmammi preparing hot pot or cleaning the porch. I even wanted to see them stinking greedy goats. Weren't a good moment for me standing there, no place to go, shivering like I got some fever.

I never got to drop any tear though, because just at that moment, a voice came booming out from above the rattling exhaust of the buses.

-2-

"If it ain't Pam Davis. Raas look at you windswept hairstyle."

"Thomas Smith?" says Pam.

"Hello Angel, look at my baby," he said to me, trying to pick me up but thinking again as he saw I weren't no tiny doll no more. "What are you doing here?"

"Looking for your brother," Pam said, hitting Thomas across the chest. "He a bumbaclot meant to be coming to meet us at the station no sign, walked our heels off trying to get here. He got some explaining to do." Pam was breathing fast.

"William, he in the hospital," Thomas said, not looking sympathetic. "A couple of stitches that's all. Got a broken nose. Small fight. Get over here." Thomas grabbed Pam and pulled her into his arms so that her skirt swayed out like a wave. He went to kiss her but pulled away. "Shit, I'm not putting my mouth near your face, you taste of saltfish."

"What you think I do, Thomas, walk here? Just got out of the ocean you rassclot."

We was making a spectacle of ourselves, people stopping and staring. I didn't like this and pulled Pam's sleeve.

"Don't leave us standing here, take us to William's house or your house or anywhere. Show some hospitality for your daughter."

"Can't go to my place," said Thomas. "Got a landlady hates colored. Only reason she is letting me stay is because I fixed her staircase and boot cupboard door."

"Then to William's, Thomas. Got to go now, Lynette needs to pee."

Thomas raised his eyebrows and I shrugged.

"William he's got a better situation, no landlady but you got to watch out for bed bugs. He's got no one cleaning his lodgings, his place dutty."

We walked along the narrow pavement past white couples holding hands, old ladies pulling shopping trolleys, piles of rubbish strewn across the pavement, empty bottles and cigarette packets, across a zebra crossing. Thomas and Pam walking ahead of me, Thomas's arm linked into Pam's like they was young lovers.

William lived in a four-story house up concrete steps and through a chipped black front door. Thomas rang the bell and stepped back as a window opened two floors above.

"What time is it?" puffy black head called out.

"I make it 8.30 o clock, Robert," Thomas said. "You due on your shift in 15 minutes."

"Shit," said Robert slamming the window shut.

We waited for the door to open and made way for Robert to run past us, sweeping back his tight curls and straightening his British Rail shirt collar. "Don't go keeping them passengers waiting," called Thomas patting him on the back.

You know, we was brought up on tales of England. Back home we knew more about Britain than we did about Jamaica. About coals from Newcastle, Lancashire shoes, kings and queens but that weren't what we saw when we went into William's digs that evening. It was like someone taken the insides out of a pig's gut and smeared them all over the walls - - that was the stink that met us. There was smashed window panes filled with cardboard, wallpaper green with mold and the carpet was just threads of wool clinging on to holes in the floor. Weren't no china teacups or Victoria sponge.

"This it?" said Pam.

"Good as it gets," Thomas said. "Only the best for the Caribbean guests. There's a bath tub upstairs and a WC outside through the kitchen, you can freshen up. Careful of the third step. If someone paid me I would come fix that."

William had one room in the house called his own and in that room there was a bed and a pull out sofa bed. Down the hall was the bath tub, a green, stained affair, which weren't sanitary as there weren't no more than a drip out of the hot tap and the cold tap missed the bath tub altogether and watered the floor sodden and slimy.

Pam done what Pam always done when she entered a living space, she cleaned. She made up William's narrow single bed, spreading her clothes and my clothes across the mattress, as we was going to sleep here and no skin of ours going to make contact with no royal British dust mites, she told me. She pulled out the sofa bed and put William's thin sheet across that, as that was where he was going to sleep. She swept the floor of loose hairs and dust and washed the sooty windows.

When William arrived back an hour or so later with his nose askew and stitched across the bridge, we was sweating like the Caribbean sun beating down on us.

"What the raas?" asked William walking in and seeing us, our clothes hanging off the door of the wardrobe.

"You late, William," said Pam. "Due at the station four hours ago."

"Shit, that was today wasn't it?" said William. "Had it in my head it was tomorrow otherwise I never would have...." he stopped.

"Never would have gone got yourself a beating last night?" said Pam. She had her hands on her hips and she looked like she had a lot to throw William's way.

"Isn't like home here, Pam. Don't know what you expecting but we got to watch our backs. White people don't like black people on the streets." He blinked over in my direction catching sight of me brushing down the curtains dotted with cigarette burns, "Hey Lynette, girl, look you grown," he cried giving me a big hug, pleased for the distraction. "School for you just round the corner from here. That where you going to be when your Mammi and me get our tailoring business up and running. You going to be happy here English girl. Soon as the money comes in we can get out of this stink hole house, you can find a place of your own with your Mammi and maybe your daddy too, if he ain't too busy schmoozing the white girls."

"That enough of that," said Pam.

Four days later I started the school at the top of the road. I had to go my first day in a skirt and T-shirt I brought over from Jamaica because I never had no school clothes. My first day was a good one. Everyone was curious about me. There was already one West Indian boy in my class but I was the only girl and so all the girls wanted to come touch my skin, feel my thick hair like I was a novelty. Second day, now that was bad. The school uniform given to me by my teacher was too big and everyone bored of my looks started noticing other stuff about me like the way I talked, English but not English anyone understood, hair in typical Jamaican cornrows.

While I knew all about the ship that brought me from Jamaica to England I knew nothing about the buses that took people from Notting Hill to Maida Vale or West End, everyone laughed that I didn't know nothing about Notting Hill.

Day three, four, five people decided they didn't like what they saw and began to call me names. It only takes one child and the rest are off. At first it was just darkie then it was negro and nigger and gorilla. These names stuck. I was offered bananas at lunch and when I accepted everyone made monkey noises and scratched their armpits.

Day eight, I had my first fight, which to me weren't no big deal. Everyone in Jamaica fights. Ain't no hard feelings afterwards. Here you fight and you get summoned to the Headmistress's office. That's what happened to me. Two girls pushed me in the playground and I fought them both at the same time, left them with bloody noses. Headmistress called in Pam. Pam asked whether their noses were broken. When the headmistress said no, Pam asked what the problem was? I got to have three days off school hanging around the flat, as a punishment.

So, about Thomas, he was my dad but at the same time, he weren't my dad not in the traditional sense of looking after me and bringing me up. That weren't what Jamaican men did them times. They made the babies and it was the women carried them.

Thomas, he loved women, particularly white women. Them days white women going with a black man were spat on, rejected by their families, called nigger lovers. You got to admire them women who continued on regardless. Thomas was a good looking man, a charmer, smooth on the dance floor. He was also confident which a lot of black men weren't them times. Most men of my kind felt unsettled living in England but Thomas, he never did. He believed he had every right to be here after helping fight in the war.

This was the time of teddy boys. Boys who wore them drape jackets with the velvet trim and drainpipe trousers. Pam knew about them clothes because that was what William decided she should be tailoring. "Got to be at the head of the trend." That was William's favorite saying.

Teddy Boys, they hated black men like Thomas. They hated the way he took white girls. Used to be fight ups in the street. Hating the black man who takes white women, that was a trend. Problem with Thomas, he never made a good name for the black man. He liked to play the field, weren't ever any particular white woman, just anyone he picked up at a dance. He was getting white women pregnant and moving on. Sometimes I would come home from school and see Pam bottle-feeding some half-half baby Thomas dropped off after being dumped on by the white mother. "Your kid, you look after it," the white woman would say. He never had no interest in bringing up kids. Pam was normally too busy to look after Thomas's "drop off kids' as we called them and so she would hand them to me to play with when I got in from school. They was light relief for me after being bullied all day at school, having some kid looking up to me felt good.

I was lonely them times. Never had no one to play with and Pam too busy to talk.

She was such a hard grafter. She was determined to make it work for her in England. She had promised everyone back in the homeland that she would send money and she had promised me she would get us out of William's stinking room and she had promised herself that she weren't going to mess it up. She worked night and day even when there weren't no money to pay the electrics, she worked in darkness tailoring clothes to order.

After eighteen months, though, we weren't nowhere. I was permanently scratching fleas and coughing asthmatic lungs, stuck as we were in that same damp room. Pam worked and I helped her cut up the fabric, pin the seams. William, he stayed out most days and nights but when he was there, there was frost formed between him and Pam from the balance sheets never adding up.

"Our bumbaclot landlord putting the rents up every day," said William. "Materials to buy, raas, be patient, Pam."

"I'm turning out five items a week selling at £14.10s, you paying £4 rent, £1 fabric, where the change William?"

"Not just the fabric, got the selling and word of mouth. You think our customers just come out of the sky?"

"Don't cost that getting five customers a week, raas, William. Where's the profit?"

They argued like this day in day out. Never made no sense the numbers. William showed Pam the books but Pam weren't able to read the figures, she could only add in her head. She just wanted to know if there was money enough to send home and make a living in London but there weren't even enough to pay the light switches to come on.

"Shit, William, what you doing with the money? You gonna bring pound notes here for me to see. Raas, Lynette better at babysitting coins than you are."

Tanya put the letter down and took a break. She had said she wouldn't start reading till the baby was born, but it was better than staying on top of Jerome all the time or missing him when he was selling shoes, so she read. She knew about racism, too, but this of course was just plain all over the place and damning. She couldn't imagine how her grandmother and great-grandmother were going to get on their feet.

-3-

There was fifteen of us lived in the five-bedroom house with only a camping stove for cooking. The outside toilet was through the black wooden door that you had to drag shut as there weren't no hinges and it never flushed unless you poured buckets of water down it from the tap in the kitchen. It stank worse than cattle troughs, nobody done nothing to care for it, as everyone working too hard to survive a living.

Problem was, nobody wanted coloreds in their homes so we was limited with where we could go. Landlord, he was son of the devil. I ain't kidding you. He crammed people in, shoved up the rents, never fixed nothing and if you complained, he kicked you out with an eviction fee. He knew he had us trapped well and good. Only thing kept us going was backitive. We all looked out for each other.

One of the tenants, Reggie, used to be a banker in Kingston, he established a pardner, everyone paying into a shared pot any coins they had so we could help each other out with clothes or furniture we might need. Reggie kept the coins hidden away in his room on the top floor and managed the books fair and square. Every month one of the tenants was nominated to receive a pay out from the pardner if they was able to justify what they needed. That was how I got my school shoes and Pam got her sewing machine.

At first we paid into the pardner with the money William bought back but when the money stopped coming we was no longer able to contribute. Reggie, he was a kind man and he helped Pam and me out when he could, bringing extra food, paying our contribution of the electricity meter but weren't fair to give other people's money if we weren't putting in the pot.

Truth was, William weren't being honest with the money but we never knew London well enough to understand his crafty ways.

It was with Robert that the apple cart upturned. Robert worked the graveyard shift for British Rail. He was one confused man. In the winter months he never saw no daylight, ate his dinner at 6am, grew fat and grumpy but always paid his way and never made no fuss in doing so.

He used to jump at the sight of me if we passed on the stairs like I might be a character in one of his nightmares. That was how rarely he got to see other people.

Robert got home from his night shift around 5am one morning, went into his room and found all of his meagre possessions strewn on the floor like they got up and danced without him. He kept his earnings in a jar in a box in a drawer in his cupboard. The jar was out on the floor upturned and empty. Robert, normally a hushed up man, made a mad ruckus an' woke up the house. We thought someone been murdered. It was every penny from three months wages, gone but not only that, also a silver cross been given to Robert by his Mammi before she died that meant more to Robert. That was sentimental value and ain't no replacing sentiment.

Wasn't any point in calling the police because they didn't care nothing about the West Indians in their patch. We was inhabiting a separate district far as they was concerned.

We was all in Robert's room, Pam, me, Robert, Reggie,
other tenants. Not William, he never came back that night but
the rest of us, we was hunting around not for the money, that
was clear gone but for the cross until Reggie told us there
weren't no point, a silver cross worth as much as wages.

"If you going to steal you going to steal," he said, patting
Robert and shooing us out the room.

It was me discovered the burglar, same day. Wish I hadn't
but often kids more observant than adults because they don't
need to be always yabbering polite yabbers. I was back from
school and removing the cardboard from the broken window
panes to let some air into our room, always got so stuffy in
there but no one 'cept me noticed. Pam was at her sewing
machine as usual but she was sleepy from the burst of
sunshine coming through and kept jabbing her fingers with
needles. William, had been in, Pam said, but only to change
and go out again, "on business."

Got a knock on the door from Susan, one of the tenants
lived in the room beside ours. She often came in after her
cleaning job to gossip about life. She always made an effort at
talking with me about my day, what did I learn in dem books
but quickly moved onto talking to Pam. Pam was a better
listener than me. As Sarah and Pam was talking about the
burglary, I flopped myself down on the sofa bed shoving a pair
of William's trousers out the way.

As I done that my eye caught a sliver of silver. First I
thought it was a belt buckle, but when I looked again I
realized it was Robert's cross fell out of William's trousers
lying there beside me on the bed. Checking out Sarah and
Pam not paying no attention my way, I stuck my hand in
William's trouser pocket. Empty. He must have taken the
money and scarpered. I should have said something straight
off but Sarah, she was a gasbag and I never wanted her to go

shouting it out loud that my uncle was a thief. I stuck the cross in my pocket and waited for Sarah to leave, all the while my heart racing like I sprinted a mile.

Straight after Sarah gone, Reggie came in to discuss his sister getting married in Kingston, next Robert come by on his way to work to say he hadn't slept a wink all day. By the time I got Pam on her own she was fussing about getting food on the table and sending me off on errands to buy peas and beans.

When I come back to the room, William is there. He is merry. Full of his successful day getting lots of "potential new customers" and, "don't you look pretty Lynette," and haven't you got "fingers like fairies, Pam." Pam, she ain't got the same level of mirth and is complaining at him to show her the money. "Ain't no food come from chitter chat, William."

I am all the while wondering if William even knew about the silver cross when he stole Robert's stash and, if he did, when would he notice it missing? Had anyone mentioned it to him? I wondered if he just stuck all the notes in his pocket along with the cross, next, took the notes out, leaving the cross there, unaware. You don't need to be smart to be a burglar just greedy...or desperate.

Tell you, I was tense, I wanted to say something alone to Pam but William he was settling in for the night. I tried to act normal but I was jumpy like a cat. When a car horn honked outside I nearly fell off the bed.

"What wrong with you tonight, Lynette? Dem kids at school again?" said William laughing at me. "You need to get a thick skin, girl. Let it all run off." I had to do something about the cross burning a hole in the pocket of my school tunic. I tried any excuse I could come up with to try and get William to vacate the room but he weren't budging. One moment when I thought he was asleep I sidled up to Pam ready to show her the cross but he started humming and shifting and

reminiscing back to them days on the porch with the crickets and the warm white rum.

In the end, I decided all I could do was return the cross to Robert's room while he on his night shift. Could just put it back on the bed and run away. Would mean Robert would know someone in the house the burglar but he wouldn't know who and William wouldn't get in no trouble, which meant Pam and me wouldn't run out of business. Everyone happy.

It must have been round 11 pm when I crept out of my bed and made my way to the door to go downstairs to Robert's room. I had to go past the bathroom making sure no one in there. I weren't good at creeping. It didn't come naturally to me. My feet was too flat and I never had nothing to hide before today. Robert's door was tightly shut like no air allowed seep through. The door handle was long and slender and rusty. First off, I knocked in case Robert came back from work early. When no one answered I pushed the handle. It clicked mid-way causing a crack as loud to me as if someone dropped a box of tools. I hesitated and continued.

There was the cross inside my clenched fist ready for me just to place it respectfully on his bed and run away. The door opened silently and I stepped inside with the floorboards screaming out at the padding of my feet. My hand was sweating and the cross stuck to the sweat. I flicked it onto the bed and stepped back round. Standing behind me in the doorway, big as a bear, was William.

"Pick it up," he whispered.

"What?"

"Pick up the cross."

"No."

"Pick it up or I'm going to yell that I just found you in here."

"It's not ours."

"Pick it up."

I grabbed the cross back off the bed.

"Now out," William said, making way for me to squeeze past him.

I strode out into the hall defiantly but all the while trying to figure out what game William was playing.

"Don't tell no one about this. Got it?"

I shook my head.

"Mention it and I'm going to tell everyone it was you who stole it and people going to believe it because people believe adults not kids."

"Why do you want it?" I whispered.

"I don't want it but I need it, got some debts to pay."

"What kind of debts?"

"Debts that got people after me."

"Cross belongs to Robert's mum."

"Yeah I know, don't you think I feel bad enough about that?"

"Then give it back, find another way."

"Can't or I'm dead and you're going to be dead too if you say anything because I am going to take you with me so everyone seen your face."

He shoved me in the back, "Downstairs."

"What?"

"Downstairs, we're going now."

"But it's night."

"Stop talking." William was poking me to walk forward.

We left the house, me in my nightdress. William dragged me down St Stephen's terrace. "You stupid girl, what you go get involved for?"

"I was going to return it and not say it was you took it."

"That weren't the point, though, Lynette. Point is I took it because I need it, got debts to pay."

At the top of the road there was a group of men, white men hanging around, smoking cigarettes. When they saw William and me coming their way the jeering began.

"Look, he's bringing a chimp. Don't want none of your women, nigger."

"We want the money, not the monkey."

"Here you go," said William handing the silver cross over to the shortest of the three men.

"That it?"

"Yeah, that's me, fair and square."

The men took turns to weigh the silver in their hands, bit it with their teeth to check it.

"What about the girl?"

"What about her?"

"Either got to give us another £3 quid or hand her over."

"I haven't got any more money."

"Then hand her over."

"She's my niece."

"She's my niece," said one of the men mimicking William's accent. "Then what you bring her for?"

"Company."

"Yeah? Well, we want her company now."

"What you want her for?"

"Nothing naughty if that's what's on your mind. That ain't what we're into."

"What then?"

"Hand her over or give us another £3."

"Ain't got three quid."

I was grabbed by the arm and yanked over. "In that case, she going to earn it for us. You gonna watch."

The men pulled me away from William and clasped me fast not letting me go. I kicked and I spat and bit whatever hand came to rest near my mouth. The men laughed. "You're a wild animal from the jungle. Ain't you? You can fucking go back there, make our lives easier." One of the men hit me on the head with his fist causing me to stumble.

"Come on," they said.

I was dragged away up the pavement. William sauntering along behind, only there because he was shit scared of what Pam was going to say when she realized it was his fault I was missing.

They stopped dragging me once we was outside wide grey detached, grand homes with balconies and chimneys and big bay windows, proper residences with golden doorknockers.

"What you do is you go up them steps to the front door, take the milk bottles and smash the windows," one of the men said, the tallest of the three pushing me into the garden. "Go."

"No," I said.

"Go or I'm going to smash your teeth in," said another of the men, who didn't have many teeth himself.

I was shoved up the stairs shaking all the while but there weren't no going back I knew this, no way I would get away from these men unharmed. I took a bottle and threw it feebly at the window, my arms all jelly. The window stayed intact but the bottle smashed to the floor.

"Harder."

Picking up a second one I threw it with all my might causing the window to shatter, the milk sprayed everywhere, all over me.

"Look, black kid turned white," laughed the men. They were hiding in a bush by the gate.

"House next-door. Go on."

I looked around me trying to find some way of escaping but the only way out was the gates and the men had these covered. Running up the steps of the house next-door, I done the same although the milk bottles were empty. The window smashed.

"And that house too."

The third house I smashed the window almost effortlessly. I ain't going to lie, it felt good like when you slam a wicket in cricket.

When I turned around, the men was gone. I saw the shadow of William running towards me.

"Run, Lynette," he shouted in a whisper.

I trotted down the steps but I was scared, I couldn't distinguish between the gates and the fences and kept running into dead ends. I raced back and forth across the lawns as lights came on all about me and front doors opened up.

"Over here," shouted William. I spotted him just as the first figure brandishing a bat came at me.

"Quick."

From another angle came a running figure holding a metal pan. I was being got at from all sides.

"Through here," William grabbed my arm and pulled me out onto the pavement.

I heard a voice shout, "It's a colored."

"Colored vandals!"

"They went that way," the three men that put me up to it, suddenly appearing like they had been innocently walking along and fallen upon us.

William and me we ran along the pavement, William being careful to dodge the streetlights, me just running in my white nightdress, not caring where I ran so long as it was away.

"Niggers!"

"Going to pay for this."

When we got back to our place, Pam was still asleep. Pam slept like the dead since arriving in London.

"Don't say nothing about this, any of this," William whispered, as I climbed into bed absorbing Pam's slow, steady breaths.

I ignored him and simply turned over. I was mad but at the same time more exhilarated than I had ever been.

The next morning Pam was all up in arms about my stinking like a dairy farm but I explained nothing. Just shrugged it off like I had no idea how I came to stink like this either. Problem was, I had to stink like this for the next week with a crusty white neck, until it rained when I went out and got myself soaked.

The next day in the newspaper and for a few days to follow there was headlines complaining about the blacks taking over, stealing white man's jobs, "wreaking havoc" as they put it. I felt like it was me they was talking about.

This incident changed me. Up until this time I was a good girl, helping Pam, keeping my head down at school learning dem books, not drawing no attention but after this incident it was like some wild animal crept in and I craved drama. I came to realize I was more than a quiet kid from a small island. I was someone strong, able to do harm, fight for myself and for Pam.

Around about this time I stopped going to school, why had I never thought of this before? I hated every moment I was there cooped up in the classroom considered dumber than the white kids in the class, laughed at for my spelling.

I began hanging out with William. He didn't like it but I stuck to him fast. Wanted to see where he spent Pam's hard-earned pound. I knew he weren't never going to give Pam her share of the money and so I had to get it from him direct. At first he clung to the rule book buying fabric, looking for customers, "schmoozing for new business" as he put it but he never kept this pretense up for long, there were too many temptations for William. He had a business going on which never included Pam and me. His was a business he was running with Thomas and he was using this business to fund his gambling habit. Bottom line, William weren't up to no good and I was about to get myself in deep.

Them times there was two minorities in Notting Hill, black men and white prostitutes. Thomas, he knew how to milk this, getting white prostitutes together with black men hungry for love. That's how it was them days, most black men came across to England by themselves from the homeland and they wanted female affection. Not many white women going to risk getting together with a black man without some recompense so black man got to pay for affection.

Thomas, he made a fair packet dealing women, a share of which he gave to Mary, the white landlady, who let him run her house like a knocking shop. William, he was the headhunter, used to bring the men to Thomas for Thomas to match up with the women, that was how he earned his packet and once the women got their pay, Thomas got his cut, the biggest cut of all. Yeah, ain't proud that my Dad was a ponce but them times it was all about survival.

Thomas, perhaps because he was my dad but more likely because he was charming, made me feel like it was acceptable to be hanging around his business. At first he done all the "should be at school," and "what about your mam?" lines but we both knew they weren't going to work so he quit caring about the ethics. Instead he saw me as somebody who could enhance the business. Told me men like having girls around especially slim beauties.

Mary, Thomas's landlady, she had her head screwed on like no other woman I'd met in London. She knew how to make a business from the white hostility to blacks, keep the respect and keep Thomas under her thumb. I liked her and she put up with me mainly because I was useful, ran her errands, kept the place clean.

Her house in Colville Terrace was big enough to house all the prostitution upstairs while at the same time, running a shebeen in the basement. She ran the shebeen all day, the illegal drinking and gambling den for blacks and, because she was a white lady, nobody suspected her. She done up the shebeen all comfortable with low armchairs, jazz LPs and a kitchen table where she used to lay out all the beers. Entry cost two shillings and a bottle of beer, two shillings. Room next-door was the gambling den where people played five-card stud poker betting away their weekly wages, sometimes stakes as high as £100. It was a happening place for blacks but Mary was in control.

That was why I respected her, she knew how to manage the men in the shebeen, get the most out of them and then get them to clear out at four or five in the morning. No one ever played her up as they knew they was onto a good thing having her place to spend time. Often fights broke out on the street outside when the pissed men was making their way home. They would bump into white men jealous that the black men was pissed and they weren't and there would be scuffles but Mary's lights would be out in Mary's house and no one would suspect nothing about what her house was used for.

It's strange, stuff that becomes the norm once you do it enough times that is why I can sit here and write all casual about prostitutes and ponces and gambling because that became normal to me. The people I was spending time with, they was people, not labels. There was Irene. She had mountains of blonde hair and eyeliner so thick it ran like trenches you could just about make out the slivers of her light blue eyes. She was clever, always reading books when she wasn't working.

I liked her the best. I liked learning from her and she always had time to teach me. She loved history and taught me all about stuff I didn't know like the Egyptians and mummies and the Vikings. Stuff kids learn in primary school. She said she wanted to be a teacher that was why she done paid sex to pay her teacher training but that was six years ago and she was still on the game.

Irene never sat comfortable with doing what she done for a living. Her dad was a bobby used to walk the beat up Bow Street. And she had three older brothers all connected to the law. What she was doing was risky. That was how we got close in the first place. I used to be Irene's "eyes." "Any coppers about, Lyn?" she used to ask me before she left Mary's house all done up like she been out buying groceries. I had to do a recce of the roads surrounding the house before she left, make sure they was clean. She used to pay me three shillings for doing this.

Irony is, it was Irene's father who led her into prostitution in the first place. He banned her from working in a decent job. "Woman's place is by her man's side. You could be a policeman's wife or a doctor's wife." That was the life he wanted for Irene, to be a wife. Used to try and fix her up with his copper friends but Irene weren't having none of it. She wanted to make her own living. She was wise like that, she knew that the only way a woman was going to survive was with her own means. That was why she moved out of her family home to live with her spinster aunt and worked under Thomas's watch in Mary's house.

Irene's best friend was Gwen. I liked Gwen too but she was harder than Irene, harder to read. She had been on the streets most of her life since running away from a kid's home. She never knew no proper love, only love you got to work for. She weren't blessed with any of the easiness Irene possessed. Had to work hard to get a smile from Gwen and when a smile did come, it never stuck around. She was like a rat, always watching, eyes never still. Irene, she was more like a rabbit, silky and soft with laughing eyes.

Gwen was funny though, that was why I liked her. Never known someone able to sum people up better than her. She had names for all the fellas. William was Welder, Thomas, he was Prince, there was Burgess, she called him Pants, because he used to breathe like a dog, Evan was "Bitch yeah Bitch,' because that was what he cried out in the sack. Hadley, he was called Fingers, because, yeah, well you got the message.

I used to arrive at the brothel around nine most days in my school uniform because that was how I had to leave my house so that Pam would never suspect.

I spent the day helping Mary tidy up the basement or making the beds, doing laundry, buying supplies. Every bedroom in the brothel was split into two rooms with a screen or curtain across the middle so that there was eight bedrooms altogether. In each of the eight bedrooms, there was a picture on the wall to make the room a bit cheery, trees or flowers, a church or birds.

It was a full time job keeping the house spic, as Mary called it, with just a short nap on one of the beds in the middle of the day to make up for the sleepless night. Mary paid me a few shillings for my work. Every shilling I earned I stored in the zip up pocket on my school belt, dropping it into Pam's purse when I got home in the afternoon. "William asked me to give you that," I used to say. She never questioned how it was I kept bumping into William. In fact, had Pam had time to look up from her fabric she might have noticed many things weren't quite right. Like, the schoolbooks in my school bag never changed. Like, I never sat down to do any homework or spoke about my day. Like, I kept leaving in my school uniform even when it was weekends and school holidays. Neither she nor I ever kept much track of the days.

I was always home with Pam around four to give her a hand with the sewing, run any errands she needed doing, make us a plate of food. Got to the point though when I wondered why I bothered. Pam barely registered me. Had I been a bit more observant or perhaps kinder, I might also have spotted stuff weren't right with Pam. Like......she only ate a corner of the food I made, left the rest hidden under her fork. Like ... she had big bags under her eyes and a face sunken into her cheeks. Like ... she never spoke no more about Jamaica or about making a living for us. Like ... .she had a cough that never left her chest just hung around in her lungs.

Around six in the evening I would be off out again fibbing that I was going to see my school friends. Really I was back at Mary's tending to the needs of the prostitutes, the drinkers, the gamblers, or Mary who used to make me do all "up and down" the stairs work as I had "young legs." When Thomas was there, he would sneak me into the kitchen and pour me whisky. "Don't call me your Dad for nothing." He taught me how to knock back the liquor in one so that the burning sensation lasted only moments. "Go sit with Randall," he used to say when my cheeks were hot, "He's a bit homesick right now, tell him stories of the homeland. Go now." He would push me out of the kitchen and down the stairs to the basement to find Randall who was sunken into an armchair, eyes glazed with rum. "Sit nice and cozy, make him feel loved, Lynette."

Everybody done what Thomas told them to do, me included. If it weren't Randall I was telling stories to it was Rutledge or Harold or any number of men passing through the shabeen. They liked hearing my stories, at least they told me they did, but all the while they was listening they was feeling my schoolgirl thighs, breathing down my schoolgirl neck and because they done the same to all the girls, I never thought to slap them.

The reason everyone listened to Thomas was because Thomas always made sense. He never let no liquor run around his head making him woozy. He was a professional. At 4am, when Mary began rousing the household to "fuck off back to where you live", he always made sure I was safely returned to Pam. Normally it was Thomas himself who borrowed Mary's car to drive me the five minutes home, never letting the conversation run much beyond small talk, which suited me too because 4am weren't no time to run deep.

Pam never stirred when I got back home and crawled into her bed but she always had me awake by 6.30 am poking me in the back with her bony knee to get up and make her tea.

This was how I done my life for a year or so never took note of the passing of time, locked as I was in my routine.

-4-

I wonder often how life might have worked out if I never, one particular night, broke the routine and stayed the night at Mary's. Might things have turned out different?

Ain't good to blame people, we should always stand up for our own wrongdoings but, this particular occasion I've got to blame Thomas. He gave me a grass laced cigarette to smoke along with three shots of whisky. I told him I never wanted to touch no grass but he said it was "one in a million,' going to make me soar.

I was so far gone I never knew which man I was story-telling to that night. Was it Blakely or Randall or Archie? I was swimming and flying at the same time, laughing and moaning. When I came around it was broad daylight and I was in the basement with a blanket across me alone except for Mary who was clearing bottles into bags.

"You alright there duck?" Mary asked. "Took a turn for the worse I would say."

"Where's Thomas?"

"At work in the Sorting Office, love."

"Is he going to take me home?"

"It's past 10 in the morning he's got another hour left on his shift."

I staggered around at Mary's that day helping her but not getting much done. When it came to four pm I set off for home concerned that Pam might be wondering where I was. In normal circumstances I would have thought up excuses to explain away my absence but it felt like my head was disconnected from my shoulders. Weren't able to think things through.

Perhaps because my mind was foggy it never occurred to me as strange that Pam should be in bed fast asleep when I came home that afternoon. Truth was, seeing her there under the covers was the best outcome of all as I was longing to go back to bed and sleep off the narcotic. William's sofa bed was empty so I crawled in to his not wanting to risk waking Pam and getting a tirade.

It was dark when I woke up, 9 pm on the clock. Pam was still asleep. I crept up and was about to leave to go back to Mary's when I noticed Pam's cup of tea beside the bed. It was untouched. Next to the cup were the two aspirin I had delivered to Pam the morning before after she said she weren't feeling well enough to rise.

That was when I got the uneasy feeling. It crept up my back down my shoulders and into my gut. I went over to Pam and shook her gently. She was stone cold. "Mam-mi." I said. "Mam-mi." I shook her again roughly but she just lay there, all stiff.

"Mam- mi," I yelled, my hands shaking. I ran out of the room and up the stairs and banged on Reggie's door so loud. "Reggie, it's Mam-mi. Reggie."

Reggie came hurriedly to the door, eyes bewildered pulling his tie straight across his collar. I dragged the old man down the stairs. "Please, Reggie, what is wrong with her? What is it?"

Reggie went across to Pam and touched her softly, laid a hand on her wrist. He looked across at me quivering in the doorway. "She's dead, Lynette. I'm sorry, yeah."

Very gently he wrapped the blanket back across my mam and taking my hand took me out of the room and upstairs. "We'll have to call my cousin, Doctor Johnson."

Everyone was out of their rooms now wanting a news bulletin. They all crowded into Reggie's room behind us.

"She weren't looking well,"

"Had a bad cough."

"God bless her soul."

"Died peaceful, best way to go"

Words were swimming around my brain as I sat at Reggie's tiny wooden table next to his bed. I should have come back before. Should have made her take those pills.

Reggie was in organizing mode sending someone off to call Doctor Johnson, someone else to go track down William or otherwise making tea. People were patting me and petting me and rubbing my head. I couldn't look at any of them. Pam was dead, dead? How did that happen? Dead?

Thing about West Indians, we can create a party out of the most tragic of events. Within minutes of Pam being found, Reggie's rooms was filled, the rum was flowing, music playing, bodies swaying. Everyone was in a sad, mad groove. That was when I crept out. Only one saw me going was Robert who escorted me down the stairs. It was unusual for Robert to be around in the evening, normally he was on his shift, not that I registered this at that moment.

He followed me back into Pam's room and stood beside me as I sat down on my bed beside my dead mam.

"She worked too hard," Robert said shaking his head. "Would never have happened if she'd stayed in the homeland. This country kills its finest."

I said nothing, just laid my hand across the blanket covering Pam.

"S'why I'm going back home," Robert continued. "Got fired from the trains."

"Why?" I asked. Robert weren't the type to get in trouble.

"Talking to a white girl; the boss's daughter." He vigorously rubbed the stubble gathering on his chin. "It was in the depot. She only wanted to know where her Dad was I told her I didn't know but said I expected him back soon. Her Dad walked in as I was answering her and just yanked her from me like I was breathing fire. Next thing I know I'm out of a job for harassment."

"That's bad, Robert."

"Yeah, that's why I can't stay here no more, what with that and now Pam, shows you got to do what your gut tells you."

"I'm sorry to hear that, Robert," I said. "Ain't fair at all."

I sat in silence, Robert beside me all awkward, doing the best he could at sympathy.

"Could you do me a favor Robert?" I said. "Go over to Colville Terrace, get my dad, bring him here?"

"Yeah, that's fine. Do you want me to tell him what's happened?"

I shrugged. "If you want." I didn't really care. Truth was, I just wanted to get rid of Robert. He stank of stale beer and piss. It didn't feel dignified having him stand so close to Pam's corpse.

Doctor Johnson arrived with his black leather doctor's bag filled with tools that would never bring Pam back. Reggie accompanied him into my room as the doctor sat on the bed next to Pam, pulling back the blanket and feeling for her pulse much like Reggie had done thirty minutes before. He pulled a form out from his bag and filled it in. "Keep this," he said handing the form to Reggie. "Call this number for the undertakers. They going to come take her away." He got up, shook Reggie's hand, nodded at me and left the room. Reggie nodded at me too and followed his cousin shutting the door behind him.

I didn't leave Pam. Found stuff to do in the room putting piles of fabrics into new piles, undoing the piles, folding the fabric and unfolding, rolling balls of cotton and unrolling balls. From time to time the door knocked softly and one of the residents came in to sit beside Pam, stroke the blanket, offer me more tea.

After an hour or so, Irene and Gwen turned up, filling the room with the scent of cheap perfume and tobacco. They was done up in headscarves and long Macintosh coats but still looked every bit the whore in their make-up and high shoes. I was surprised Irene had come out without changing her shoes at least. She was taking a risk on my behalf.

"What's going on here my love?" she asked sweeping over, "we got word your mum's passed?"

"She's there," I said pointing to the bed. "I thought she was asleep."

"Best way gal," Gwen said, rubbing my arm. "I tell ya, I've seen a lot of suffering at death's door, gimme a calm passing any day."

"Thomas said he don't do death, sent us instead and Mary said you can have a bed at hers for a bit until the dust settles and all that." Irene perched on the edge of William's bed. She didn't look comfortable being here, close to death in a house of black immigrants, kept glancing at the door like she was expecting an ambush or something.

"You don't have to be here." I said. "I can come to Mary's later on when my mam's been taken."

"No, you're alright," Gwen said. "We can stay can't we Rene?"

"Yeah, course," Irene replied. It was stuffy in the room but none of us thought to remove the cardboard panes. Irene took off her headscarf and pushed her hair into shape.

We must have looked a strange combination to the undertakers as they came in all polished up, two whores and a scrawny black kid. They never said nothing though to indicate surprise, kept their eyes lowered all dignified. There were two of them, an old man with grey hair and a younger one, maybe his son. They done their business lifting Pam, all tiny and breakable into a plastic coffin. I'll never forget how I felt when they done up the clasps on the side with Pam in there. Still get claustrophobic just thinking about it.

We sat in silence, Gwen holding my hand for comfort. I was pleased they was there with me but I wish they had never come because of what resulted next.

The two men carried the coffin out of the room. The older man said his goodbyes and went out first. As the younger man followed carrying the foot of the coffin, he looked from one to the other of us and spat on the floor. "Say hi to your brothers for me, Irene," he sneered and shut the door.

We was all stunned.

"That fucking bastard," said Gwen under her breath.

Irene was sitting completely still and pale staring at the stained floorboards. "I can't believe he just done that," she said eventually.

"I've got a good mind to go after him and whack him one with me handbag." Gwen jumped to her feet, suddenly all fired up.

"Leave it," said Irene. "What you going to achieve doing that?" she pulled her friend back onto the bed.

"Satisfaction for a start. This girl's just lost her mum."

"Well, one thing's for sure," said Irene. "I'm busted."

"He ain't going to say nothing."

"He is, Gwen, I recognize him now, he drinks down the Legion with Ken and Shirley. Ken's one of Mosley's boys."

"Which one's Ken again, oldest?"

"Second oldest, Bill's me oldest brother. He's just as bad. Anyway, safest place to be right now is back at Mary's. Come on, Lynette, let's go." She refitted her headscarf and lit a cigarette. "Need to get some business tonight. I reckon danger's looming."

I grieved Pam's death, not like I grieve Alicia's, that's fresh grief, ain't never going to recover from that. Thing about death you don't just grieve it for a set period of time, you keep grieving. Intensity wears off after a while but not the grief. Just speaking about Pam and your mam-mi brings tears to my eyes. We done the whole nine nights, everyone drinking around Pam's casket and eating a feast provided by Reggie to celebrate her parting so I reckon her dubby found peace. Thank God for that mercy.

Most of what I feel though is anger at myself for messing up. I never looked after Pam. So big on everything I was doing I never paid no attention to her, stuck away in that stinking hellhole, other side of the world from her sisters. Maybe my neglect was payback for her bringing me to England. When I think that, though, I feel bad as she came here to give me a better life. Oh, I don't bumberclot know.

Well, Tanya would rather live here than in Jamaica so she, for one, was glad Pam made the trip, sad as her life here was. It would have been better for her in Jamaica, but Pam must have had a sense that the future generations, just like the one Tanya was carrying, needed to grow up somewhere else.

-5-

So, after Pam died the shit bounced off the fan. That was what happened, all as a result of Gwen, well, Thomas too and Irene. And Mary she was to blame and most probably if you break it all down, so was I. It was Gwen, though, most of all. Gwen was a kind-hearted girl but she never had no stability in her life, made her fickle. Irene trusted her too much and that was her downfall.

Thomas, he done a good job managing his side of the brothel business but when it came to women, as I told you before, there weren't no stopping him. He loved the feel of women's skin. Rumor was he shared a bed with several different women a night but the one he showed himself to care most for, was Mary.

Mary and Thomas, they never admitted to being an item and no one discussed it public but they were. Mary accepted that Thomas was a philanderer so long as he always slept and woke up in her bed. That was why she done the whole brothel business, to keep Thomas by her side. She loved him that much.

What Mary didn't realize was that Thomas was also seeing Irene, sleeping with her of course, that was a given but also seeing her, courting her, whatever you want to call it, Irene had his heart. During the day, when Mary and me was cleaning up the house and Thomas was supposedly off at work down the Sorting Office, what was really happening was he was canoodling with Irene.

Irene's aunt lived on Kensington Park Road. She had a cleaning job out all day. Irene used to sneak Thomas into her aunt's house when his shift finished at 11.

Course, Gwen found out about Irene and Thomas because Irene weren't good at keeping her mouth shut. Gwen swore to keep it secret but, deep down, she was jealous. Got it into her

*head that due to this alliance, Irene was getting a bigger cut of
the dough than her. So, what Gwen does, she lets it sit a couple
of days and then lets that cat out of the bag to Mary. She just
slipped in a passing comment. I heard it because I was there.*

*"Wonder how long it's going to last between the Prince and
Irene?"*

"What do you mean?" Mary asked, stopping her dusting.

"Seeing Thomas' smitten."

"Where you getting this?"

"Well they meet down her place every afternoon."

"That so?" said Mary.

"Yeah, her Aunt works all day, house is free."

*That was all was said. Mary carried on dusting while
Gwen continued applying her make up. All appeared calm
'cept I could see Mary was ruffled. She weren't dusting with
any logic after that. Just kept redoing over and over the places
she'd already done.*

*A few days later as Thomas was leaving Irene's house, a
crowd of teddy boys confronted him, grabbed him by the
jacket and beat him with their fists and feet and
knuckledusters until my dad was vomiting blood up on the
pavement.*

"Leave our white girls alone, nigger."

*Irene tried to run away, get help but they got her and
slapped her up, tore off her clothes, called her a cheap whore.
Irene's only mercy was an approaching police siren, which
scared the men into running away. Irene waved her arms as
the police car approached. When the police saw it was a black
man writhing around the floor they done nothing just drove
on left him there. They never wanted to get involved.*

*Thomas lay there for thirty minutes, while Irene ran off to
find help. Passersby just stepped around him as he lay there
like he was a mound of rotting vegetables. They kept their eyes*

averted avoiding the pool of bloody spit dribbling out of his mouth.

It was William and Burgess lifted Thomas into Mary's car and took him round to Mary's house. Mary, she was all tender and shocked, but it was just a mask because it was her Uncle Eddie beat Thomas up. Irene recognized him. Irene knew all the white youth round them parts. Uncle Eddie must have been put up to it, how else would he have known where to lie in wait to make the attack.

Mary never let on to Thomas that she knew about his thing with Irene but she didn't let him out of her sight. Every place he went had to be accounted for. Enough to drive any man insane particularly Thomas who was used to getting stuff his way. After a few days of nitpicking, the fighting began.

"Just going down the Apollo to get a pint."

"I'm coming with you."

"Fetching a paper from the newsagents."

"Expect you back here in five."

Thomas grew mad at Mary and that led to the beatings. First off the odd slap but then widespread abuse often leaving Mary in need of stitches or bandaging up. Everyone turned a blind eye particularly Mary because that was what you did them times. We all knew we was onto a good thing having Mary's house and the business and no one wanted to make no waves.

The way Mary coped was by letting off steam on Irene and me. She might have banned Irene from coming to the house altogether but that weren't good business as Irene was a popular whore. Instead, what she done was make sure Irene got all the drunks or dirty old men. The ones normally reserved for the new whores as a rite of passage. Irene, she never made no complaints, though. She just took what came her way. She could have left and done her whoring elsewhere but she said she liked being with black men because they was more grateful for what they could get. I reckon it was also so she could stay close to Thomas. Even unavailable, he was like a magnet for women.

The only indication that Irene was suffering was in her attitude to Gwen. She severed all ties with her best friend. Where they used to arrive and leave together, now they came separately. They never shared make up no more or drinks or stories.

Towards me, Mary turned cold, like it was me caused my father's infidelity. First off it was my cleaning she took offence at. My dusting weren't thorough, beds saggy, toilet stained. Next it became my living there.

"Got to start paying rent, kid," she said one day through a thick lip brought about by a heavy night of Thomas abuse. "Three quid a week or you can bugger off."

"Three quid?"

"Yeah, you better start whoring. Thomas will line you up with your first fella tonight."

"Don't do it," said Irene when I told her. "You need to be back at school. Get yourself an education. Education means freedom. Don't go on the game else you'll be stuck on it like I am."

"What's the meaning of this?" Irene asked taking Mary off to one side on the staircase. "Setting a kid free on the street. That's worse than Borstal."

"What's it to you, Irene? Why do you care about Thomas's kid so much?"

"I don't care about her because she's Thomas's kid. I care about her because she ain't got no one else to care about her."

"Yeah, well with me that's one less. Get back to the dishes. Lynette, stop ear wigging and you, Irene, fuck off to work. Got a deaf, drunk pervert for you to fuck tonight."

Truth is, going into whoring weren't no big deal for me. I only knew that kind of life now. Seen Irene and Gwen on the job enough, knew what it entailed and I weren't no stranger to having men rub me up and down, Thomas had seen to that enough times when he sent me off, hammered, to tell stories. I got it, a woman's purpose was to please a man and if it meant getting paid, that was a bonus. Course, I ain't proud now of what I done. Ain't a path in life I would have chosen for myself but, as much as I liked Irene, I weren't going to listen to her on this one. I wanted my own money. That was all I'd wanted since coming to England, enough money to get Pam out of the shit infested hole, enough to send back home to her sisters and enough to get me a life of my own. Aged fourteen, I had it all mapped out, except the bit about Pam dying. That weren't part of the plan.

It was end of August 1958, a Saturday night that I was lined up to get my first penis-come-knocking. I can't say I was scared, most probably more apprehensive as there was a lot of tension that evening round Mary's place. For several weeks now the mood was heightened around the city, men arriving at Mary's with tales to tell of street fights and white youths shouting abuse at any passing black face. We had to be on our look out all the time, as white people was angry.

My first "customer" was Randall who was a regular round Mary's house. He was a gentle old man who wanted to make a big deal of it being my first sexual encounter and all that. He showed me how men like to be touched and aroused and different ways of prolonging their interest. He was patient and affectionate and most probably lulled me into thinking that all men was kind in the sack.

Weren't the case round two or three. These experiences was all hands and fingers and shoving and pushing. I was knackered after an hour and desperate to go find a drink.

I was just coming down the stairs for a break, legs all wobbly when this shouting and yelling began outside Mary's front door. It was the sound of men's voices, deep and brutal.

"Fuck off home niggers."

"We kill all black bastards."

"Watch out, nigger hunters about."

"Shit," said Randall. He was standing at the bottom of the stairs as the hallway window smashed and a brick landed with a thud on the carpet followed by another and another. There was glass shooting off in all directions.

We was surrounded by a crowd of scared black faces gathering from various rooms around the house.

"Go out back to the kitchen," said Randall pushing me down the corridor. "Stay out of the way."

Behind me was Irene and Gwen and three of the other white prostitutes all in different states of undress, screaming as iron bars smashed down the wooden front door.

"We're done for," Irene shouted.

"Out the window," yelled Gwen.

"Are you fucking mad?" one of the other prostitutes shouted. "It's like an eight foot drop."

"I'd rather have a broken ankle than a smashed in head," said Irene removing her high heels and pulling the window open. The kitchen window overlooked a small back garden that, in turn, led to a high fence with a wooden gate leading onto a narrow alley.

"Don't Irene," I said. "It ain't safe out there."

"Ain't safe in here either, Lyn."

"Let me go first." I had always been Irene's "eyes", that was my role. It was thanks to me, I believed, that Irene had stayed safe this long.

"No, Lyn, you stay here. It's black people they're after. They'll lynch you if they catch you."

But I weren't having any of it. Pushing Irene out of the way, I stood on the windowsill for a split second and jumped. It weren't as high as eight feet maybe more like six feet but it was enough for me to land awkwardly, twisting my ankle as my bare feet hit the spiky gravel.

"Stay there," I called up to the faces looking down at me. Hobbling through the garden, I opened the gate and peered up and down the alleyway. It looked clear for now.

"All right then, Irene, now jump outwards so you land on the grass."

She did that and landed neatly, both feet together like a gymnast.

"OK, I'll go first, you follow," I said.

I'm making it sound like I was some brave heroine or something. Weren't like that, I was shit scared. It was just that I had always looked out for Irene and I really cared about her staying safe. She was like the only mammi I had in the country and, well, I weren't going to let another mammi down.

We ran through the garden, the two of us and out the gate. I was just following my ears for sound. Where there was shouting I ran the other way. We raced in bare feet down to Westbourne Grove and along the pavement to Portobello Road, which is where I ran, head smacking full on into a gang of white boys. They was coming around the corner at me, at least seven of them holding glass bottles. I tried to turn back but caught the edge of my thin bathrobe on a thorn bush.

"Ey -ey, grab her," shouted one of the boys smashing his glass bottle on a brick wall. "We're going to do her well and good."

"RUN!" I shouted to Irene coming up behind me. "The other way."

"Who you looking out for, nigger?" they yelled at me. "A group of you, are there? Running away from the crime, nothing new there then...ha."

At that moment, Irene appeared holding her high-heeled shoes over her head ready to lash out at any one taking a swing her way.

"You leave her alone, you bullies," she shouted, waving her heels.

"Oh-oh, a nigger lover, a white bitch whore."

"No, a copper's daughter actually and I suggest you leave her alone."

"A copper's daughter then you're wasting your breath cos the coppers don't give a shit."

"Grab her too," shouted one of the boys but Irene, she was quick and she made a race back the way she'd come throwing her shoes behind her so they wacked some of the fellas in the face.

Left there, I knew I was done for and the number of attackers was swelling as onlookers came to join in to "whack a black.' They damaged me bad and they punctured my lung. More than dead after they was done with me. It could have been curtains for me for five days they told me at the hospital after I woke up. Touch and go. The only good thing about being out for the count was that I missed the next four days of rioting when every street in North Kensington was ravaged. Would have been good to see the black man's comeuppance, standing out on rooftops slinging down petrol bombs and kitchen knives, that must have scared the shit out of them white boys.

I stayed in St Mary's for three weeks as they tried to put me back together. Irene, she came to see me, in fact all the girls did and Randall, William, Fingers, Pants.

The hospital weren't happy though. They wanted my mammi to come visit but when I said my mammi was dead, they wanted my dad but I knew there weren't no chance Thomas would come. He never saw himself as my dad, not in any paternal sense. So I told them that Thomas was dead too.

They wanted to know what school I went to, where I lived. I couldn't answer none of the questions. What was I going to say? I live in a whorehouse and ain't been to school for two years?

"They are going to get the authorities in, you'll see," said Gwen. "And when they do you got to make it all up. Tell them you live with your aunt and you go to All Saints School and you love arithmetic the best. If they doubt your story they'll slap you in some home and you don't want that."

When the authorities came to see me, I weren't able to make up stories. They was throwing all sorts of questions my way and I was floundering forgetting names and all sorts. In the end, what I done in desperation was I gave them the name, Grace-Ann, name of the bird helped up when we first arrived.

"I live with her," *I burst out.* "She said she was happy to help."

Strange me thinking of her, after seeing her for those first few hours when we arrived in London. I must have clapped eyes on her maybe three more times in passing, enough to nod and wave but the name just popped out. That was because in my head she was a motherly kind, someone like mammi who had kids of her own. I gave the authorities her address as I remembered it. I considered giving a different address and running away but part of me wanted it to be Grace-Ann who took me in, she had been so kind to mammi that day.

Three days later, Grace-Ann turned up at the hospital. She looked almost the same to how I remembered her except her hair was greyer and it was shorter on her head in a bun. She looked smart in a red dress with black buckle shoes and a pair of expensive white silk gloves. I was really embarrassed to see her, as I don't reckon she knew who I was. Bet she was wondering why some kid using her name in vain.

"You Lynette?" *she said to me, not sitting down but standing a few feet away from my bed.*

"Yes, remember, I'm Pam's daughter. We met you that day and went together on the bus and you said if we ever needed anything you'd be happy to help."

"I did?"

"Yes, we was just arriving here from Jamaica, you also got relatives in St James."

I could almost hear the cogs in Grace-Ann's head clunking around trying to make connections all the while questioning the truth of my tale.

"Your mammi called Pam, you say?"

"Yes that's right.

"Met you near Waterloo, that right?"

"Yes, you was coming back from a day's work at the hospital and I needed to pee."

Not sure why I said that last bit. It was like the memory just popped out.

"So, where's your mammi now?"

"She died," I said my voice shaky.

"Sorry to hear that," said Grace-Ann. She hesitated, stroking the gloves before suddenly looking around for a chair. There was one a few steps back, which she pulled over and sat down in close to the bed.

"Look, Lynette, I......"

She was about to say something but was interrupted by the authorities coming in to the ward, a social worker called Jean and another woman I had never seen before with small spectacles, all dressed in a grey suit, official looking.

"Grace-Ann," Jean said as Grace-Ann stood up politely from her chair. "Nice to meet you again. I see you have been reacquainted with Lynette here."

"Yes, that is correct." Grace-Ann had sat back down and was perched awkwardly on the edge of her chair.

"So...?" said Jean looking quizzically from me to Grace-Ann.

I was squirming awkwardly under the covers. Shit. If they'd met each other already that means the authorities knew I was lying to them saying Grace-Ann looked after me.

"So, we are just making plans," said Grace-Ann authoritatively like she knew how to handle officials.

"Well, if no plans have been made by tomorrow when Lynette is due to be discharged from here, we will need to transfer her into the Children's Home managed by Sister here," she motioned to the officious looking lady standing beside her with spectacles hanging off a chain around her neck.

"I am sure we will have managed to reach a decision by then," said Grace-Ann with a short smile.

"Good, then shall we arrange to meet back here tomorrow at 10 am?"

"We shall," said Grace-Ann standing up and giving a nod of her head by way of a dismissive farewell.

As soon as they were gone, Grace-Ann sat back down beside me. "Lynette, I..." She was fiddling nervously with her gloves.

"Stop," I said. "I don't need you to look after me for real. I will be fine. I just needed someone upstanding to pretend they was going to. I've got friends who will help me."

"No, Lynette, I can't have that. You must come and live with me just for a bit while we see what else is out there for you."

I wanted to cry. Really, I did because I wanted so much to go and live with Grace-Ann just for a bit, get some routine in my life. I could stay on the game earning my way as I didn't want Grace-Ann paying for nothing. Stay independent, that was mammi's values and I wanted them to be mine too.

"You won't need to pay nothing for me," I said.

"We will see, Lynette but first, you got to get better, go back to school, keep learning dem books. I'm going to come get you tomorrow morning. You be ready and dressed."

That afternoon Irene came to see me. She had a black eye and bruises up the side of her face.

"What happened?"

"Oh, just my bullying brothers. They're gits that's all, Lyn. So what's your news?"

I told her about Grace-Ann and going back to school.

"Great, Lynette. I'm really pleased to hear that. Soon you're not going to need me any more to teach you stuff, you'll be the smart one."

"I doubt that," I said.

She reached into her coat pocket and took out a ten shilling note. "This is from Thomas. He said he don't want you going back on the game as it might get him busted, selfish git. He's says he's keeping his head low for a bit until all the hostilities die down." She handed me the money. "That's what Thomas says, what I say, Lynette is stay off the game, yeah because it ain't brought nothing for me but trouble."

So, I had been living with Grace-Ann for three months trying to fit in with family life but I was a bit untrained. Living in Mary's house all that time I had forgotten about sitting down for meals and going to school and saying prayers and sleeping at a proper time. I was also not entirely sure how to treat men as my experience was based on making them feel good and flirting with them just like Thomas taught me to do. This made me always awkward around Louis, Grace-Ann's husband, as he weren't like Randall or Pants, he was an upright citizen who dressed smart and never drank or smoked. He used to say that I needed to be disciplined like their boy Tommy, over now from Jamaica. He never said it meanly, more matter of fact. He was a very religious Methodist man

223

with good morals. Becoming disciplined meant I had to go to church each Wednesday and Sunday and Grace-Ann got me singing in the choir and sent me out after school to visit the sick and needy of the community to read them bible stories.

No one ever questioned my background, where I was that time between Mammi dying and getting beat up. I think they just assumed I was with school friends, not hanging out with whores.

So, three months in, I start feeling really ill. I am getting pains in my stomach and throwing up and headaches and all this kind of stuff.

Grace-Ann, she is worried about me, thinks maybe I'm having some sort of relapse from the beating at the riots so takes me to the doctors. They run some tests and discover that I am pregnant.

That weren't good news.

Well, Grace-Ann, she don't know what to do with herself. She is so agitated leaving the doctor's surgery that she almost gets knocked down by a bus. She steers me into a café, orders me a glass of milk and says, "Lynette, I want you to tell me everything."

So I done that. I told her everything, bit like I am telling you now, Tanya. I tell her about the silver cross and throwing the milk bottles and Thomas and Mary and Irene and the undertakers spitting on the floor. I tell her about lying to Mammi that I was going to school when I weren't. I tell her about the drugs and the alcohol. I tell her that the people I knew from Mary's are all my friends, Pants, Fingers, the lot.

When I was done, I looked up at Grace-Ann. I had avoided her eye for most of my truth telling but when I was finished talking I expected her to say something. That is, after all how conversation works, ain't it?

Well, she don't say anything, not for about five minutes. She was black and I don't mean color. I mean she was exuding blackness out of every bit of her holy white soul.

Eventually she speaks, looking me directly in the eye she says to me, "I never put you down as a sinner, Lynette."

Well, I was taken a back. "I'm- I'm not a sinner, Grace-Ann, really I'm not they was the only people took me in, that's all."

"I understand this but you can't be in our house, anymore, I hope you will understand. I will continue to care for you but we will need to find you an alternate place to live. You know how Louis is an upstanding man, he cannot be seen to be accommodating... ladies of the night."

I wanted to say something here, defend myself but I reckoned there weren't no more words to say. I had stated my case and she had found me guilty.

"Say nothing about this to anyone," she said removing coins from her red, leather purse to pay the bill. "I will make enquiries tomorrow."

I didn't see Louis or Tommy again that same week or the next and when it came time for me to leave Grace-Ann's house, they were nowhere to be seen. Grace-Ann told me to pack my nightdress, three dresses, underwear, my bible and a toothbrush in a red and yellow suitcase, which I did, taking care to unpack the ten shilling note Thomas had given me from my underwear drawer and place it discreetly inside the front cover of Grace-Ann's bible. I hated that I had humiliated her and wanted to make it up in some way.

I followed Grace-Ann to the bus stop. She paid for my bus fare and gave me an address. "I will come and visit you," she said.

I had no idea where I was going. I could have rebelled and not gone where Grace-Ann was sending me but I didn't have it in me. I was sick all the time and I was scared. I weren't ready to be a mother. I weren't even grown up myself. The bus traveled away from West London into East London. The address I had was for the Redford Hotel close to Woodford Bridge in Essex.

It took over an hour to get there. As the bus pulled into the depot I was the only one along with the driver still sitting there.

"Out you go, girl," the West Indian bus driver said, "end of the line."

I showed him the address I had and he directed me on my way with a fatherly squeeze of the shoulder. I nearly cried at this affection. I felt alone and scared and, for two hoots, I would have stayed on that bus all night.

It was approaching dusk when I eventually found Redford Hotel. In my mind I pictured a guest room with a hot bath and warm bed waiting for me but it weren't like that. Instead, I was met at the door by a harassed looking white lady, hair askew with a red and shiny face.

"Downstairs," she said when she saw me. I followed her down two flights of stairs, each step we trod getting thicker with dust.

"In there."

She showed me into a dark, damp room with moldy walls and ivy covering the inside of the windows. "Toilet outside, bucket to wash your face, dinner on that plate." She pointed to a china plate with a lump of bread and a piece of cheese next to a thin mattress on the floor. "I'm Val, Head of staff. Report for duty 6am tomorrow morning." She turned to leave, "Oh," she said turning back, "Don't bother to dress nice, ain't going to be clean work tomorra."

I looked about me on the edge of a sneeze as the dust shot up my nose.

"Excuse me," I said as Val trudged back upstairs, "but I think I might be in the wrong place, I was sent here by Grace-Ann?"

"Yeah, I know. But we don't have no coloreds working the top floors, puts the guests off, no offence yeah. Your living and working quarters are down here until the time comes when your belly is too large then we dispatch you to the Lodge to give birth."

"Lodge?"

"Yeah, Horsefields Lodge. You have the baby there and the state adopts it unless you got some kind of a fortune to bring it up yourself, which judging from..... no offence but you don't look like you got much to offer a baby."

"But I don't want to adopt," I said more thinking than sharing.

"Tough luck."

Val gone, I made a plan to get out of there. Stuffing the bread and cheese down my throat like some starving orphan, I took my bag and crept back up the stairs. The door at the top was locked but it was only a loose bolt and after a few knocks, I had it off the wall. The main reception area of the hotel was quiet even though there was lights on and the sound of voices in the small room behind the front desk. Clutching the handle of the red and yellow suitcase, I made it to the front door forgetting that there was a bell went off when it opened.

"Yeah, where you going?" said Val from behind me.

"I-I'm leaving," I said in as grown up a voice as I had. "I don't like it here."

"Yeah, well don't tell me that. I don't give a shit. Tell my boss."

"No, it's OK," I said. "I'll just go."

"Go where?" came a man's voice.

"Oh, hello, Reverend," I said as a minister dressed all in black with a dog collar round his neck appeared from the room Val just came out of.

"This is the new girl I was telling you about," said Val. She raised her hand and whispered loudly, "Going to be trouble I reckon."

"Where exactly do you intend to go?" he asked again. "It's a cold night and if I am correct, you do not know this area too well."

"I'll be all right," I said. "I can take a bus back to Notting Hill. I know which one goes there."

"At this time of night, no, no buses," said the minister glancing over at Val. "Have you another room she can go to, Valerie, just for tonight until she's better settled in?" He spoke in a clipped English voice, like a newsreader.

"Well, I suppose she could have that empty one in the attic but don't go letting anyone see you there. People funny round these parts to... new faces."

"Perfect," said the minister. "Tell you what, why don't you show the young lady up there, Valerie, and I will be a perfect gentleman and bring up her bag."

I nodded. It weren't what I wanted but it beat being stuck out on the street all night in the cold. "I'll sleep here tonight and then leave in the morning," I said following Val up the stairs.

"Only after you've done your chores," Val said tutting, "Ain't free boarding here ya know."

The room was small but clean and there was a proper bed and a small washbasin, with a toilet outside the door. I waited a while for the Reverend to bring my bag. Thinking he must have forgotten, I collapsed onto the bed not bothered about switching off the light or washing my face. I just wanted to sleep.

I can't tell you what time it was when I was woken up but judging by how alert I felt it can't have been much past 9 pm. My bedroom light was off but the curtains still undrawn. There was something tapping my leg. I leapt up expecting to see some rat but instead, there was the reverend sat on the end of my bed, smiling at me.

"Sorry, didn't mean to wake you. Just brought up your bag. Where would you like it?"

"Oh," I said rubbing my eyes, "Anywhere is good. Thank you."

"Give, and it will be given to you. Good measure, pressed down, shaken together, running over, will be put into your lap. For with the measure you use it will be measured back to you." *He hesitated.* "Luke 6 verse 38."

"Oh," I said.

I was grinning at him all the while with a kind of "good bye' face expecting him to leave the room but he never did. Instead, what he done was sat down on the end of my bed and began tapping my calf again moving up to my knee and onto my thigh.

He was most probably expecting me to flinch and all that but I didn't because I'd been having my legs felt up for years of my life. That's men, ain't it?

"Rescue the weak and the needy; deliver them from the hand of the wicked," *he said moving his hands up towards my pants and yanking them down.* "Do you wish to see my wicked hand?" *he said.*

I shrugged.

"Do you?" *with the palm of his hand he slapped me hard across the face so that my cheeks were pounding.* "I said do you want to see my wicked hand?"

"Er yes," *I said holding my cheek. The strength of his hand had opened up one of the gashes on my cheeks from the riots* and there was blood on my fingers. I weren't liking the look in his eyes. They was wild and unhinged.

"Right answer," he said, "because only by showing you my wicked hand can I rescue you from weakness and need."

As he was speaking he was undoing his black, holy trousers and slipping out his white man's cock and while he is waving it around with one hand, he is punching me in the fanny with his other fist. "Let each of you look not only to his own interests, but also to the interests of others, it says in the Philippians chapter two," he yelled. "You are looking to my interests and satisfying me and I am looking to yours, curing you of your past sins."

He was thumping real hard at my fanny. I tried kicking him off but he just came back like some man-eating puppy. Then out of his inside pocket, he pulls out this rope and I was all confused. Remember, I'd hung out in a whorehouse but it was only straight sex, whatever went on behind the closed bedroom doors was out of my domain. I was naïve.

He tied the rope around my neck, a thin rope, there was not much more to it than a shoelace. It was cutting into my skin and I was trying to kick him off me but he was on top and he ain't going nowhere just pulling the rope tighter and tighter as with his cock, he enters me and starts pounding like some mechanical piston.

Shit, well I am seeing both stars and stripes. I can barely breathe but at the same time I am rasping with the pain of his advances, cutting off the blood to my brain. I'm gasping for breath and writhing around and he is shouting about God and Helping Neighbors and Casting out Demons, interspersed with high-pitched hysterical laughter like some mad man.

Somewhere along the way, I was out for the count, Passed out. Can't tell you how that whole sick, sordid abuse ended. All I know is that when I woke up I was tucked into my bed, curtains drawn, pants returned to their correct position and *blanket pulled up across me. When I turned on the light, it was still dark outside, the only evidence of any of the indecency went on before was the blood still on my pillow from my bleeding cheek and the feel of the rope marks around my neck red and raw. Oh yeah and the fact my fanny was so numb and bruised I couldn't piss.*

I tell you, I was out of that house before dawn broke. Oh yeah, forgot to say, by the bedroom door there was a little stack of shillings next to a note saying, "And my God will meet all your needs according to his glorious riches in Christ Jesus. Philippians 4:19." *I tore up the note and took the coins and was gone.*

I got off the bus in Notting Hill, back in my familiar territory but feeling so much like a stranger I never knew which way to turn. Who would have me? Where could I go? I wanted so much to be with the people I loved, Mammi—dead —or Irene or Grace-Ann, but one was out of bounds and the other one had banished me. There were no other women in my life now, except Mary and she hated me. I looked about. Everyone was busy going places, stuff to do. I had nothing, no one, Tanya. I was way down rock bottom.

Dragging the red and yellow suitcase, I followed my feet back to my first house with the chipped black front door. Maybe my room, the one I shared with Pam and William would still be there, untouched. Perhaps I could catch a waft of Pam's aroma lingering on her pillow. I climbed the steps and rang on the doorbell. A head shot out of the window.

"Who are you?" the man yelled down. He was a black man in a British Rail shirt but it was not Robert.

"Is William here?" I called.

"No," said the man.

"How about Reggie? He here?"

231

"Hold on," said the man.

He came down the stairs and opened the door.

"Top floor," he said flattening his curls and running out of the house past me to catch his shift on the trains.

I had not been back to this house since Pam died. I didn't need to before, I had people to care for me but now it was the only place I could think to go. I wanted my belongings, everything that I had brought across from Jamaica with me, even my old battered suitcase complete with the loose grains of Jamaican sand. The sand. That brought tears to my eyes. It was the sand I wanted to feel most of all, sand all the way from home.

I made my way up the flights of stairs feeling my way along the greasy bannisters, the stink of mold making me want to retch. I stopped outside my old room and knocked on the door. Nobody answered so I turned the handle and looked inside. It was gone. There weren't nothing the same no more. Not the bed covers or the floor rug or the smell. There weren't Pam's pile of fabric in the corner or our collection of clothes hanging off the door of the wardrobe. We weren't there no more. Even the dust looked different in the sunshine seeping through the panes of glass. We was gone like we never existed.

I continued climbing the stairs until I got to Reggie's room. Standing outside his room, I knocked. Had he ever wondered where I was?

"Coming," he said and I heard the sound of feet shuffling on the carpet.

"Lynette," he said on seeing me standing there. If he was surprised at my suddenly turning up he never showed it. Instead he was fixating on my chin. At least I thought it was my chin but it was my neck where I had the rope marks. I had forgotten all about them.

"What happened to you?" he said.

"I-I got attacked," I said.

He looked at me with pained eyes like he was reading into my broken soul.

"We need to get you treated," he stood back to let me enter into his room. "My cousin's daughter is a nurse, let me see if I can get her around here. You are in a bad way."

It had not crossed my mind to look at myself in the mirror. I touched my face; it was caked with blood. At the feel of the blood, the pain between my legs came flooding back and I collapsed onto the floor both sobbing and light headed all at the same time. Reggie, he was flustered, not used to emotional young ladies.

"Wait there, Lynette. I will be right back." He went out of the room to the phone box. I dragged myself onto a chair and held myself tight rocking back and forth in an attempt to soothe my misery.

I never knew I'd gone to sleep but I must have because I came to with the feel of a warm hand on my face. When I opened my eyes I saw Grace-Ann crouched down next to me. I jumped in horror. I was in shock seeing her there. She was going to shit bricks at me for leaving Woodford Bridge.

"I had to go," I said speaking all quickly. "The priest there, he..."

"It's OK," said Grace-Ann.

"Yeah but, it weren't the right place," I said.

She was rubbing cream on to my neck and on to my cheeks.

"I know, I'm sorry, Lynette." She took a hold of my hands. "It was recommended to me by a colleague at work but I only found out today that there were..." she hesitated, "unsuitable elements. I'm going to take you home with me." She continued with the creaming. "I think one thing we have learned is that this city is no place for a young girl to be wandering around on her own."

Reggie brought tea for Grace-Ann and me and we all sat together in his small room sipping silently.

"What about Louis?" I said to Grace-Ann as I tottered down the stairs out to Reggie's car with Reggie carrying my suitcase.

"He will have to learn to be flexible with his views. I would imagine he will not look at you or speak to you but at least he will not harm you. I am sure of that."

Grace-Ann was right. Louis paid no attention to me. It was obvious that he was as awkward around me as I had first felt around him. He kept himself hidden behind newspapers or running errands for the church, anything to keep him away from a "lady of the night."

Course, that all changed when my darling daughter, Alicia came along.

"So, what is it?" I heard him asking Grace-Ann outside the bedroom door the day that she was birthed.

"A girl," Grace-Ann replied, "a big girl."

"Healthy?" he asked.

"Looks it."

When Grace-Ann walked in to join me in the room where I was lying with your mammi, Alicia, on my lap, she was smiling. "He wants to know when he can get the cricket bat out. He is hoping to have more luck teaching cricket to this little thing," she said rubbing her matt of black hair, "than he has ever had with Tommy." She took a deep breath.

Things was good after this, Tanya. I was part of a family, Alicia grew up to love cricket, which meant she was adored by her LouLou, as she called him. Me, I was sent back to school and Alicia was shared out in the family while I done my nurse's training. She was a spoilt girl my Alicia with so many people looking after her. That was why she done good at the cricket, she had natural skill but she also got bags full of encouragement.

I saw Thomas a few times after this. Weren't good experiences on the whole. He got in with Malcolm X and turned political and angry. All into black man's rights with one hand while screwing black and white girls over with the other. I tried to avoid him but you know, Notting Hill ain't a big place.

Every time our paths crossed, he tried to get me back on the game, told me I could be a pimpstress, get young girls into prostitution in return for a hefty cut. Told me I was pretty and good with men. Ain't going to lie, at times I was tempted. That's how it is when your old man praises you, you would go to the ends of the earth for admiration but I had too much at stake. Being a nurse has done me proud. Get a lot of admiration for that job and what's more, I got a place in society. That was all I ever really wanted from the moment I set foot in the motherland, just to fit in.

There's a lot more of course but I ain't ready to talk about that yet, anything to do with Alicia still too raw. Might need to wait another twenty years for that. Just make sure you don't go getting in with a bad crowd. I know life ain't always been easy for you and we haven't always seen eye to eye but one insight I hope you got from this letter is, if you find someone solid and reliable with a good job prepared to stick by you, go with it. Remember the saying, it ain't who you go to the party with but who you got waiting for you when you come home. That is the person going to treat you well.

Grand-mammi Lynette

REBECCA MEETS LEVANA

July 2014

Rebecca pushed her airport trolley into the arrivals hall at Tel Aviv airport scanning the scores of people for her mother. It had been two years since the two women's paths had crossed. Ever since Levana and Johnny had returned to Tel Aviv a decade before for "Johnny's work," as the story went or in truth to stabilize Levana and patch up the marriage, communication between mother and daughter had been scant. Even scanter than usual; there had never been a bond. Levana was too cold and Rebecca too hot. If it had not been for Johnny and his patience and determination in maintaining family ties, Levana and Rebecca, at Levana's insistence, would most probably have drifted fully apart.

"Why else do you think I do stand-up comedy?" Rebecca used to say to her friends. "Because I crave love and feedback."

Levana was standing a few rows back from the meet and greet barrier. Her hair was cut short and Rebecca couldn't help but note how Jewish she looked, traditionally Jewish. Just like Helga's father apparently looked traditionally Jewish. A wave of anxiety gripped Rebecca. Now everything is starting to come in for her, all the clues to her own life, in full color.

She waved in Levana's direction waiting for Levana to spot her, and when she did, Levana waved back. Half a wave, of course; she would never give more than that. Well, by the sound of Helga's letter, Levana never even got a wave at all.

It was hot in Tel Aviv, as hot as New York. Both women, sitting side by side in the front of the car, Levana driving, hid their eyes behind dark glasses. Both stared straight ahead in silence. There was so much big stuff to talk about yet so little small stuff to say. Levana drove the car through the automatic gates of home and parked up in the driveway beneath a palm tree. Neither woman made any attempt to move. Levana left the engine running and the air con on.

"So, am I inbred?" Rebecca asked eventually in a quiet voice. She could smell the scent of her step-father all around the car and it brought her courage.

Levana fiddled with her wedding ring. Her fingers were small and splattered with sunspots, early signs of ageing.

"You are Austrian," she said.

"Oh God. I think I need a drink."

"But no, he is not my father."

Rebecca let out a long, slow breath.

"Thank fuck," she said running her hands down her cheeks. "But how can anyone know…?"

"We can't with what she went through. But it seems from people I met that I physically remind them of Karl Knox, a printer from Vienna. I found that out because their family contacted me, which was very awkward, to see who was left alive. Karl had a son called Max whom I believe knew my mother at school. When they met me, they thought they could see Max…"

"Max…" Rebecca scanned her brain for the name. It sounded familiar. "Max Knox. I know him," she cried. "I mean, I don't know him but Helga mentions him in her letter to me. He rescued her once when she was being bullied." With a burst of excitement, Rebecca suddenly clasped Levana's hand. Levana didn't pull away. "She said after he rescued her he made her heart all jittery or all fluttery, I'll show you the letter, I remember the bit. How weird is that?"

Levana was looking straight ahead. "Does she mention his father at all?"

"No but ..." Rebecca stopped. Tears began to roll down Levana's cheeks. Rebecca had never seen Levana cry.

Neither woman said anything and Levana made no attempt to wipe away her tears.

After a short time she said, "It's funny, my mother always used to lie to people that my father was a respectable man and that he had been the love of her life. Turns out in some distant, obscure way, she might have been right. Max was most probably the only human being who ever made her heart flutter and it's more likely it wasn't Max but probably his father because Max would have been out working since he was young but, well, somehow the story is not so shameful." She wiped her face. "At least he was Austrian."

At this Rebecca laughed at the wit of it, and Levana laughed too.

"A small blessing," Rebecca said, "I guess. Not a Nazi."

"Max is still alive," Levana said softly. "My possible half-brother. He survived the war and lives in Jerusalem. I am sure we will never meet each other but he has written a letter to me apologizing for his father's actions.... And I have forgiven him. I only wish my mother could have known."

"She left it to us to find out," said Rebecca, "That was her legacy." She opened the car door and the heat of the midday sun flooded in a welcome relief after the relentless chill of the air con.

"Look Mom," Rebecca squeezed her mother's hand. "It's all out there now OK, our past, our present, everything. You can read the letter. Helga might have fucked up with us both when she was alive but she's tried to fix things now she's dead. It's going to take years to digest and we can't ever get back what's gone but please, no more lies, no more hiding from the truth, no more stone hearts and no more goddam shame. OK?" She clambered out of the passenger seat. "Now let's go have a drink. We both deserve one. I don't care what it is but it better be bubbly and come with a cork."

Levana smiled and, when she did, she had a dimple on her cheek. Rebecca had never seen the dimple before.

"I might have just the very drink cooling in the refrigerator," she said, checking her face in the mirror and getting up to follow her daughter inside.

MAYA RETURNS TO RONNIE

July 2014

One month was the longest Maya had ever been away from Ronnie and she was pleased to find herself excited to see him. He had gone into a strop after her last phone call to him en route to Manchester and refused to answer any of her texts but she knew it would be easy to snap him out of this. He was not a complicated person. It was just a case of cooking him a curry. She just had to stop off at M and S foodhall on the way back, slip into a comfortable piece of lacy nightwear and within moments of the hot chili sauce touching his lips, he will have forgotten she had even been away.

Maya often wondered if she chose a man like Ronnie to marry because he is so uncomplicated. He didn't harbor resentments or become emotionally confused. Having grown up surrounded by women, these attributes were appealing. With Ronnie, she never had to explain herself or analyze her behavior. He sort of reminded her of a dog with simple needs—eat, sleep and love.

It was the love part that Maya had on her mind as she paid the taxi driver and walked up the steps to the apartment. She longed to feel Ronnie's soft, warm skin up against hers and feel his chin nuzzling against her cheeks. After hunting around the bottom of her handbag for her key fob, she entered the lobby of the block and walked along the red and white striped carpet to the lift.

She had texted Ronnie to tell him she was back today but heard nothing, of course. He was still at work but home soon, so Maya was on a tight time frame to get everything ready for the perfect evening. As the lift door opened, she was struck by an unfamiliar odor that rammed into her nostrils. It was a mélange of rot and feet and fried fat and sweat and sewage, worse than any aroma she had encountered on her world travels. "Oh God," she said slamming her hand across her face and checking she was at the right door. Tentatively sticking her key into the lock she pushed open the door. It slid halfway and then stopped, something was blocking it. Squeezing through the narrow gap, Maya saw garbage sacks, a row of them lined up against the wall and overflowing, feasted upon by flies. Ronnie's football trainers and kit were discarded in a heap next to a pile of dirty laundry and junk mail also seemed to be piled everywhere. Leaving her suitcase at the door, Maya side stepped over the mess and into the sitting room, only to be confronted by dirty plates, cups and saucepans stacked on the arms of the sofa and the coffee table. It was the same as she glanced into the kitchen, the only visible worktops, smeared with grease.

Maya crossed her arms, too repulsed to touch anything in the flat that she so prided herself on keeping clean and tidy. She held her breath to defend her lungs from the toxic stink.

"Hello? Maya?" came Ronnie's voice suddenly appearing behind her as he slid open the front door. "I came back early... You're home." He bounded into the room and Maya recoiled. His normally soft, boyish face was hidden behind weeks old stubble, the previously crew cut head of black hair was hanging lank over his ears and he had food stains down the front of his creased, blue shirt. "At last!" He raced over to Maya, arms outstretched, all evidence of any previous strop seemingly wiped out. Maya stayed put.

"What?" said Ronnie, then rubbed his chin, "Oh yes, not shaved for a while. Do you like my halfhearted attempt at growing a beard?"

"It looks horrible," said Maya through clenched teeth. Butterflies had appeared in her tummy from nowhere and she was not sure why.

"It's not that bad," said Ronnie. "I ran out of shaving cream and so decided, why not let it rip."

"You could have bought more," she said.

"Oh yes, didn't think of that. Anyway, aren't you pleased to see me after neglecting me for so long?"

"I would be, Ronnie, but the flat's a shithole. Didn't you do any cleaning when I was away?"

Ronnie looked offended and Maya instantly felt badly. She hadn't expected housework to be the first topic of chat.

"I was going to clean up but then thought that we could do it together when you were home. Sort of a bonding experience."

"But Ronnie, it stinks." Here I go again, thought Maya.

"Alright," said Ronnie. "It's only a bit of cleaning and hoovering. Sheesh, you're ratty." He kicked off his shoes and slumped down on a dining chair pulling off his tie.

"I just hoped that, I don't know, you would have made the flat nice for me to come home to, that's all," said Maya. She wanted to flop down onto the sofa but, amongst the empty cans and crisp packets, there was nowhere to flop. She stood rigid, pinned to the spot.

"But you know I hate cleaning," said Ronnie. "And anyway, it was you who ditched me remember."

"Only because my grandmother died," said Maya. "Hardly a vacation."

"Yeah, well, you were gone so long I sort of didn't know how to cope." He stuck out his bottom lip and looked up at Maya with big, glossy eyes. He paused two seconds then jumped up. "Look, here's the plan, quick shag on the bed, I'll go and empty it of all my clobber and then we can discuss the cleaning rota after that. Please Maya, my balls are bursting."

Maya felt sick. The flies were gathering around her knees, honing in on a sticky patch of something red on the carpet. She didn't want to move from where she was and she had no desire to go into the bedroom and see her lovely, Egyptian cotton duvet cover stained with the remains of takeaway food. On top of that, the idea of a "quick" shag with her grubby fiancé made her inwardly gag.

"I'm not sure I can," she said.

"Look, it's only a bit of mess. Why are you so uptight?"

"No Ronnie. I am not going to stay here until you have sorted this place out. It's disgusting." Maya put her hand to her mouth to suppress a sob. "I'm going to stay at Emma's."

"Well fuck you," said Ronnie. "I had hoped we could have a special evening together but if that is how you want to treat me, then I'll go out and you can stay here. I've been working hard all week, not swanning around the world so why should I clean up?"

Grabbing his jacket and shoes, Ronnie careered out of the flat slamming the door behind him.

Bursting into tears, Maya took out her phone and instantly dialed Rajika in Calcutta. "The house was like a squalid dump when I got home," she cried as soon as Rajika answered. "And when I asked him to clean up, he just stormed off."

Rajika yawned. Maya had forgotten to do a time check. "Oh no, sorry, Mam-mi, did I wake you?"

"It's midnight so yes but don't worry about it. So..... what are you going to do?"

"Well, I'm going to have to tidy everything up myself and it is so disgusting I don't know where to begin."

Rajika paused. "OK. And what happens next time?"

"Next time?"

"Next time you come from being away and the house is like a tip, then what? You tidy again?"

"I love this flat, mam-mi. I don't want it all dirty like this."

"I know my darling. Who wants a dirty apartment?"

"Exactly and that's why I'll clean it. Ronnie doesn't like cleaning and I don't mind it so I'll just make it my role. Everyone has roles in a marriage, don't they."

"Yes, and what will Ronnie's role be?"

"Well, he can work and..."

"But you work," Rajika interrupted.

"Well, he can do the shopping... oh wait, he hates shopping. Well, when we have children he can take them out and look after them and..."

"And while he's doing that, what will you do?"

"Well, I guess I'll be cleaning up."

"And shopping."

"Yes and shopping but that's OK, I like shopping."

"And what about cooking?"

"You know Ronnie doesn't cook, mam-mi. I'm going to teach him. I'm sure once we're married he'll get into the whole home life thing. Although that's more likely to be me as he has said he doesn't want me to work when we have children so I'll be at home to look after everyone."

"And how do you feel about that?"

"Mam-mi, stop it," said Maya absently sitting down on the sofa, squashing a half full box of Pringles. She jumped up and wiped the back of her skirt. "You're suddenly making me doubt Ronnie and I don't want to doubt him. I love him. He's funny and good looking," Maya paused. "Actually, he looked pretty ugly this evening with his long hair and beard but normally he's handsome."

"I haven't said anything," said Rajika. She went silent for a moment. "Do you remember reading about my grandfather, Shakti?"

"Course I do. He was evil but that's because he drank. And you can hardly compare him to Ronnie."

"And my father, Rajeev, he was really good looking as well and funny. That was why my mother fell in love with him. Not that she would admit that."

"And he was intelligent," added Maya. "Look, that was all in the past. Ronnie is a modern man. He would never treat me like any of the men in those letters."

"OK," said Rajika. "I've only met him once, so what do I know? I trust your instinct, Maya. The only thing I would say is, if he properly loves you, he will clean up. So why not wait and see," she yawned. "Now…" another yawn, "perhaps I should get some sleep."

It's a test, thought Maya, as she wrote a note on the kitchen table informing Ronnie that she was going to stay at Emma's until the house was the way it should be. If he loves me, he will clean it. She didn't like to admit that Rajika's idea was a good one but it was. Picking up her suitcase, she wheeled it back into the lift and pressed the button for two stories up. Emma was surprised to see her friend turning up like this out of the blue but also delighted. She had so much to tell Maya. "Come in, I will go and make up the spare bed." The flat was clean and tidy and smelt fresh, a saucepan of food was simmering on the hob. Maya flopped down on the sofa. This was not how I intended to spend my first evening back, she thought, as she stretched out her arms and relaxed, but it has certainly turned out to be a preferable option by far.

Three weeks later

"You knew all along, didn't you?" Maya was making herself a cup of tea in her own clean kitchen, phone perched on the polished window ledge.

"Knew what?" came Rajika's voice down the loud speaker.

"That Ronnie was wrong for me."

"Is he wrong?"

"Oh stop it mam-mi, you know he is."

"I thought he was the perfect match," Rajika said, joking.

"No you didn't. You hated him."

"Hates a strong word, Maya."

"Well, you didn't like how he treated me." Maya lifted out the tea bag and popped it into the recycling caddy.

"I just felt you deserved better. And so did Nani-ji."

"So she was in on this too."

"On what Maya?"

"On the whole "let's teach Maya about men" adventure." Maya carried her tea into the sitting room and plonked down on the professionally cleaned sofa.

"That's not what it was, Maya."

"What was it then? Sending me off to deliver all those envelopes."

"It was just a sort of time experiment."

"Meaning?"

"Meaning, if a relationship is meant to work, it will last the test of time."

"And mine didn't survive the month."

"Well, you answer that, Maya."

"It might have survived if he wasn't so blind. He literally came back and picked up one pair of socks, which he brought up to Emma's flat and stood dangling it on her doorstep."

"I know, you told me."

"Well I'm telling you again mam-mi seeing you instigated all this."

"I...."

"So, he dangled the sock and, when I asked him what he was doing, he said, 'showing you that I love you.' And I said, have you cleaned up and he said, 'No because I don't do cleaning.' Then he puffed out his chest and walked off."

"So, thank goodness for these modern men," said Rajika.

"Stop it mam-mi, you know I'm sensitive right now. Breaking up is hard to do."

"Very hard, my darling, but you seem to be coping amazingly well."

"But how did you and Nan-ji know he was wrong? You hardly knew him."

"You just weren't saying the kind of things about him that a woman says when he is right."

"What are those?"

"Things like … 'He made such an effort when I returned from my trip,' 'He wants me to be successful in whatever I do and he will help out.' Those are the things, Maya."

Maya smiled, just taking in how her mother and grandmother loved her.

"The right man wants you," Rajika said, "to be happy, like we want you to be."

REBECCA WRITES TO MAYA

November 2014

Writing to Maya was something Rebecca had been intending to do ever since Maya had breezed into her world and broken the terrible silence between she and her mother, but Rebecca just hadn't got round to putting fingers to email. So much had happened since discovering who she was or more importantly, coming to understand the lingering threads of pain that were handed down to her through Helga. Rebecca was not even sure she was keeping up with all she had to process. Just like her mother, she, too, would have to learn how to open up, and not hide, as she had in comedy.

Right, now's the time, she said to herself putting aside the article she was writing on "Global Warming and its Effects on Men's Pajamas."

> *Dear Maya,*
>
> *So, I'm not inbred. Yippee.*

It was a strange way to start an email but Rebecca knew Maya would get it.

> *I've discovered I'm Austrian, which is good because it is a beautiful country but bad because of its behavior in the war and its fascist leanings. I've also discovered that my grandfather might have known my grandmother, at least, his son was acquainted. Do you remember the name, Max Knox?*

*The one who saved Helga in the playground? Well people feel
he could be my half uncle. All a bit f*** up. (Apparently we
look like the Knoxes.)*

*The good news is, now I know my past, and some doors
opened to a de-frosting in my family, and I am no longer
screwed up as in I have a boyfriend. First one ever, which at
my age is amazing. I didn't realize how messed up I was when
it came to men until I read Helga's letter and spent some time
bonding with my mum. When I did that, I realized the
pleasure in sharing and trusting and letting myself connect.*

*It seems all the suppression and shame and guilt they
carried had a knock on effect on me. I did not even
understand what someone caring deeply about me would feel
like. But now that I understand what Levana went through
and Levana has opened up a bit, I've just kind of let it all go
and I'm in love. He smells good too, which won't mean much
to you but it's important to me. In fact, all men smell good
now. Might need some therapy to explain my olfactory issues.*

*Purpose of this email is just to thank you for enlightening
me. You did a good thing bringing me that letter from so far
away (and I'm pleased you read it so you have a clue what I'm
talking about). Hope you too have been educated by your
"grandmother"' story. Just wish I'd had a chance to meet mine.
She seemed very strong and very independent. That these
women who suffered so much also chose to come round to do a
loving thing for us grandchildren, took the time and opened
up their pain, also makes me feel loved. And feeling loved
makes me want to give.*

*Ah well. If you are ever back in NY look me up. I don't do
stand-up anymore – seems I get enough love at home.*

All the best and thanks again
R

MAYA MEETS UP
WITH TANYA AGAIN

November 2014

Maya was not sure how Tanya would react to her calling Tanya out of the blue but she just happened to be in Manchester for work and was intrigued to see how Tanya had got on reading the letter. A baby was crying in the background when she answered the phone, but Tanya sounded genuinely glad to hear Maya's voice.

"Yeah, come round right now," she'd said. "We're here."

Jerome was clutching the baby to his chest when he opened the door instinctively bouncing her up and down.

"Hey, good to see you again." He was dressed up smart in a suit and tie with a muslin tucked between his shirt and the baby's mouth in case of any unexpected vomit.

He held the door open for Maya to enter, requesting she remove her shoes to keep outside mess from the sitting room. "Of course," said Maya accustomed to the habit from her own home life.

Unlike before, the sitting room was immaculate. Watery November sun was shining through the windows and the flat was warm and welcoming. There was the smell of something meaty stewing in the kitchen.

"I just popped back in my lunch break to bring some diapers and check my little girl all right," said Jerome, kissing the baby's tufts of black hair. "Ain't she a beaut?"

Maya peered into Jerome's chest. "We called her Alicia after Tanya's mum." Alicia was fast asleep snoring quietly.

"She's gorgeous," said Maya.

"Hey," said Tanya coming out of the kitchen wiping her hands on a tea towel. "Good to see you." She smiled a broad smile.

"I'm going to leave you two, get back to work now," said Jerome kissing Alicia on the head and handing her over to Tanya. Giving Tanya a kiss and Maya a wave, he turned and left the room.

"So, how have things been?" asked Maya sitting down on the sofa.

"Pretty good," said Tanya. "I had a few revelations."

"Really."

"That letter you gave me. I read it as soon as you left. Couldn't resist." She paused. "Made me cry you know." She glanced at Maya. "You read it too I am assuming, that right?"

"I did," said Maya. "Sorry."

"S'alright," said Tanya. "Never knew my gran was a prostitute. That really shocked me when I read it. Not that she done all them things but that she got treated so bad. She went through so much." The baby gave a whimper and Tanya stroked her head. "Thing is," she continued, "the letter showed me that not all men are bad, even at the whore house, some of them was kind. My gran just fell in to a bad situation, my mam did too." She gave a deep breath. "That ain't going to happen to me. I'm going to make sure I stay on the straight and narrow. And so's this little thing," she said bouncing the sleeping Alicia on her knee. "I used to think Jerome was too boring and straight for me but, having read my gran's letter, I've realized, he is a good man and a kind man and he ain't going to let us down. That counts for a lot when you got kids don't it?"

Maya nodded.

"You know when you came round last time," Tanya carried on, "I was just about to break up with Jerome. Thought I wanted a bit of danger in my life. Thank God you come with that letter when you did. It was like my gran and my mum was speaking to me from their graves. They made me reconsider everything about my life and I don't want to tempt fate by saying it but, I'm really happy. Me and Jerome never been so in love."

"I'm so pleased for you," said Maya. "My grandmother's letter made me want to end it with my fiancé. I realized he was a lazy slob and to marry him would be a disaster." Maya laughed and Tanya joined in.

"Shit, bet you weren't expecting that," said Tanya.

"I'm very relieved, that's for sure," said Maya. "You know," she paused, "the purpose of our grandmothers' writing the letters was to enlighten us on their pasts because they believed these would help us make sense of our present. They were enlightened women, weren't they, because it seems their letters have made a very profound difference."

Tanya sat down on the couch, holding the baby. "I think about the time it took to write that gargantuan letter, and how she wanted to tell me something about life. The caring of it. And what sticks out is when someone in her story was caring to her. Like Irene, the prostitute. How things in the story shifted when someone took an action of help."

Maya said, "That's interesting. Kamla had the women at the refuge to help and help her and that probably saved her."

The baby started making sounds to draw attention to herself and both Tanya and Maya laughed. "Alright," Tanya said, "you're part of the conversation."

Maya looked off. "Conversation..."

"It was all in opening up what they had been hiding and then all those feelings..." Tanya said.

"Freed something in us. Well, if they could survive, we will," Maya finished, standing up.

Tanya nodded.

"I better go."

"Thanks for dropping by," Tanya said. "Come again. You're generous, you know, like your grandmother in coming back. I appreciate it."

"It's a great thing," Maya said hugging her, and both of them knew exactly how much was meant with that simple phrase.

MAYA RETURNS TO THE TREE

February 2015

A year later, Maya found herself once again traveling. She visited Rajika and then now she was another trip, once again to a tree.

"Oh Nani-ji, look what you have done to me," said Maya to herself, as the taxi halted outside the big ugly house that Maya now knew had once belonged to the abusive landowner, Mohan Lal. "You have made me superstitious like you."

The dogs behind the gate barked as they had done before and the taxi driver retreated to the far side of the road.

"Pick you up here," he said not taking his eyes off the snarling teeth.

Clutching the goddess in her hand, Maya climbed out of the cab and made her way along the path past the houses filled with curious eyes and friendly waves. She was grateful that she was wearing her trainers this time instead of those flimsy little pumps and dressed in her casual jeans and T-shirt, she didn't look anything like the city girl she'd looked when she'd come before.

"Namaste," waved Maya, her palm wrapped around the disintegrating clay turning sticky.

Following the track at the back of the houses, she approached the small forest of trees until she was at the edge of the forest, beside a tall banyan tree with a hole in its trunk.

Here she stopped.

"End of the road for us, goddess," she said taking one last peak at the lump of clay with the dip for the eyes and the chipped off paint. "I will never know whether it was you or Nani-ji that helped me come to my senses but in case it was you, I thank you. Nani-ji told me to trust you and I'm pleased I did."

She shoved her hand inside the hole in the trunk and reached in as far as she could, laying the goddess on the soft, warm bed.

As she withdrew her hand, something tugged at Maya's elbow. She looked down to see a group of young girls, aged seven or eight, gathered around her looking curiously up at Maya with dirty faces but big, shiny eyes.

"What are you doing?" said one of the girls.

"I'm just returning an old friend to where she belongs," said Maya.

"Is it the goddess?" said another of the girls.

"Yes," said Maya. "How did you know?"

"My mother told me about her," answered the same girl. "She told me never to tell anyone that the goddess lived here."

"And how did your mother know?" asked Maya.

"Someone told her a long, long time ago. The same lady who planted this neem tree." She pointed to the tree next door.

"My grandma planted that tree," said Maya her face turning red with surprise. "In memory of her mother."

"My mam-mi said we had to look after that tree and, if we did that, the goddess would look after us."

Maya brushed the soil from her hands and made her way back along the track with the girls beside her. Stopping suddenly she said, "Do any of you know how to read and write?"

"Yes we do," said the girls. "A little bit."

"Do you know what the goddess likes best?" asked Maya. "She likes people to write her letters, letters telling her all about your lives. Perhaps you could do that for her. Pop a letter in the tree and leave it there. Maybe one day someone will read it and find out all about who you really really really are."

"And the goddess will protect it," said one of the girls.

"Or eat it up," said another.

"Here," said Maya rummaging in her handbag. "Take this pen and notebook, go get started..."

One of the girls grabbed the book and pen and ran off, the other girls close behind, but then they turned around toward Maya.

"Did you do it?" one of the girls asked. "Did you write letters?"

"No, but I might one day. Somebody I loved did it. And then others did it and everybody grew to love each other more."

"Really?" asked a girl with big eyes. "How?"

"You mean, why..." her friend corrected her.

"Well," Maya said, now that the girls seemed to have returned to her, "you learn about people that way and why they are the way they are and, through that, you learn about yourself."

And then the girls went to their current favorite subject.

"Are you married?"

Maya laughed, "No, are you?"

Then the girls laughed.

"Do you want to be?" one asked.

"Of course," she said, putting her hand in the tree, deciding to refinger the goddess one last time. "Why?"

"Come meet my uncle. He works in the city in London, he's visiting. He's here helping people in Mumbai and seeing us. We're just over there," she said, pointing to a group of flats.

And then the girls began pulling her.

Does Nan-ji and the goddess have something to do with this? Maya wondered.

One girl said to the other, "We can write about it one day if they like each other."

"It better be a good story," Maya said.

"Of course," one said, laughing. "We met you by the tree … Come on," the little girl said, "Follow us. You never know what can happen."

THE END

… CAN ALWAYS BE A BEGINNING, TOO …
FOR EVERY MOTHER AND EVERY DAUGHTER.

ELITA

Protagavo
VT Zapload
October 12 2043
{ Sooz, Angelina, Bo }

   Has been a while tracking everyone down, EntonDS in glitch mode right now. Hope you are all receiving?
   Have been pinged a LoopIn to activate this project. It might mean something to you depending on how *au fait* you are with your Heirloom data and voca: Holocaust, famine, bumbaclot, DNA tests, COVID-19, nanoBlack ...
   If you are not up to speed, let me fill you in. You don't know me but I am the granddaughter of Maya, great-great-granddaughter of Kamla. As I transmit you should be airloading "the Granddaughter Project", which should make this VT Zapload make a bit more sense.
   Please read through the 'Granddaughter Project" (it is going to take time) in order to get the purpose of our four-way. It is our turn now to recreate the next set of communications of our lives as women in the 2040's for +2 generations from now.
   I am up for doing this. These letters from the past are emotional. Not sure I have that

much helplessness to convey—or that much
strength to channel—but maybe I have? Let me
know if you are up for it too and ping me
your schedules. I will set up a Round Table
in WingDrop for us all to meet face to face.
   Looking forward to sharing and baring …
   Checking out …

   Elita

ABOUT THE AUTHOR

Shaheen Chishti is an Indian-British author, world peace advocate and thought leader. Shaheen is a member of the London Literary Society and Muslim-Jewish Forum in London. He is also the founder of the Jewish Islamic International Peace Society. He is a descendant of the revered Sufi Saint Khwaja Moinuddin Chishti, whose shrine is also known as the Ajmer Sharif Dargah. Shaheen studied in Mayoor School, Ajmer before moving to London with his family at the age of 15. In London, he went to Holland Park School where he completed his secondary education. Thereafter, he pursued a degree in accountancy from London Guildhall University to become a professionally qualified accountant.

Shaheen's writings—fiction and non-fiction—primarily focus on the upliftment of women and the emancipation of Muslim women in particular. He believes that the "empowerment of women is at the root of Muslim teaching." *The Granddaughter Project* is Shaheen's debut novel.

An ardent believer in the Sufi philosophy of "Love towards all, malice towards none", Shaheen endeavours to promote the message of peace and solidarity of the Chishti Order of Sufism. Shaheen was born into the Syed Chishti family in India which traces its ancestry directly to Hazrat Ali, the cousin and son-in-law of the Holy Prophet. Shaheen had a multicultural and liberal upbringing, and he grew up with ideas of peace and harmony to all of humanity.

He currently lives in London and has two daughters, Yasmeen and Saima.

Made in the USA
Middletown, DE
25 July 2021

44507555R00155